Storm Frost

P. M. Sabin Moore

authorHOUSE®

AuthorHouse™ UK Ltd.
500 Avebury Boulevard
Central Milton Keynes, MK9 2BE
www.authorhouse.co.uk
Phone: 08001974150

First published by AuthorHouse 3/21/2009

ISBN: 978-1-4389-5995-5 (sc)

Printed in the United States of America
Bloomington, Indiana

This book is printed on acid-free paper.

Cover photograph: Richard E. Moore
Cover Design: AuthorHouse

FOR MY SONS

GERARD AND RICHARD

ACKNOWLEDGEMENTS.......

my husband, Christopher, who fought the computer into submission

my friends since university days, Steinunn Einarsdottir and Hilda Butler (nee Vivian), who lent me their names and have given me so much more

my father, the late Rev.Richard H Sabin, who believed in educating women

my father-in-law, the late Rev. Ivan E Moore, who first took me to Sutton Hoo; he was a friend of Basil Brown, the first archaeologist there

the Sutton Hoo Society, and those responsible for the National Trust Exhibition at Sutton Hoo, where I have soaked up so much

Dr. Sam Newton of Wuffing Education for answering so many questions

my wise and helpful friends: Gary and Jennifer Sanford; Terry and Jennifer Maidens; Andrea Eichhorn; Anne Hartnett; Sally Goodwin; Roy and Jo Thatcher; Mark Mitchels; Valerie and Jack Constable; Dee Higgins; the captain of the Puffin Cruise boat, who sailed us round Coquet Island, sharing his local knowledge: I wish I knew his name!

the Wisbech Fenland Museum, and the Librarian at Amble, who helped with my research

I am very grateful for your knowledge and advice. Any short-comings herein are mine alone.

AUTHOR'S NOTE

It is important to recognise that this tale is set in pre-Christian England. Pope Gregory's mission landed in Thanet in 597 AD, one hundred and eighty-seven years after the Romans withdrew their governor and army from the province. Raedwald introduced Christianity to his kingdom in 604 AD.

I have, therefore, been selective in my use of the poems, some of which may well have descended in an oral tradition, prior to being inscribed by monks, possibly in Crowland, and included in the Exeter Book. The Exeter Book was given by Bishop Leofric to his cathedral there, in the 11th century.

"Beowulf" concerns tales of earlier centuries, and began first to be written down as late as the 8th, culminating in the (Cotton) MS of about 1000 AD. One of Raedwald's ancestors, Hrothmund, is one of the characters in it.

I have changed the spelling of several place-names to conform to the period of the late 6th century. The name Coquet is a Norman version; the original appears to be from the Celtic "coch", meaning "red", as its waters flush reddish when in spate. Pronounce it with a long 'o', to rhyme with 'crow'.

Tyttla, Eni, Raedwald and Aethelfrith are historical figures. Their actions in this novel, and all the other characters are entirely fictional, though I have tried to remain true to the period.

(P.M. S.M.)

STORM-FROST

It is about 592 AD and two princes of the powerful kingdom of the East Anglians travel west to forge an alliance with the tribe of a king of Middle Anglia. One is Eni (known as Wulf) the other is Raedwald (who will one day become High King, ruling the east from Sutton Hoo). They meet and fall in love with the king's daughter, Niartha.

This is the story of her disastrous love. It is based on Anglo-Saxon poems: the first love-triangle story in English literature.

LIST OF NAMED CHARACTERS

Niartha   daughter of a king at Wedresfeld

Eadwacer   steward to the king; (pronounced Edwacher)

Edgar   Niartha's uncle

Gerda   Niartha's bondwoman

Guthlac   horse-carl in the court

Aescgar   stepmother's brother

King Tyttla   King of the East Anglians

Prince Eni   also called Wulfgrim or Wulf, elder son of Tyttla

Prince Raedwald   younger son of Tyttla

Gurth   cousin to the princes; Eni's chief thane

Hardric   dweller at a mere-side shrine

Hilda and Hubert   hospitable couple, living beside the fens

Ulrica   girl being taken to her wedding by her unpleasant family

Oswald   Ulrica's husband, living in the Lindsey wolds

Edmund   keeper of riverside inn at Barmby, living with his elderly parents

Steinunn   kindly headwoman of family at Keldholm

Morwyn	the wise-woman of Ugglebarn
Eric and Ailwyn	Gurth's followers from the Northern Isles
Lukas	a merchant seaman
Ricberht	a baby
Bertha, Haesel,	fisher-folk of the River Cocket (now Amble)
Aethelfrith	King of Northumbria (Bernicia and Deira)
Wilhelm	a sea-captain's son

RAEDWALD

"You are wanted, my lord. Wake up!"

The young man uttered a soft groan and turned his head. The girl's leg sprawled across his thigh, and her arm and her long, dark hair tumbled over his chest, her face nestling in the hollow of his shoulder. He screwed his eyes against the sunset streaming in through the barn door and pushed the girl aside, ignoring her sudden cry.

"By Thunor, Gurth! What do you think you are doing?"

"The king calls for you. I am sent to fetch you to the hall."

"Is it so late? Have I missed supper? I've hardly had a bite since they called me at dawn."

"Oh come, prince," Gurth replied with a grin. "You've taken your fill. She's a tasty morsel."

Raedwald smiled. "Let's hope our efforts are fruitful." He smacked the rump of the girl smiling dreamily beside him, so that she gave a little shriek, half surprise, half laughter.

At dawn a group of young girls, not yet wed, or bedded, had come, singing and dancing, and pulled him, the chosen man, to greet Nerthus, the goddess-mother of the earth. Her effigy, accompanied by these maidens, was conveyed on a four-wheeled wagon, painted and gilded like herself and drawn by two yoked cows to the fields. Following a damp spring, one field had been stricken with a blight. The priest had called for the *Aecerbot*, a powerful act of magic, and the king readily agreed. On that day, all weapons were securely put away, no man to touch arms of any kind.

The priest, in his role as healer, led the wagon in procession to

1

cut turfs from each of the four quarters of the diseased land. In the squares of exposed soil he left the runes to mark east, west, south, north, creating the signs with twigs from the rowan tree. He carried the four turfs to the shrine beneath the sacred hawthorn growing beside the spring where they drew their water. Here he kept the holy place of Nerthus.

On the underside of each turf he laid clippings from all the soft plants that grew in this place. The green stuff was mixed with lavender oil, honey, water and milk, and dropped thrice on the underside of each square. The people returned to the field to watch as he laid each turf exactly in its original spot. The healer turned to face the east, towards Asgard, home of the gods, and called on Nerthus to bless the ground and make it fruitful.

He chanted his spell three times, turning in a circle, and fell to the ground, kissing it and laying his hands on it tenderly.

The plough was brought, ready with its oxen, carrying in its beam special oil, spice and fennel. The prick of the plough was laid to earth. The men of the village stood in a circle around it and, while the squealing girls danced outside the ring, the priest spilled his own seed over the corn grains lying in the body of the plough. Now it was ready to impregnate the earth as she arched toward it.

The priest spoke the words of the marriage-blessing: *Be well, oh earth, mother of mankind; grow large in the god's embrace; fill with food for men to use.*

The furrow was cut, the plough pushing steadily into the cleft of the earth. The seed was planted and the singers begged the goddess to bring a fruitful harvest. The priest with his acolyte, accompanied by two slaves to drag the wagon, moved alone to the little pool nearby, a secret place where none but they dared go. There the goddess would be cleansed, before returning to her shrine. Meantime, only the holy ones could look upon her body. The two slaves would never be seen again. The sacrificial pool had claimed them, men believed, their bodies to lie for a thousand and a thousand years, enclosed in the black silt of the pool.

Back at the homestead, the fun began. After the effigy of the goddess had been borne back, under cover, to her shrine, the chief handmaid and the chosen man went laughingly through a mock marriage before being led to the great barn where the act of coupling would complete the rite.

The priest recited the blessing, though all present knew that this act was symbolic – the boy and girl, though at puberty, were wed only for the day. The girl was already betrothed, but still a virgin, and her man, a horse-carl, would not object to the offspring, if any, of this holy ritual. In this case, with King Tyttla's son as the chosen man, she would be well cared for.

Ribald spectators were pushed back to the door of the barn. The priest and selected elders stayed long enough to see the pair disrobed, and that the young man was suitably aroused. Then they left them in the dim light shafting in through the timbers, dustbeams rising around them. Raedwald lifted her onto the bed of straw prepared for them, covered in deerskins. In the warmth of Midsummer Eve they needed no coverlet.

After the first, immediate, urgent act, where the youth found quick release, they sipped at the mead left for them, and nibbled honey-cakes. Then he turned to her again and began, more gently to show her how best to honour the earth-goddess. As dusk fell they slept, to be awakened by the thane, Gurth, who pounded the ground at the door, with his staff.

"What's the hurry, Gurth? I thought to be here for the night."

"Your brother has returned, lord. The thanes are gathering to hear his news."

"Eni Wulfgrim? He's home? Then we must make haste." He gestured to the girl, who slipped from the straw and covered her pliant body with her dusty, green robe. She picked up a garland of fading meadowsweet and held it to her rumpled hair. Her lover clipped on his belt over a fine, blue tunic and reached for his boots. "You will make Aelfric a good wife," he said. She bent her head and smiled, blushing. He tossed her a gold piece. "To bring you luck!" he said, then turned, one arm flung over Gurth's shoulder, and strode out into the evening light.

She kissed the gold and clasped it to her breast in one hand. She bent to stroke the skins, still warm, where they had lain: stained with her blood and his seed. The priest would be pleased, too. At the door she gazed up at the rising moon and whispered a plea that her body would bear the fruit of this day, and of this man.

He had not even asked her name.

WULF

With gladness I return to my father's hall. I have fulfilled his command to greet our kin across the eastern sea. He is wise, King Tyttla. He knows that, as his heir, I must be known to those men, and know them, myself, and their ways.

So I have journeyed upon the paths of the great fish and through far lands, seeing the wide earth extending before me. Some men have welcomed me warmly in their halls, and I found praise and generosity. Others were more cautious, even hostile and I worked to melt their animosity, earn their trust and create peaceful alliances between our peoples. The tales of my travels bring pleasure to the feast, and I have often spoken of the wonders I have seen, the harper strumming to accompany my words.

I tell of rare beasts: the crusty-coated whale who lifts his huge body from the deep; the shining, black panther with his amazing voice and perfumed breath. I speak of great, blue ice-caverns and rivers of green ice that topple from high cliffs into the black sea. There are forests of pine, where huge deer roam, and no man may reach their end. I have heard of vast wastes of sand where live extraordinary creatures and wise men of many skills. These I long to see.

As for now, I shall return to this, my home. I know that my father looks to see his kingdom secure before his death, and he is old. My mother is dead. I was given a wife, and she is dead. The babes are young, frail and housed elsewhere to be nursed. I know my father hopes to wed my brother to one of the kingdoms

5

in the west of our lands. That would cool his fire, and bring us strength. For me, who knows? I miss the pleasures of the bed, but find solace in travel and music. It would be wisdom to look to the Geats or the Scylds, but the daughters of their queens are too old, or mere babes. There was a maiden in the land of the Scyldings, but a daughter of a thane might not be high-born enough to suit my father and his counsellors. She must bring power and wealth, who comes to the Wuffings as their queen.

In this matter, and on this occasion, I shall follow my own heart.

NIARTHA

1

I did not wish to meet his eyes, so bent my head to receive the small packet wrapped in cloth.

"This token was engraved at my lord's command," said Eadwacer, "and the jewels were impressed upon the gold. See? The hedge-rose twisting around the curving lines of the great dragon? There are letters here to represent your names." He pressed it into my hands.

I saw it very clearly, though I could not read the letters. It was undoubtedly the same brooch Raedwald had given me at the time of our betrothal. So, he remembered it now? After all this long age of silence, why did my husband now think of me?

"With this token," Eadwacer continued, "he sends words. He is now king in the lands claimed and ruled by his father and his grandfather. Now he owns horses, fine goods, some small hoard of gold and he is rebuilding the great hall of his grandfather. It is his wish –"

"Why should I care for his wishes? I have enough of my own!"

"Niartha, listen. He says that what happened between you was long ago, and times have changed. He wants you to –"

"I do not want him!"

"He wants you to come on the next ship at the coast, sailing to the south in the spring. Come, he says, when the cuckoo calls and cross the calming seas as summer starts. Join him where he waits upriver, not far from the sea. I am to –"

"You are nothing!"

"Princess, how can you say that? Have I not been your friend in the past? Did I not loyally serve your father, and have I not proved my devotion to Raedwald? He offers you so much – the restoration of his regard and the place of honour at his side as he rewards his men with gifts of gold, rings, armbands, horns –"

"Can you see me, Eadwacer?" I cried." Look at me!" My gown was threadbare. I was thin and stiff from constant toil. " Look at this place. Who would respect me, honour me, once my story were known?"

"Niartha, forgive me, my lady. I cannot bear this. I have taken many months seeking you since I heard that you left your father's hall. Why did you go? What has happened to you? Are you living in this – this hovel?"

"Everything – everyone had gone whom I loved. I became an outcast. Who would have helped me?"

By now we were walking over the heath, purple and gold in the autumn sun and a strong west wind blowing our hair and our cloaks. He stopped and turned on me.

"You could have turned to me, surely. You know how I –"

"I know how you put your duty to Raedwald before your care for me – your care for our family."

"I would have come, Niartha, if you had sent me word."

"Sent where? I did not dare to approach Raedwald. We had no news. And you would not have cared to come, even if he had allowed you."

"I would have come."

But you betrayed us and then you went away. I did not say it, but he read my eyes.

"I would never have let you come to such a pass as this," said Eadwacer. "Tell me what has happened to you."

I stared at him. Just as tall and lean as I had known him, but with a touch of grey in his hair and lines of weariness at his eyes.

He stood there, waiting, as if he were still my father's hall-thane, obedient to my wish.

Memories crowded. In my mind I could hear the subdued clamour as servants hurried to the table, bearing dishes and goblets. The great fire crackled. Wooden pieces clattered on the game-board and a man swore. Then came the rustle of dresses over the dusty floor and the clear voice of the lyre.

I sat down on the trunk of a fallen willow. How could I describe to this man what I had lived through? Thanks to Eadwacer I had lost Wulf, the man I loved, and Raedwald, the man to whom I was married, as well as the security that being the king's daughter had given me.

Suddenly the griefs, old and new, which I had suffered since I was a child, were swamped by the fresher afflictions of the past. I dropped my head into the folds of my coarse and tattered cloak and let the tears flow.

He came and knelt beside me, the bracken snapping beneath his weight and his body shielding me from the wind, but he did not touch me. He never had, once I had grown, though I knew he wished to do so.

"Lady," he said, "let me take you back inside." He gestured towards the place he had described as a hovel. Locally it was known as an inn, as signified by the bush of thorns tied to its door-post. I knew all too well how little privacy it afforded.

"No. Let us walk on. I will tell you exactly why I am here. Then you can tell your lord and mine why I can never return to him again."

How dared he, I was inwardly screaming, how dared he send – and by this man of all those who served him – word of 'the restoration of his regard!' How like Raedwald that he should hope instantly to kindle a flame from a spark that had never blazed for him.

Anger makes many women weep and it was with difficulty, choking back more tears, that I turned to the messenger.

"I will tell you, Eadwacer. Never, never in my life have I been free from grief. At every turn I have met with pain and rejection."

2

When I was born, a month after the shortest day, my mother lay cold on her bed, as white as the snow, which coated the chilly land, but the sheet was red with her blood. Hearing of her death, said my nurse, my father handed me back to be wrapped in lambswool and turned his back, as icy as the north wind itself.

I swear he tolerated my presence in the hall only because I was an obedient child. As I grew, my only use to him must have been as the prospective source of power – some minor king or noble would gladly forge an alliance in exchange for a relatively easy dowry. I was not unattractive: my nurse called me her 'little beauty' and taught me what she could of dress and behaviour.

It was as well she did as there was no-one else. When my father took a new, outlandish wife, my stepmother kept me distant and, like my father, spoke rarely to me and usually on formal occasions, or when I could be useful. I knew she would gladly be rid of me.

Often I asked the nurse what she could remember of my mother. If only I could have known her.

"She loved you," said nurse.

"How could she? She died," I answered.

"She wanted you." I thought about this doubtfully. Why should she? I was of no use to anyone, being too young to work except at trivial tasks, which might not demean a princess or call down scorn from my stepmother. Still, I watched the servants as they spun yarn, sewed, prepared food and treated animal skins.

My father's steward, Eadwacer, was about twelve years older than

11

I and allowed me to sit quietly in a dim nook in the hall and listen to the storytellers, as they chanted their tales. Quietly, he saw to it that I was present with the queen's retinue when important envoys visited. So I learnt of life and events beyond our bounds.

Sometimes the talk was of skirmishes on the boundaries of my father's kingdom. Near the limits of the fens, at Wedresfeld, it was in an important position, guarding the old way that led to the great markets and large rivers, flowing to the north-west, where the wool could go for trading. Our allies to the east depended on our fighters to hold the boundary. At the feast, men with swords, shields and spears left them at the entry to the hall. Valour was rewarded ceremonially with gold coins, ornamented drinking horns, finger-rings or decorated arm-rings.

When the noise rose from the drinkers or arguments broke out, I was led away to the women's quarters and found my small, unlit corner with its bed and chest where I kept my few possessions.

Sometimes I envied the children of the hall-servants and the serfs, especially the girls, who could - it seemed to me – run about where they wished, free to wander in the fields and along the edges of the woods. I had to seek approval, and was always accompanied by my nurse or a maidservant – even occasionally by Eadwacer.

Somehow I learnt about the plants, herbs and wildflowers, and those fruits, mushrooms and nuts it was good to gather. I watched as wounds were bound with herbal poultices, as tisanes were forced down the throats of coughing children. I saw the men at work outside the homestead, carving up the red deer and wild boar caught in the hunt and throwing onto the midden any scraps that could not be used. I even helped to scrape the skins and soften them, until I was rebuked.

However, it was deemed fitting for me to learn to sew cloth and to learn some of the crafts of the kitchen, so that eventually I might oversee the work of servants.

I never dreamed how much use to me would be such knowledge, nor that these few skills might save my life.

As I grew older I hardly ever let myself dream at all. How could I ever hope to achieve the sort of position held by my stepmother? Kept in a state of almost perpetual loneliness, lip-service paid to my status as the king's daughter, I had no close friends. My father generally ignored me, while his thanes and their wives preserved a courteous distance in deference to his example. After my beloved nurse died when I was thirteen, only Eadwacer spoke gently to me, steering me from any impropriety, protecting me (I realised later) from any uncouth behaviour inside the jovial hall or without. He comforted me in moments of childish distress.

I remained largely unaware of his attention, so restrained and apparently deferential. He was integral to the running of our lives, seeing to it that the king's commands were issued and obeyed, that the queen's requirements were met. Always he called me 'princess'. I liked him. He was steady and reliable. My father had employed him since Eadwacer had been sent to him as a youth to join the household. The son of a chieftain of the fen country, he was taught some of the crafts of soldiering and to master the more diplomatic skills of the great hall. He became hall-thane. He seemed both able and content. Never to me, probably never to my father, did he reveal how much ambition was lodged beneath his calm demeanour.

Only after my own heart was stirred, surging in its own turmoil so that I felt as if I were in the grip of a whirling torrent, did I see in his eyes that he was capable of similar passion. By then he had betrayed me.

3

In the spring of my fourteenth year, I was gathering bluebells in the fringes of the beech wood a few hundred yards from the homestead. Sunlight played on the gleaming bell heads as a slight breeze set them nodding and swaying.

It felt safe enough here, in broad day. I could hear the goatherd singing in a clearing not far off, and the bleating of the animals. But I would not have taken many steps further into the wood. Who knows what creatures might lurk in the shadows of the mighty trees?

It was not only the fear of boar, stag or wolf that held me close to the track, but the knowledge that the gods of the place would need to be appeased before any human ventured into the deep shade. Our hunters took care to perform the propitiatory rites and make offerings before treading the forest paths. Tales were told of the great black dog we called the 'Shuck' who leapt, threatening, into the path, and was impossible to escape. No man ventured near the marshy swamp at the western edge of the trees for dread of him. Even the trees were feared – they were, after all, living things. A few of them were worshipped, each in his own right, as local gods. Only with the agreement of the priests could an axe be laid to timber. I always felt as if I were being watched, but never dared to turn my head. What might I see? I shook myself gently and, as I straightened up to hand the plants to my bondswoman, I heard hooves drumming on the trackway.

"Put these in the trug, Gerda," I said. "Have them taken to the queen's quarters. Are these horsemen expected, have you heard? Has

Edwyn said anything?" Edwyn was a horse-thane, and I knew he had his eye on Gerda, to wed her if the queen allowed me to spare her in a year or two. I think Gerda liked him well enough. She was a lovely creature, shapely, even at thirteen years, and with a ready smile.

"Not that I know, lady. Perhaps they bring news?"

I stepped out from the dappled shade of the trees, catching my headband on a slim twig budding into clear green shoots, so that I paused to disentangle it. Then I stood on the grassy verge and watched as a troop of horsemen, about twelve in all, cantered up.

The leader raised his arm and they slowed. I thought he was about to speak, when he spotted the palisade and tall gates of the homestead.

"There!" he called, and with only a slight inclination of his head to acknowledge that he had seen me, he rode on, followed by his companions.

I stepped down onto the track, the wind gently blowing my skirts about my legs and casting tendrils of hair across my face. As I raised my arm to clear them, I saw one rider leave the rear of the group, turn his horse and trot back towards us. I stood still.

He was older than I, by several years: a young man, full-grown, not a boy. His dark hair shone in the sunlight, his skin was wind-tanned, and his eyes were an impenetrable brown. I met his look and opened my lips to speak, but he circled silently, looking from me to Gerda and back again, a steady gaze, no smile, no words. Then he bowed his head, flicked the reins and leapt forward to catch up with his fellows, now disappearing through the gates.

"Well, lady –" began Gerda, but I dropped my arm and walked on swiftly towards the hall. The mild sunset of mid-May reddened the skies, and I was eager to know the cause of this visit, and who this man – these men – could be.

They were brothers. The younger was named Raedwald, a prince of the Eastern Angles, and the elder was Eni, but his brother, laughing as he clasped his shoulder with affection, told us that Eni was known as Wulfgrim, or Wulf for short: a favourite nickname of their forebears, it seemed. My father knew theirs; their grandfather's lands had lain not far from ours before their family moved back to strengthen their kingdom at the eastern coast.

Apparently they wished to endorse this former friendship and empower an alliance that would help us all against the constant threat from the west or from the coast. I was young and naïve, then; I did not understand what this could mean. As Raedwald talked eagerly with my father and drank wine from the horn brought with the usual ritual by my stepmother, my eyes were once again held by those of his brother.

Wulf.

That night I could not sleep. After tossing in vain for several hours, I crept out of bed, pushing aside the leather curtain at the doorway and tiptoeing past the other sleeping-quarters. I paused at the entrance to the great hall and slid cautiously by it, hoping to avoid the guard. He was nodding on his stool, the spear held precariously in his slackened grip, and I crept past him towards the old apple tree in the corner of the yard. Moonlight slanted in and a chill draught caught my gown. I drew my blanket closer, but before I could move, there came a quiet voice.

"Princess, what are you doing?"

"Eadwacer. I could not sleep. I needed air. I need – "

"It is too cold outside. You cannot stay here. Our guests' men are sleeping in the hall. Let me get you a warm posset. I will bring it to – I will get Gerda to bring it to your room."

"Eadwacer, wait. Tell me, what do you know of these guests?"

"You heard their story in the hall tonight. They are noble by birth and Raedwald has already proved himself in battle. He is likely one day to make a good leader – a warrior for sure."

"What of his brother?"

"Eni Wulfgrim. He is a different sort of man, though no-one speaks to dishonour him. His father has sent him abroad, taking messages and gifts to other courts across the sea. Doubtless he is brave."

"He does not say much."

"Unlike his brother! There is one to entertain you with tales of valour."

But I wanted to hear the tales of the man who had wandered on the lonely seas. I sighed.

"Goodnight, Eadwacer. Leave Gerda to sleep. I shall rest now."

Of course, I did hear some of the tales of this sea-faring prince. My stepmother dutifully conversed with him the next day, and I sat

17

beside her, listening. He made little of the struggles with wind and waves, but could not conceal how lonely he found those embassies, so many days and nights out on the cold waters or in strange halls.

When the business of our own house called the queen aside, he sat still, his face half-shadowed. Then he stood up and bowed to me. As he turned away, I spoke.

"Wulf. Pardon me – I meant to say Lord Eni –"

"Wulf will do well. No-one has told me your name."

"I am Niartha, daughter of the king."

"Why did your mother not introduce you to us?"

"She is my stepmother. My mother died when I was born."

He sat down again, half-sunlit, half in shadow again.

"My mother died, too. My wife, also. It happened three winters ago when I was visiting the king of Kent."

So we began to talk. I had never known such an hour. The prince told me that his wife gave birth to twin boys, only a year after the birth of their first son, Onna. This time she died in the childbed. The infants had all gone into the care of cousins nearby, as there was now no grandmother to see to their care. The king, to counteract his son's grief, had taken to sending him away on missions across the sea. Wulfgrim began to tell me some of the adventures he had. I was gripped in a kind of still excitement and found it hard at first to find words of my own. In fact we communicated our thoughts as much by looks as by words. Once when I gasped in amazement, he took my hand and pressed it gently. Then there came a sudden interruption.

I had given no thought to where the other menfolk had gone. There was the stamp of feet and hooves outside the door of the hall, and calling voices.

The serf at the door ran towards the women's quarters and the queen and the other women, Gerda among them, came in haste to huddle over a wicker hurdle.

On it lay Raedwald, head bent forward and gripping his leg with taut fingers. His face was white.

"Brother!" cried Wulf. "What has happened?"

"It is my fault. I fell clumsily. That cursed nag threw me. I think my leg is broken."

I stepped aside as the inevitable hubbub ensued. It was Eadwacer who pulled the bone straight. The queen herself poulticed it with the nine herbs, including chervil and fennel, uttering the charm as she did so, and bound the leg to a splint. At her command, I administered a restorative drink to the fainting prince. I sent Gerda to fetch a bearskin to lay under his body on the pallet by the hall-fire and laid a blanket gently over him.

"I thank you, " Raedwald murmured, and looked at me for the first time. "Your name?"

"This is my daughter," replied the king. "Her name is Niartha."

"My lord is fortunate to have so gentle and beautiful a child." He gritted his teeth against the pain.

"Indeed," was my father's reply.

"May I beg the favour of her company for a little while? If she has no other duties."

I glanced at Wulf.

"I shall go and see to your horse, brother." He left the hall, taking several of the men with him.

"Sit, Niartha," said my father. "See that our guest has all that he needs. Gerda, wait here."

I saw the look he gave me, then the one he exchanged behind Raedwald's head with the queen.

"I will send a message to your father to tell him what has happened. He will need to know of our talks, and must be reassured that all is well."

"Send Eni," said Raedwald. "He can take this ring in token of our alliance. It is the one you gave me last night in the hall." He sighed.

"You should sleep," said the queen. "I will send another draught to reduce the pain and aid rest."

"You are kind, great lady," said he, and rested his head on the bolster I had placed for him. He smiled at me. His blond hair was a reddish-gold in the firelight and his eyes were dark blue, but dulled just now with pain. I sat and picked up my sewing, neglected for the last hour.

"Gerda, go and fetch the drink from the queen's maid, then bring your spinning here. Will it disturb you, prince, if we work quietly?"

"I think I should like to be disturbed by you." He smiled a little and lay back with his eyes closed.

A little later there was quiet in the hall. Two men played their board-game at a table set in the sunlight by the door. Maids moved to and fro. The king and queen had vanished. I saw and heard nothing from outside except a sparrow that fluttered in only to escape, a minute later, from the door at the far end of the great room. Gerda, sitting just behind me, pulled the flax rhythmically from the distaff between her knees, twisting the yarn with monotonous repetition.

I stitched with apparent diligence, but my pulse was racing. I could barely comprehend the experiences of the last hour or so. I longed to speak – but to whom? I longed to go outside, to be alone, to explore these feelings.

I raised my eyes and with a shock met Raedwald's. Again, he smiled. Then he held his finger to his lips, pressing it with a kiss, then twisting it into the sign which means 'silence!' I held my peace, but heard Gerda's movement behind me. I bent my head and stabbed the cloth so suddenly, I pricked myself. The pain brought me back to an equally sharp awareness. The drumming of my heart steadied and I collected my wits.

A sudden, easterly wind slammed the hall door shut.

4

And so it began.

The king and queen saw to it that I was responsible for the care of Prince Raedwald, and I gained some respect in the hall as I made possets of warm milk and honey, herbal concoctions of rue and comfrey, brought strengthening meats and had warm ointments of saffron and wax brought for his body-carl to use on his bruises.

Each time I visited, he stirred himself to thank me and smiled. He was not exactly an easy patient, however, always sending men to see to his horse, check on his spears, calling for Beorhtfyr, his sword, to have it polished or honed. Soon he demanded to leave his room and be brought to a bench in the hall. I sent for wolfskins to be laid for his comfort and ran my fingers into the deep pelt.

"Wulf," I thought. By now he must have returned to his father, King Tyttla, with the news of Raedwald's accident, and reassurance of the alliance holding between our tribes. Surely he would be sent back to fetch his brother home. Two weeks had passed – another to return here – perhaps two more while the legbone healed strongly. We could have – but my reverie was interrupted.

"Lady," said Eadwacer, "here is the prince." Raedwald approached, hopping awkwardly with a crutch. " Let me help you, lord." He helped to lift Raedwald's leg onto the comfortable couch and placed a small wooden table beside him. "Shall I fetch wine, princess?"

"Thanks, Eadwacer. Will you also ask the queen if I may use her crystal globe and some comfrey and self-heal to make the drink efficacious?" The steward bowed and left. I turned to ask someone to bring my stool but at the same moment Raedwald signalled to his men to withdraw. I stood quietly beside him, waiting for Gerda to appear.

My hand was gripped suddenly and I was pulled firmly to the side so that I sat on the wolf-fur cover, close to the body of the prince. Instinctively I made to leap up, but he held me down, smiling but strong.

"Let me go," I whispered, looking round. "This is not right!"

"Don't squirm so. You will hurt my leg."

"Please," I begged. "At least let me move." As his grasp slackened I stood and stared angrily at him.

"Forgive me, princess. That was a stupid thing to do. Show me that you forgive me. Do sit." He gestured toward his feet, one leg still heavily bound to the splints. "I am so bored. I hate being tied to a bed, and there is no-one to talk to."

Reluctantly I sat. He smiled. "Thank you. In fact, I have much to thank you for. I do not wish to seem ungracious, but I long for news from Wulfgrim. I long to be out with my horse and hound." I, too, longed for these things!

From outside I could hear the sound of scuffling feet and clash of metal as thanes practised swordplay in the forecourt. He shifted restlessly.

"I should be out there with them, not stuck here with my strength dwindling away."

"I can understand that. But it will not be for long now. In a month –"

"A month!" He slammed his fist down on the table at his side. "Sorry, princess."

Gerda appeared, carrying a wooden tray, which she placed on the table. She poured wine from a bottle into a goblet. I sprinkled into it some herbs from a small pottery bowl and lifted the crystal on its delicate chain, dipping the globe into the wine. I had seen my stepmother do this and heard the words she used to welcome guests and warriors as we dined. "Waes hael," I murmured. "Be well, Lord Raedwald."

"Assuredly, princess. With sweet Niartha to offer such comfort, who could not be well?"

"Gerda," I commanded, as she stood there, looking demure but missing nothing. "Bring our spinning." At least I could concentrate on that and avoid the blue eyes that searched my face.

"Tell me of your home, prince," I said. "Is it far from here?"

Each day for many days passed in this way. I listened to his tales of how he and Wulfgrim grew up. What freedom they had, compared to me. What adventures, as they explored streams, forests, shorelines. I asked him did he not fear the gods of such places? Raedwald said carelessly,

"For my part, I do not let such thoughts trouble me. Wulf, now, will perform the odd sacrifice, or make the correct signs against evil fate, but he does not lack courage."

They had learnt to ride, to train dogs and hawks, to use the bow and the spear, to sail and to fight with swords. What began as play became earnest as they grew older and stronger. They had taken part in skirmishes and raids to the west and come back undisgraced.

One day the door-thane helped Raedwald to hobble to the door of the hall, propping his weight on the cleft stick, until he sat on a bench in the sun. It was a warm summer and the light southerly breeze lifted my headcloth. Raedwald flicked a strand of hair from his eyes and laughed.

"I need to get this thatch trimmed," he said. "Which of your father's serfs clips the king's mane?"

"I do it for him."

"You, princess?"

"Yes. He says I have the touch and he knows I will not hack his ears off at the same time."

"Will you do this for me?"

I felt shy and bent my head away. "If you wish it."

"Yes, I do. Can you do it now?"

"I will send Gerda for the trimming shears and a cloth."

So we pulled the bench away from the wall and I stood behind him, glad that he could not see how my fingers shook and my cheeks burned. I lifted a lock. "How much should I cut off?"

"Hold it down by my ear." I did so, feeling the warm pulse of his neck.

"A little lower. Just above the braid of my tunic. There."

At my sign, Gerda wrapped the cloth around him and stood back. I began to lift and trim.

"The front is still too long. I like to have it cut short above the brow."

I came round, stood before him and bent to the task, trying to concentrate. I felt his breath on my arm where my sleeve had loosened from its wrist-clasp. He raised his eyes and laughed softly.

"This is the nearest you have been to me, Niartha. Is it so terrible?"

"Keep still, please, or I shall cut crooked."

And then we heard a call from the square watch-tower at the gate: "Horsemen!"

Men ran into the hall and out again, carrying arms. Usually we had word of who might be approaching but no strong guard had been set to the east, as there lay the lands of our allies.

It was Gurth, Wulf's chief thane, with a troop. My heart stopped thudding and I stood quietly beside Raedwald, who had risen and waited for his brother's man. Gurth approached the hall, a tall, strongly-built man, blue-eyed under thick brows, a band wound round his head, wearing silver arm-rings below his broad shoulders. He and his men were escorted by our warriors, to be taken to my father, the king.

"Greetings, my prince."

"Where is Prince Eni?"

"Your father has sent him with messages to the south and then across to Jutland. King Tyttla had heard of stirrings to the north and wants support. I came to warn our allies here. Are you well, my lord? Your strong arm may soon be needed. Is your leg healed?" He looked doubtfully at the stick on which Raedwald was leaning.

"It is mending fast. Only another week or two. The travelling months will not be over, and I should be fit to ride, even if I cannot run. I will come into the hall with you." He took Gurth's arm and began to hoist himself indoors. "Thank you for shearing this woolly pate of mine!" he called, as they passed into the shadowy doorway.

"Clear this up, Gerda," I said and wandered off, disappointment choking me.

Outside the gate I followed the track blindly, stepped onto the grass and sought the shelter of the trees. Grief made me forget fear. Cow parsley was giving way to buttercups and then the grass thinned and grew cooler under the beeches. I sat on a root coated with moss and let my tears fall. Wulf had not returned. He had been sent away, for many months, it seemed. Could he not have sent some message? I had been so sure that he would do so. How could I have misinterpreted his reactions to me? What a fool I was.

A twig cracked nearby and I looked up to see Gurth crossing the glade. He halted and bent his head deferentially as I wiped my eyes on my sleeve.

"Forgive me, lady. Your maid said you had been seen coming into the wood, and I need to speak with you. It seemed best to take the chance. They have no further need of me in the hall."

He put his hand into the scrip carried over his shoulder beneath his blue cloak, and held out a small wooden box. On its lid was carved out the shape of an animal – a wolf.

I met his gaze and he answered my unspoken question.

"Yes. I have brought this from my lord, Prince Eni. He felt much regret at his sudden departure. His heart is full of sorrow now that he has to complete the embassy at his father's behest, as it prevents him from returning here. He says – he says – " He stopped.

"Say it."

"He told me to say that he loves you. Please do not be angry."

"I am not angry!" My tears threatened to spill over again, but this time because I was overcome with a deep joy. "Gurth, I thank you. I will send a message in return before you leave – but you will stay a while, surely?"

"Much depends on what happens here. Your father may need our help, as there is trouble brewing on the northern border. I hope Prince Eni may soon –"

"Princess!" Startled, I saw Eadwacer with two carls, pursued by Gerda, all hastening towards us.

"Lady, what are you doing here?" He looked from me to Gurth. His face was dark.

"The princess was seen coming this way. I felt she might need an escort, and offered to see her safely home." Gurth spoke courteously, but calmly stared Eadwacer down. "Thanks, Gurth," I said calmly and passed through the little group. "There was no need for anyone to feel anxious. Come, Gerda." We returned to the homestead. I felt annoyed at Eadwacer's presumption, but he was only doing his work, I supposed.

There was indeed a lively discussion, taking place round the great table. Wide gestures and excited voices covered my entry and I slid away to my quiet room.

I fingered the little box and lifted its lid. Inside there was a small piece of folded cloth. I unwrapped it, and my breath caught in my throat. On my palm there lay a polished orb of amber with a dark speck near its centre. I pressed it to my cheek, cradled it and held it back towards the light. It was just the colour of my hair.

"He did not forget me," I whispered. I rewrapped the shiny nugget, restored it to the box and traced the carving with my finger. Then I hid it under a tunic in my clothes press; at night it would lie under my pillow. It was all I could do to steady myself and return coolly to the hall. Hiding my happiness was harder than ever it had been to hide my grief. I could feel on me the eyes of the queen, as she sat beside my father. The steward handed me a small cup of wine. My maidservant stood behind my chair. Prince Raedwald raised a large drinking-horn, ornamented with silver wire.

"Wish me health, princess," he called across the board. "We are raising a force of men, and in less than twenty days we shall ride to war."

5

Three weeks later they left, taking all the men who had been amassing in encampments round the homestead. The hall fell silent. Some women wept, Gerda amongst them. I thought it was for Edwyn, but she told me, with unusual shyness, that she had longings for Gurth. He had noticed her in my company and had begun to talk to her in the occasional moments she could snatch aside. She felt confused, uncertain now of her feelings for Edwyn. I could not blame her, though I was not so sure that Gurth was as interested in her as Gerda hoped. Still, Gurth was a strong, lusty figure of a man, and gentle with it. We whispered together, giggling, at what it must be like, to lie with a man and feel his flesh. Only one man featured in my longing dreams.

Other women moved briskly around, chivvying children, restoring order and harrying boys and old men. Soon animals were re-penned, and mud scraped and brushed away. Blankets, hangings and garments were scrubbed, beaten and hung out on fences and hedges to dry in the hot sun, until a sudden thunderstorm sent everyone under cover.

Then we waited.

As usual, my stepmother largely ignored me except for a word of rebuke if she noticed me 'idling,' as she saw it. If I missed the odd meal she made no comment. Even when I wandered over the sheep-meadow one whole afternoon and Eadwacer reported my absence, she waved him away. On my return she did not summon me to her. Instead she followed me to my room. She had not done this since I

...s a child to be punished.

"I suspect you have something on your mind," she said. I stood, wondering how she knew, how she could have guessed. I had just spent two hours dreaming of Wulf and forgetting everything else.

"I am sure that Prince Raedwald will return safely. He is young and strong, and with your father's guidance – "

"Of course, lady," I responded. She must have read my relief as eagerness.

"He is very interested in you." She studied me, as if in surprise. What could a man like that see in me? "When they return, it is likely that your father will approach King Tyttla with a view to a settlement."

"You mean - ?" The shock came like an arrow.

"Grow up, little girl. It is high time we had you off our hands. This is a golden opportunity. The boy seems besotted. They will not require too large a dowry."

"But –" I stopped.

"But? But nothing! Your father will have your interests at heart." And yours, I thought. "His mind is made up." She would see to that. She turned to leave, then suddenly bent and lifted the lid of my chest and riffled through the various layers of cloth. "We shall have to sort out your garments." One sleeve fell over the edge of the chest, and my precious box fell out onto the rushes. I forced myself to breathe and kept my eyes on the queen. Gerda moved so that her skirt shielded the little object from the queen's sight. "While they are away," pronounced my stepmother, "we shall prepare your linen and do something about this sorry assortment of goods. You must not disgrace us."

She swept out and I heard her call for Gerda and her own maid to see what flax was ready. Wool was needed, too: they were going to be kept busy.

I crouched down and retrieved the little box. Clasping it to my breast, I gasped for breath, still feeling winded. "Oh, Wulf," I wept. "Please come quickly."

Five days later the army returned, wild with victory. A series of raids, counter-attacks and defensive stands at the Mercian border had sealed a truce, more than temporary, it was hoped. There had been a few deaths, not many serious injuries, and the mood of jubilation was high. A banquet was called.

Later (though it is not easy to recall happiness when you are wretched), in my loneliest, most desolate and deprived state, I would try to picture our hall at Wedresfeld, always at its best in feasts. The earthen floor was raked and swept, and fresh rushes were laid against the dust. Three long, central hearths were stacked with kindling and logs, and lit so that sparks flew and smoke fingered through the high roof-ridge above. Torches, slung from wall-brackets, vied with the bright flames and candles glowed along the tables running alongside the hearths. The warriors' shields hung high on the silvery, adze-smoothed timber walls, jewels glistening on the finest warriors; their spears were stacked, leaning by the hall doors.

On the dais by the central hearth sat the king on his carved and gilded settle. The queen was beside him, and the scop, the hall-singer, perched on a curved stool to one side, lyre at the ready. The jester waited nearby. Opposite, across the fire, was the guest-stool on its dais, but my mind would sheer away from that memory.

Inside the hall was noise: men's voices clamorous in drink, calling for the great drinking horns to be refilled and passed on. The lyre sounded, sweetly plucked, or thrumming with a vibrant sound, as the singer lifted his voice in a chanting tale. Gaming pieces rattled on the boards. Inside the hall was torchlight, fellowship, conviviality, security. You could even hope for some reward for duty done. That was, after all, one of the greatest roles of a successful king, to acknowledge loyal service.

Outside the hall, as I was to learn all too cruelly, was darkness, isolation, hunger and terror, not only of the invisible spirits of the dark places.

Women, of course, were responsible for the provision of the feast and the maintenance of the finery that went with it, bright clothing, shining dishes, the greatest possible variety of delicious foods. It was hard work for us all, but fun was to be found. It certainly seemed to me that the serving-girls had the best of it, their giggles and wanton shrieks hushed only by a stern rebuke from the hall-thane, or the queen's furious glance. It was her task to control the feast, welcome the guest, prompt the king in his familial or diplomatic duties. Eventually she would call a halt to the formal proceedings before withdrawing to her quarters, the thane-wives and I trailing behind her.

It took a woman of common-sense, with knowledge of what was going on in the land, a powerful character who could organize and dominate. A wise queen looked for ways to keep the family peacefully united, and ensure harmonious relationships with outsiders. It was possible for me to admire her for this, but I could never love her. Her sexuality and, possibly, her wealth, held the king to her, but I do not think she loved my father warmly and she resented me ever more acutely as her infertility became clear.

Now her chance to be rid of me was come. I could be given to Raedwald. Three days of the home-coming feast would be enough time to work on my father.

Ale flowed, and wine. Oxen were slaughtered and deer. The tables were covered in great bowls of apples and nuts, and the smell of bread was sweet. The dairy was hard put to supply enough cheese and butter.

There was much coming and going. Men bade each other hearty and noisy farewells as squadrons of horsemen broke away and left for their homes. Gifts were bestowed, of rings, horns, bows – even swords; the armourers and smiths had been busy before, during and after the conflict.

On the third day my father summoned me. He sat on his great, carved settle, the queen on his left, and Prince Raedwald standing beside him.

"Daughter," said the king, "I am sending a messenger with the thanes of King Tyttla. It is Prince Raedwald's desire to take you in marriage, and I seek an arrangement with his father. When I receive his reply, you will accompany the prince."

I glanced involuntarily at Raedwald. Was he staying here, then? Not returning home with his army? I fixed my gaze on the dusty rushes at my feet. I wished I could sink into the earth.

"I shall enjoy this time of waiting," Raedwald said. "Our time together was so pleasant, and now I can walk with you and ride out, as well as enjoying the pleasures of the hall."

"Young man," the king laughed raucously, "you will take care to enjoy only those pleasures suited to a couple hardly yet officially betrothed!" I blushed hotly and turned, but the queen gripped my gown and prevented me.

"You have not yet thanked your father and this noble prince for the honour they do you. Speak, Niartha."

I swallowed, then opened my lips, seeking words that I could use. Raedwald smiled his confident smile.

"She is quite overcome. Do not fear, princess. I will not force the pace. We shall talk, as before, and you will come to love me. Here, I have had this made for you." A golden brooch, with a curving, bejewelled, flowery stem intricately interwoven with a twisting dragon. "This marriage will strengthen the alliance between our families and kingdoms. This symbolizes your beauty and my strength. See? The jeweller put runes for our names." Raedwald pinned the brooch at my neck, his hand barely brushing my breast, but his glance was hot. I held still. Surely, this was the sort of gift a man gave his bride on the consummation of their marriage? The morning-gift, we called it. Raedwald was very sure of me – or of himself! My father stood and beckoned Eadwacer to approach.

"Have horsemen prepare to ride. Send my cousin's son. We will have gifts to offer as part of her dowry – fine Celtic bronzeware, gold, of course, and silverware from the east. There is much to do. Negotiate the number of cattle. It may be some weeks before Tyttla replies, and longer before our trading is complete."

That was, naturally, all it meant to him – a trade. I was an object in his possession, worth less than his horse, his sword, his jewels, his warrior-thanes; yet I could still be used like a piece of merchandise. It was lucky for him that Raedwald placed some value on me – but for me…

The king almost pushed past me, bustling through the hall, calling up this man, then that, his hand going often to his purse. The queen rose, took my hand and laid it in Raedwald's palm. "There," she said with soft satisfaction, and left us.

As I made to snatch my hand away, the prince caught it in both of his.

"I am happy, Niartha, with this day's work. Often, while we were away, I thought of you. You will bring joy to our people – and to me." He lifted my chin and kissed me. I trembled. All the time they had been away, I had been free to think of his brother. Now, with Wulf so far away, I did not know where, I was faced with this. In spite of myself, totally confused at my own reactions, I felt my body respond, my lips softened and I swayed toward him. Then I pushed away.

"I must leave you. There is much to attend to. Gerda!" I called.

He laughed gently as my maid approached. "We shall meet tonight at the feast. The minstrel has prepared a song to celebrate our battles, but I shall enjoy more the music of your voice."

The music, however, was to be broken. At the moon's height, blue shadows in the forecourt, and with the merriment loud in the hall, golden with fire and lamplight, there came a shout from the guard, a response, a flash of mail, and out of the shadowy night into the hall strode Wulf.

6

Raedwald leapt up and ran to meet him, clasping his brother warmly and leading him to the guest-stool. Gurth moved to stand behind him.

Eagerly, Wulf ate and drank and listened to the voices telling him of the battles, the victories, the riding, the comrades. When there was a lull, Raedwald asked him,

"What of you, brother? Have you completed your embassy for father?"

"Yes, indeed I have. At last I have. I went south into the lands of the East Saxons, and on into Kent. Our relations with these people are good, lord king, and I told them of your concern to maintain our alliances. Then I crossed the sea and visited the lands of our forebears in Jutland. They will spread our news to the eastern tribes. I sent word to the king, my father, with the shipmen, when I put in at Sheringham, and came here as fast as I could."

He still had not, it seemed, looked at me. Luckily for me no-one noticed how I stared at him. I could not have turned my gaze, as he sat there, turning a chunk of bread in his fingers. I had mixed dough that morning, blending the dark flour with five different grains and a little honey so that it tasted tangy and sweet.

"It was a pity, brother, you could not have joined us sooner. You would have enjoyed the strife – and your arm would have been welcome. We –"

"You were fit to fight then? Your leg was healed?"

"I think I was limping still, a little, but I could ride. All that

33

training Gurth put us through, horse, sword and spear, certainly paid off. But the healing was thanks to this lovely lady, our princess." Raedwald gestured toward me, and at last Wulf acknowledged me. His smile was slight and cool, but his glance came like a hot knife.

"Speaking of alliances, Prince Eni," came my father's voice, "I have today sent out some of my kinsmen, together with thanes of your brother, to propose a bonding of our own. I am happy, if your father agrees to the terms, to give my daughter in marriage to your brother."

There was a brief pause and Wulfgrim straightened up. "I wish you joy, brother," he said. "Lady, you have put the time to good use. You have obviously made my brother both well and happy." He stared at me then, and I shook my head infinitesimally, trying to pierce his mind, to pass to him the pain and longing I felt.

"Be more gracious, girl," snapped the queen. I felt my face twist, and with an effort I mumbled, "Forgive me, I wish only to give happiness." Then, under the pretext of re-stocking some bowls and clearing the more precious dishes, I excused myself and left the table.

People listened to the minstrel's song or chatted quietly in the further reaches of the hall. As for me, I escaped to my room and sat in the light of the candle, holding the smooth nugget of amber in my cold hand.

In the morning, I rose from my restless bed and went to supervise the waking of the fire and the baking of oatcakes. It was hot work at this time of year in the holy month of harvest. Offerings were made at roadside and lakeside shrines, and feasts were held, when crops were garnered. Now there was the extra preparation for a wedding feast.

I stepped outside to seek a cool breeze and, turning the corner of the building, I collided with Wulf. He flinched away from me and murmured an apology. I seized his arm.

"Lord Eni, no, Wulf, please, please." Words drowned in my throat. "I must speak to you. I have to tell you how much your gift has meant to me."

"I know exactly how much it has meant to you. Nothing. How else could you turn to Raedwald?"

"No!" I cried, and lowered my voice hastily. "This betrothal is forced upon me. How could I prevent it? I am in my father's power – he is my king, I am his daughter. This suits with Raedwald's wishes – I shall be useful to him. But he cannot truly love me. It is you I love, and I know –" I faltered. "I know that you love me."

He watched me, silently, his face losing its bitterness, but his dark eyes deep with some strong feeling.

"Come. We are too open here. We must speak." He led me quietly past the stables and into the barton, where the hay was being gathered for the livestock in winter. He pushed the door almost shut and we stood in the half-light.

"You did receive my gift, then?"

"Oh yes – Gurth served you well."

"And no-one knows?"

"No-one. Oh, I have longed for your return. I could not believe that I meant nothing to you. I have held you in my thoughts all these months."

"And I have held you, Niartha, in mine." He took me in his arms. I had never felt so warmly held. I had never been kissed so tenderly or with such urgency. I had no idea of a man's strength, and at this time, he could only guess at the power of my desire, as I clung to him. Our time would come, he said. We must wait and be careful.

Of course, I had been missed, and the queen showed her displeasure when I re-appeared, holding a basket of eggs in excuse.

"I have had Gerda searching for you. And Eadwacer, too. I have decided to move you into the larger room, just beyond mine. You need more space, and it is necessary to work swiftly on the preparations for the wedding."

"You are sure then, lady, that King Tyttla will look favourably on the match?"

She was surprised. "It is what he wanted. There is only the matter of settling the dowry. Now, make haste. Your room is being cleared."

No! The little box – where had I left it? On the bed, or had I remembered to slide it under the straw palliasse beneath the lambskin on which I lay? I hurried down the passage and met Gerda clutching a pile of bedding.

"Lady," she whispered, "it is safe. I have it here."

"What? Gerda – do you know about – ?" I stared at her. She

nodded.

"Lady, Gurth tells me things. I have kept your secret as closely as he has. You should be more careful, lady. I am not sure where Eadwacer was just now." Her eyes shifted past my shoulder and she hurried on. The steward's tread alerted me.

"Niartha, I have been seeking you. Lord Raedwald wishes to go out riding. He is going to the stables. It is his wish that you will ride with him. He met Prince Eni coming in from the fields. I believe he will join you."

"Thanks, Eadwacer. Please tell the princes that I am at the bidding of the queen at this moment. I will hope to enjoy their company another time." I almost scurried towards my new room, so relieved was I not to have been discovered.

It was an edgy, nervous, thrilling time for me. So much work had to be done. There were the usual rites of harvest, as well as extra preparations, in anticipation of King Tyttla's approval. Raedwald was enjoying himself hugely, hunting with my father and the thanes; overseeing the military training of the younger warriors of his troop and ours; riding out over the meadows, marshes and open heath with hawk and hound. Often Wulf accompanied him, but occasionally, all too rarely for me, he excused himself, or eluded an invitation.

We met in the fringes of the beech wood, with Gerda waiting at a distance, ready to warn us of any disturbance. Or in the barn at early light or after the field-work had stopped for the day. One day the king and queen took Raedwald to a holy spring some ten miles away. I pleaded that I had too much sewing to do – it was all too true! And Wulf said that he had wrenched his knee.

Gerda kept the maids busy spinning and weaving in the hall, and Eadwacer had gone with the king's retinue. For the first and only time, Wulf came to me in my room.

The lamb's fleece on which we lay naked was no softer than the touch of his lips or of his hair as it caressed my body. Now I felt his strength and reached toward it.

His hand slid over my cheek; he paused to kiss the hollow of my throat and I felt his warm breath as his hand slid onto my small breast. I almost jumped, feeling a sudden inward shuddering. It intensified as he put his mouth to my nipple. As it hardened, my legs relaxed involuntarily and I felt his manhood stiff and twitching at my thigh. I moaned and shivered as he lifted his body and let his hand caress my stomach, lower and lower, till his fingers covered my softly-furred mound, and his thumb began to rub and explore. When he lowered his mouth and began to suck me, I cried out. Waves of exquisite pleasure flooded my body and I pulled him toward me. When he thrust into my crevice, I shrieked with pain and longing. He paused again, kissed my lips repeatedly and pushed again and again. My body surged, exploded, clinging to him as he, too, swelled and came to his gushing fulfillment. When our shuddering breath eased, he covered us with the soft bearskin; its depth held our warmth. It was impossible that we could return to the cold life outside this room, this moment. But, of course, we had to stir, to pull ourselves apart, to dress, leave, go out to face the busy life of the hall and the eager accounts of the riders as they clattered in.

Raedwald was true to his word. He treated me with cheerful courtesy and took only the occasional kiss as his due. I daresay he sated his desires among the house-girls, as men do. He talked of his plans to show me to his family, and how he hoped to find lands of his own and the chance to prove himself, as his forebears had done.

Sooner than I had thought likely, my cousin returned from the east coast, laden with gifts and keen to express the gladness King Tyttla had expressed on hearing of Raedwald's readiness to marry me. He was content with the proposed dowry that came with me. He could not attend the ceremony himself, being old and crippled by a battle-wound.

It was surely at my stepmother's behest that the ceremony was so hastily arranged. It may have been only a few days, but to me it felt like only hours, as the preparations were hastened, gowns were tried on and my mother's jewels were brought out and polished. The priests gathered, bringing amulets and symbols of Freya, the goddess of love, and of various denizens of local shrines.

Guests had assembled from far and wide to honour this important, inter-tribal event. The feasting was to last for three days and most of the nights, before people returned home.

We stood in the great forecourt on a wooden dais strewn with herbs. The priests waited with offerings of wine and grain so that the gods might bless this union and make it fruitful. I felt as if it was all happening to someone else. My father placed my hand in Raedwald's and the chief priest laid a finely-woven and decorated strip of cloth over our wrists. He spoke words to the earth-mother, to grant us fertility, just as folk do on Midsummer Eve. We drank from the same golden cup. I could not see Wulf's face; indeed I dared not look at him. Under my father's proud gaze, I spoke the words that bound me to Raedwald, who told all present that this day brought great happiness to him and his people. But he never said he loved me.

He took me eagerly to bed that first night and did not seem to notice my reluctance – it would, in any case, have seemed unmaidenly to behave in any other way and he did not doubt my virginity. Finally he threw out the bawdy onlookers and seized me eagerly. When he woke early and left me after another display of passion, I lay for a while, feeling bruised and shaken, silent tears soaking my pillow. Gerda provided the necessary evidence of a blood-stained sheet to the queen. She shared my secret, yearning for Gurth to show her similar passion, but her love remained unfulfilled.

Nor, incidentally, had Wulf ever said those words directly to me, although he had shown me his love. If he had said, 'I love you', we would have broken irrevocably every bond of kinship and of duty. He could not risk the fury my father would have released on me. I knew he did not wish to sever the tie with his brother. We were held helpless like a fly in amber by the laws of family and fealty to our kings. We would leave, all three of us, for the land of the Wuffings in a few days, now that all the guests had departed. Wulf and I found just one dark afternoon to take a precious hour alone together.

Eadwacer discovered us, sitting, fully-clothed, arms around each other, on an apparently innocent heap of straw in the barn, holding hands. I was laughing at some story of the great fish that leapt and danced over the waves, when his shadow fell on us and I heard Wulf catch his breath. Nothing was said. Eadwacer looked at me, at Wulf and then back at me again. His face was stone, but his eyes blazed. Then he left us. I crumpled against Wulf's chest and he held me so tightly I could feel his heart thudding. He kissed my tear-stained cheeks.

"I love you," he said. "I always will. Remember that. Come now."

Heads turned as we walked into the hall. Voices quietened. Eadwacer, the king, the queen and Raedwald were together at the end of the high table.

What followed became a blur of words: "You see, my lord?... Brother, what have you done?...Wretched girl, you have dishonoured our people...How could you repay your father like this?"

It was Raedwald who threw me furiously at the king's feet and turned on his brother.

"You are not fit to bear our name. If ever I see you again I will kill you. I banish you in my father's name from returning to our lands. You are no longer my father's heir, I will see to that. Go now - you have two hours' start. If I catch up with you, you are dead."

As Wulf turned and bent towards me, my father's thanes intervened, swords drawn. He stood, silent, looked deep into my eyes, then stalked to the end of the hall, gathered his cloak, his shield, sword, and spear, and left, silhouetted briefly against the thin sunlight. There was silence in the hall, then Gurth walked quietly out after him. No-one moved. Then, as first one, then another stirred, we heard the clatter of hooves and they were gone. I heard Gerda sobbing quietly. I was too stunned to speak.

***

"You know all this, already," I told Eadwacer as we stood on the windy bank of the river running past the inn he had described as a hovel. "You were watching me. It was you who betrayed me."

He stood silent.

"Now you come to me from Raedwald with this so-called symbol of his so-called love." I lifted my arm and hurled the token, flower, dragon, gold, garnets and all, into the river.

7

"What you do not know," I lashed out, "because you tied yourself to Raedwald – because you did not care to face me – because my father let you go, knowing a man who could betray once could break faith again – what you do not know is what my life was like from the moment Prince Eni left."

***

It was like falling down a cliff-face. The people in the court literally turned their backs on me. It was Gerda who lifted me to my feet and we clung helplessly each to other. Raedwald and my father stood apart, voices loud and gestures furious. The prince rejected me, but it seemed that the political alliance would be honoured, provided that Raedwald persuaded his father that he should brook this insult to the honour of the Wuffings.

For himself, he said that nothing now would tie him. He planned to travel, to amass wealth and find new land. Now, he swore, he could please himself alone.

Two things he requested. He wished to reward the loyalty, as he saw it, of my father's steward, Eadwacer. Now that Gurth had shown his loyalty to Prince Eni, turned his back on this prince and chosen to follow the expelled brother, Raedwald made it clear that he expected to be allowed to take his pick. Obviously he was owed something. The king's face was grim as he faced Eadwacer; he merely gestured with a movement of his arm and the hall-thane bowed.

Raedwald turned towards me. I held out to him the brooch he had given me. He dashed it to the floor. Eadwacer bent and retrieved it. He glanced at me and, with surprise, I saw sadness in his eyes. I did not care. I had sadness of my own.

The second demand Raedwald made fixed me, rigid with fear and shock. A troop of men, good trackers, led by the king's own brother, Edgar, my uncle, should be sent out immediately to hunt down Wulfgrim. When (not if) captured, he was to be taken to a remote island, as far north as could be reached, and there exiled. He, Raedwald, would stand warrant for King Tyttla's acceptance of this measure – a strong ruler had to be prepared to uphold customary practice, even against his own kin.

He would leave it to my father, he snarled, to deal with me as he saw fit. He did not look at me again.

The queen began to ask at what hour next day he wished to leave, so that food might be readied. He cut her short, barely courteous; he and his troop, Eadwacer among them, would leave within the hour. I stood transfixed in the hubbub and upheaval of their departure.

Through the doorway the forecourt was lit by the great harvest moon. This should have been a sacred time, but I had nothing for which to thank the gods. I dared not move, dared not speak.

When the horsemen rode off, there were, indeed, a dozen of our men leading the way, weapons glinting with menace in the silver light.

As the servants finished clearing the hall table and straightening benches and stools, my father and his queen re-entered. She was as straight and icy as ever; he seemed huddled inside his cloak, though the night was mild. At his word, the queen commanded those in the hall to leave. Eyes strayed towards me, and away, as heads were averted. In seconds we were alone.

I still gripped Gerda so tightly she could not have left me, even if she had been capable. Slowly the king and queen moved down the hall. She supported him as he stepped onto the dais and sank onto his seat. Then she swung round and glared down at me. It seemed that she would speak, but found no words – she actually hissed at me.

I found a shred of courage and clung to it. "Father," I began, but indeed I had too much to say. I could not utter any regret; I could not account for my lack of shame, my love for Wulfgrim, my dread of what might happen to him. A leaden fatigue weighed upon me, and I saw it mirrored in the king. He sat there, grey with weariness and let his eyes reveal the disappointment, disgust and revulsion he felt.

The silence stretched.

He spoke to my stepmother, though his eyes were on me.

"Let her not come near me. I have no daughter. She is not to leave the homestead, but keep her out of my sight."

So it was that I never spoke to my father again, or even saw him except for occasional glimpses. I ate in my room, where I spent most of my time – my old room, as the queen had me removed from the larger one I had so reluctantly shared with Raedwald; she also withheld the linen we had been preparing for me to take with me after the wedding. I sat with Gerda in the barn, but we were forbidden to pass beyond the palisade.

Apparently we were not even expected to work alongside the other women, certainly we were not welcome when we did so. From the thanes and house-carls I did not receive even the scant courtesy I had hitherto been shown. All knew of my father's rejection and none dared to risk his wrath or the queen's biting anger. Never had I felt so isolated. If it had not been for Gerda I would have been utterly broken. It seemed very unlikely that she would now be freed. She was as unhappy as I, desperate for news of Gurth, as I for Wulf.

We comforted each other, whispering that surely Gurth would find a way, that Wulf would send another message. Our hopes were built on the fact that the hunters had not returned, nor had we heard any news of them.

But when I looked at her, I saw an image of myself: thin and pale, eyes and hair dulled with misery; suffering from lack of appetite and loss of sleep, we were desperate. Life, we came to feel as three months passed, could not be more cruel.

We were wrong.

RAEDWALD

The furious gallop past fen and over heath brought Raedwald to the purlieus of his father's kingdom. He stopped only because a horse dropped, steaming and foaming at the mouth. He left a horse-carl to watch over it with a water-skin and food for man and beast. The man was told to use his knife only to protect himself. If the horse died, then he could find his way home on foot, or be lost. Of the two, the horse was the more valuable. Pausing only to let the other horses drink, Raedwald and his troop set off again at a quieter pace.

Outriders met him as, next morning, his horse trod the marls of the shallow ford almost within sight of Rendilsham. The guards sped eagerly to meet the prince's troop, expecting a gleeful wedding throng. Their greetings died at their lips as Raedwald pushed his horse between them and rode on over the watermeadows, wordless and grim. His men followed, up into the oak trees on the slope that led to the hall of King Tyttla.

A council was called and the tale was told. Pride, and not just Raedwald's, was at stake. A few hotheads cried out for a warband, but Prince Raedwald had given his word on the alliance. Who, here, was the enemy? A silly girl, it seemed, and the prince's own brother, Eni. King Tyttla, already old and stiff in his bones, was bowed with grief at the account given of Wulf's dishonourable betrayal of his brother's trust. His heir was lost, hunted and condemned. Even in his distress, he had to admit that Raedwald had acted rightly and forcefully in defence of the honour of the Wuffings, his kin. If, as seemed likely, their dubious allies failed to deal with Eni Wulfgrim,

45

then it was for Raedwald to do as he chose.

Leaning on the stout, oak table before him, Tyttla took up a slender, ivory wand encircled, mid-length, by a gold ring on which was engraved the figure of a wolf.

"This was given to my father, King Wuffa, son of Wehha, who was the first king to rule over the East Anglian folk in Britain. It bears our emblem. It was passed to me and would have been passed to my son, Prince Eni." He paused, seeming to gather strength. "I am resolved, elders and thanes, to give this into the hand of the man who will be my heir. I name him to you. Raedwald. He has proved himself strong in battle, and able to protect the honour of the Wuffings. I say he has behaved nobly in the face of his woman's dishonour. He will be fit to rule, in his time. Will any man gainsay this?"

There was silence. All eyes were on the king and the strong figure of his son beside him. No heads turned in consultation. No eyes wavered. A roar of approval broke out. The king had turned the crisis into a triumph. Questions of loyalty, questions of power were answered.

Naturally, Tyttla commanded a feast: it was already half-prepared in anticipation of a bride's arrival, but they no longer thought of her. This was a great occasion and the Wuffings would go happily drunk to bed that night.

Before the celebrations began, Raedwald called Eadwacer to his candle-lit room. The steward had stood silently behind the men in the hall, an ungreeted stranger, waiting in case Raedwald wanted him to speak out. He was given a space for his bedroll in the guards' room and had sat there, unsure what to do. He had acted, he thought, from loyalty to his king but instead of reward had met with this sudden transferral into Raedwald's service. What did the prince want with him? Bringers of bad news were seldom commended or recompensed.

He was shocked by Raedwald's act in claiming him, and hurt that the king at Wedresfeld had let him go. As for Niartha, his misery deepened. Why should he feel guilty, when she had broken all honourable codes of behaviour? Why did he feel such pangs of remorse, as he considered what might happen to her? All her life he had watched over her, protecting and guiding her. Yet she had betrayed Raedwald, her people, and him, Eadwacer. When the house-carl came to fetch him, Eadwacer was weeping.

Raedwald saw, from the reddened eyes, that the man was in distress.

"Take heart, man," he said quietly and handed Eadwacer a horn beaker of wine, then, with a lifted finger, dismissed the man who poured it. He told Eadwacer he needed a man like him, watchful, willing to speak out. He said Eadwacer would have found no gratitude or respect in his master's hall, but that he could hope for favour and reward in Raedwald's service. In due course, said the prince, would come land, a house, women. Meantime, he needed Eadwacer to travel and to bring him information.

Eadwacer protested that he was a hall-thane unused to horsemanship, and unpractised in arms.

"There is time yet," was the reply. Eadwacer would be trained with the warriors and sent out with the guards. He would even be put on the great ships that rowed downriver to trade up and down the coast and over the eastern sea.

"I need a man of many skills, who can make his way openly, as my emissary, or unacknowledged, in secret."

"A spy, my lord?" Eadwacer was taken aback. Raedwald laughed and pushed him gently at the shoulder.

"An observer. You will report to me. Some things are for me alone. Understand?"

Eadwacer nodded and bent his knee to the ground. He took Raedwald's right hand and pressed his forehead to the back of it.

"I am your man," he said. He was still not sure of Raedwald's purpose, but now he had a path he could tread.

Raedwald smiled.

8

Weeks passed and, as usual, the months before Yule were busy, even providing work for Gerda and me. Animals were slaughtered and full use was made of the meat, the skins and the fleeces or hides, as the winter grew colder and Yule approached. At midwinter the people gathered for the celebration of the Mothers' Night, and the birth of the new year, after the shortest day had passed and the sun began to grow again.

It was a time when everyone could rest from labour, except for those who prepared the feasts and kept the fires ablaze. People sang, drank, exchanged gifts, told tales, reminisced. The old were honoured and, like the children, were happy, warm and safe from the lashing rain or flurries of snow.

I felt more lonely than ever, and it was plain to all that I had no place in these festivities. I still had heard no news of Wulf or Gurth, and those pursuing them had sent no word. Perhaps they had lost the trail? Maybe they were returning by way of the court of King Tyttla, or were following the banished men into the north? I almost hoped that Wulfgrim had reached the sea, though my heart sank at the thought of the danger of braving the icy waves as the year turned. He was skilled in navigation and read the waters and the skies, but the seas were huge and terrifyingly turbulent, he had told me, and at this season were to be feared and respected. I longed for the first signs of spring, as the dark days and long nights dragged on.

Then, early one morning just before the month of Hretha, we woke to the sound of screaming. Serfs, maids, carls, thanes tumbled from their beds, and there were cries and shrieks. Gerda came back to our room to tell me what I was beginning to guess at. My father, the king, had died in the night, with no warning of illness. The queen, unable to rouse him, became distraught.

When I approached the door of the chamber, she screeched hysterically and I was shooed away. Even when the hall-thanes took charge of the situation and a kind of orderliness was restored, I was not allowed to pay my respects, to express my sorrow. My father's body was laid on a temporary bier in a cool, dark room at the far side of the hall, guarded, and lit by flickering oil-lamps.

In the hall a meeting was held. It was vital that the king's successor should be appointed soon. He had no obvious heir. I was his only child, and a daughter did not inherit, even had I been in his favour. His brother was away in pursuit of Prince Eni, and had not been heard of for more than four months. Then the queen made her entrance. Out of deference they heard her.

It had been the king's wish that a son-in-law might succeed him, but that, she reminded them, had been undone, undermined indeed. What could be more fitting, she asked, than that they should now look to another man, high-born, experienced in war, and related to herself, their queen? Her father's lands lay beside ours to the southwest, and her brother could be here in days. He was known to them, having fought and feasted beside them in days past. It would be wise to create such a new alliance. Aescgar would surely attend his brother-in-law's funeral, and they could meet with him, before any election were made.

And so it turned out.

The rites were observed. First they buried the king in the robe he had died in, wrapped in his thick woollen cloak and laid in the wood-lined pit that would hold him for the ten days before his funeral. Messengers rode off in all directions to summon the kindred and friendly kings (but not Tyttla), while the serfs began to prepare the funeral pyre and the site of the ceremonial burial.

The queen came from a family whose forebears had once lived across the grey, eastern sea in a land far to the north and east. They still clung to some strange and fearful traditions, to judge by the talk of her maids. Not so many years ago, in the days of her grandfather's father, sacrifices were made, not just of animals, as we were accustomed to, but even of serving-girls who volunteered to join their lord in the after-world. It was the work of the woman of power in the hall to see to the death of the chosen girl and to lay her on the pyre. In the absence of an elder, this death-bringer would be the queen.

I watched as the serfs built an area like a low storage barn, of birchwood. The planking was strong enough to hold the bed, or platform, on which the king would lie, on a great, furry bear-pelt. In the space below were placed bundles of kindling, hewn trees and here the sacrificial beasts would be laid after their bloody but honourable deaths.

Gerda, with the other girls was kept busy sewing the fine, colourful clothes in which the king's body would be dressed, just after it was exhumed from its temporary grave.

The queen had the new hall-thane lay forth in the hall all the treasures and finest goods belonging to my father. She planned to divide it, according to the custom of her people, so that some went to worthy members of the family, some was used in exchange for the makings of the great funeral feasts, and some choice possessions would accompany the dead man to his after-life in the halls of the gods. A mighty bronze bowl, brought with my own dead mother as her dowry, would hold the cremated remains. This would be buried with the treasure and a great mound raised over it all. Warriors and kings would circle the mound on horseback, while the king's scop sang of his master's deeds.

On the seventh day, as the expected guests began to gather, the queen, her brother and the priests met in the hall, doors closed. I noticed that the steward was called in. At mid-day the queen called for food to be brought in. Gerda and two other girls hurried to and from the bakehouse.

I met her as she left the hall. Her face was white and her eyes wide.

"Gerda – what is the matter?"

"Oh, lady, may the gods be with you! I have heard _" she stopped suddenly, seized my hand and pulled me behind the bakehouse. "I am so afraid," she whispered. "It is the queen. She wants –" She broke down again. "She claims she has the power of the death-bringer. She says the old ways are right, and the death of a king calls for the greatest sacrifice." Gerda sank, crouching against the rough timbers of the building and I had to kneel beside her, cradling her to hear her words. "She says she will choose the girl to go with your father. Lady, she says no slave will do. It is your duty –" A shadow fell on us. It was the thane who kept the door of the hall.

"You are here then, Gerda. You would do well to keep your mouth shut. Come, Niartha. You are needed in the hall. Bring this woman with you."

I recognized one or two of the holy men, especially the one who had bound me to Raedwald. He was the chief of them. He wore a boarhide cloak and used the head to cover his own in ceremonies. He and the other men eyed me narrowly, askance, not looking me in the face.

"Girl," said the queen, "you are honoured. I have decided that you will play an honourable part in the funeral ceremony. It is the custom of my people – "

"To ask for volunteers, so that one may be selected to die, I know," I found myself retorting. "But, lady, that is not the custom here. If you take this power on yourself, you will not have the support of our people. What does the high priest say?" I turned to face him. He was not the only one staring at me in surprise, but he shuffled nervously. I went on. "We sacrifice our choicest beasts on the pyre. We offer the dead our tokens of respect, honour and love. I have here the shawl I wove for him and which he loved to wear." I could envisage it now, draped in its bright colours about his great shoulders, and I held it out for them to see. "This is for him. Not my dead body!"

The high priest spoke. "Queen, it is as I said, and the king's daughter has spoken in truth. We will split the head of the great ox. We will let the King's stallion ride with him eastwards in death, but we will not now sacrifice those who have done our king no wrong. Find us one who has betrayed him."

My heart rose at his words. I feared I had no allies, but there were nods of agreement. Then I sank again into despair.

"She has betrayed him!" Her voice was as sharp and cutting as the king's sword, lying on the table among his ceremonial pieces, awaiting their removal to the hallowed mound. "This girl was given in marriage by her father to the son of King Tyttla, but she broke her pledge, as well you know, and turned to his brother. She betrayed her husband and she betrayed her father. He rejected her."

"So he would not welcome her presence at his side in the hall of Asgard, sister." To my surprise the queen's brother, Aesgar, spoke. "Only the beloved are so embraced. And it must not be one of his blood. Remember, we lie with the chosen hall-girl before her death, to give her the joy she knew with him in life, and will again in death. This love would be incest."

The wolf-priest nodded, then lifted his hand. It held the gnarled stick of holly he used in his rites, and he pointed it at me. My spirit quailed.

"If you wish to punish this girl, queen, then banish her. Cast out of the tribe, she will be gone forever."

There was silence. Eyes turned from the queen to me and back again.

"Let it be so," she said thoughtfully. "Summon the thanes, let the company be brought into the hall. Bring the wives too, so all may hear." She turned to the priests. "You will perform the ritual immediately." Then she swung on me. "You – if it had not been for you – if Raedwald – you slut!" She screamed, "You destroyed your father!" She lashed out savagely, striking me across the face.

By this time there were many witnesses to the scene. I clutched the shawl and looked at her through unstoppable tears, both appalled and angry.

"You piece of slag! You have no place here now. Priests, do your work." At her gesture the assembly moved silently to the places appointed to them in the hall. The queen moved to the royal dais, on the centre of which stood the priests, each now in his peculiar cloak. The boar's-head stared with blank ferocity at me as the hall-thane guided me silently to the place opposite, across the low-burning hearth. Here sat normally the honoured guest at the banquets. It was also the place for those receiving justice.

The voices pronounced the words that cast me out. They were hollow, growling, beastly.

"You, Niartha, are the betrayer. You are faithless. Rejected by your husband. Denied by your father. You are cast out. No man shall house you. None here shall aid you. Depart. Be forever gone."

There was no redress. To whom could I turn? I had no rights here and none to defend me. As I stumbled blindly toward the daylight, the door-thane followed me, stony-faced. Just outside he gripped one of our men by the arm.

"Guthlac, make sure she is given a horse and guide her to the stone-way. See to it that this sneaking servant-girl goes with her."

I raised my eyes to thank him, but he swiftly turned his back.

In a daze, Gerda and I bundled up some clothes, together with the few jewels I could call my own. I tied the shawl round me, and flung on top the thickest cloak I could find. In a bag on my belt I placed some gold pieces, left behind by Raedwald, and the box Wulf had given me with the amber orb. 'Oh,' I groaned inwardly,' if there was any way I could trace you, or tell you of my leaving. How shall we ever find each other again?'

Most people edged away as we moved out through the yard. I gazed round to soak in the sights, so familiar to me. To my surprise, a few hands were extended to me, and to Gerda, too, as I discovered later, when we unwrapped a bone cup or two, a knife set in a carved antler handle, a bowl of nuts and a small sack of grain. These little acts of kindness were to give us heart in the grip of despair. In helping us, these folk risked the displeasure of the priests and of the queen.

Guthlac led out my old mare and helped first me and then Gerda onto her back. He swung our bundles behind his own saddle-bags and tied them fast. A man watched from the door of the barn where I had last sat with Wulf. The last time I had been happy. I did not remember having laughed since.

I turned my head to look once more towards the great hall. In the doorway stood the queen and her brother, motionless as stone. The roof above them glittered in the morning frost. I could see the smoke from the hearth, rising high. Work stopped in the forecourt, guards opened the heavy gates and we moved the horses forward, beyond the palisade, past the fields of livestock where the sheep awaited their lambs. The hooves rapped on the icy trackway. The beeches stood, lifting their pale, cold branches to the grey sky. There was not a breath of wind.

I had not often ridden out beyond the fields and heath surrounding the homestead. I knew the holy spring splashed up where the track met the high way, which ran northwest one way, and eastwards the other, close to the treacherous fens, where marsh-monsters dwelt, and the men, it was told, had webbed feet.

I was just opening my mouth to ask Guthlac where the nearest settlement lay, when, rounding a bend between two stands of trees, we were met by galloping horsemen. We reined in, and waited while they slowed.

"My niece!" called their leader. He was Edgar, my uncle. My blood leapt. "What are you doing here? I have news for the king."

"What news, uncle?" It came out like a whisper.

"It has been a long, difficult pursuit. We were led many miles astray, more often than once, and had a fair few fights along the road, but we took our man." I shuddered and Gerda gripped me tightly. "He is where Prince Raedwald directed, safely in exile." He seemed to remember suddenly what part I had played in this tale. "His man, Gurth, escaped, but that is no matter." Gerda's breath stirred on my cheek "Do not ride out too late," he commanded Guthlac. "There are marauders raiding from the north. We had enough trouble to evade them these past few days."

He raised his arm, and the band of horsemen cantered off. For an instant I wondered what impact his arrival would have. The thanes had not yet elected their king. It was possible that my stepmother might not get her own way.

"You should go after them, Guthlac. If you go fast you can catch up and warn my uncle what lies in wait for him."

"Lady," said the man," I have no mind to leave you. You need my arm to defend you – I have no loyalties to bind me back there." He jerked his spear backward toward the way we had come. Gerda jerked involuntarily. "We will find somewhere safe." Then he couched the spear, gathered up his reins and urged the horse forward. We followed, and the voice which I found to thank him was thick with gratitude.

WULF

I feel myself to be chained here upon this rock, bound in by the tumultuous seas, my body fettered by ice, my heart frozen.

I stand on the cliff-top; below me the waves boil over the black stones. Over my head a sea-mew calls, echo of a woman's cry. At my back, the only shelter from the slanting sleet, are the fallen, broken walls, frost-covered and hung with icicles, of an ancient tower, its occupants long gone.

Time has carried them away, like the eagle or the wolf, clutching its prey, and bearing them off into the darkness. I stare out into the gathering night, huddled against the north wind, below the crumbling rampart of the men who dared to build in stone, and feel myself as powerless as they to resist cruel fate.

I am weary to the innermost reaches of my being, I who have fought the icy rollers of mid-ocean, now brought to my knees, exhausted by long pursuit and by bitter grief.

Shall I ever again find welcome in the halls of my kinsmen? Shall I ever again speak to the king, my father?

And for the woman I love – I cannot yet bear to think of her, to remember...

I lift my face to the leaden sky and let the snow fall onto my tears. A sea-eagle swoops through the mirk and surges, uplifted on his lonely path over the watery desolation. Carry my spirit with you, brave bird, as you journey into the unknown.

9

When we came to the shrine by the spring it was growing dark and Guthlac suggested we spend the night in the little, reed-thatched shelter provided for visitors, beside the priest's dwelling. He was not there, of course, still in attendance for the king's funeral.

We lit a fire, ate some wheat cakes, drank a little mead and arranged blankets for bedding. I fell asleep, too tired to think, but woke before daylight and then thoughts crowded in upon me. I would have to find a way to the north, through the land of the Mercians – long enemies to my people, but perhaps now, not to me – I was harmless to them. I must find Wulf, and Gerda longed for news of Gurth.

Except in tales told by poets and singers, I had no experience of life outside the shelter of the homestead; Gerda had little more, though she had come from the fenland to the north. Much would depend on Guthlac, who had, after all, accompanied my father on hunting expeditions and to visit neighbouring homesteads.

We set off at first light, at first towards the highway leading to the northwest. Guthlac thought it safer to travel towards the Granta crossing, and then to choose between less-trodden paths, if any there were, or even to beg passage on a ship, if we came to the coast.

Soon we found out why men preferred not to travel during these, the wettest months, the dykes filling with rain and the wind whirling, usually from the north. I longed for the cold, dry wind from the east, which would herald spring, but that would not blow for several weeks.

Only a few shepherds and cattle-guards watched us pass. Dwellers on this road were used to travellers, though we were wary. We were given shelter in a byre or barn once or twice. One night we hung a skin over some branches, bent and pegged into the soil, and lay on other skins, close to each other, hunched under cloaks and the blankets we had each brought.

We had come to one hamlet where a woman actually gave us some stew, a place at her hearth, and let us have some bread, cheese, dried fruit and nuts to take on our way. She said my father had given protection to her people and that her husband – away charcoal-burning in the woods – had honoured him. She grieved to hear of his death.

"What will happen now?" she asked. "Who is the new king?"

I could not tell her, not knowing if it would be my uncle or the queen's brother. I told her that I was travelling in search of someone who had left the court, and she did not pry further.

Warmed and restored, we pressed on further the next day, until we were halted by a river, too deep and strong after the rains for our horses to cross, as they had done lesser streams.

"The Great Ouse," said Guthlac. "Beyond, there are wide fens, but also some wooded ground, a good place to hide in, and we should be able to track across it, with care."

The night was dry, for a change, and frosty. We sheltered on the bank of the river, after placing an offering of food to placate the powerful water-god. We found a great oak, so old its trunk was riven into a kind of cave. With this as a cover, and a fire before us, we were content.

"Tomorrow," I told Gerda, "we shall search for a crossing."

"If not," said Guthlac, "I will cut some timber and make a punt or a raft. I can get us across, and the horses, even if it takes several trips."

Next morning Gerda and I took advantage of a bright day to wash linen and hang it on branches to dry. We bathed ourselves gingerly at the edge of the biting cold water, and rinsed and washed our hair, taking turns to comb and braid.

When Guthlac returned, disheartened after a fruitless search for a crossing-place, we cheered him with some broth made from roots and herbs stewed on the fire, and a hare caught in a snare he had laid overnight.

I felt quite happy to stay here another night or two. We were a distance from the trackway, as comfortable as possible, and Guthlac needed time to fell some slender trees and fashion the wooden pins to hold them together, lashing them tight with strips of leather cut from our precious hides.

He worked hard for two days, and we helped him, struggling to strip bark and twigs, snapping stiff pegs with our cold fingers, dipping the thongs in water and rubbing them, stretching them to make them flexible. We even enjoyed ourselves; it felt good to be working together. We sang a little, and remembered odd riddles. After supper we sat in firelight, falling quiet, tired in body, but hopeful of crossing the river next day.

The horses were nervous and had to be forced onto our craft; one crossed with Gerda, as Guthlac heaved on a punt-pole cut from an ash-tree. It was a struggle, and they landed quite a distance downstream from where I stood, anxiously watching, but they were on the further bank. I moved along, to meet Guthlac on his return, and he took me across, with my mare twitching and tossing her head, and my feet slipping on the wet branches. Then he had to return for our baggage.

I still wake, thrashing and sweating, as my mind pictures what happened next. A group of about half a dozen men on horseback, not warriors, but armed with sticks and knives, rode out from the trees, which screened us from the track. Seeing a man laden with baggage, alone, they wheeled round to encircle him and closed in. Guthlac hurled the bundles onto the raft and flung himself toward it.

He slipped on the mud and sprawled, as the raft slid out into the current and was quickly snatched into its flow.

We screamed, helplessly, as the band set about him. Before he could stand, or grip a weapon, they stabbed and beat him again and again. Then they kicked him over onto his back and searched him, before pitching him into the river. His body floated for a few moments and was lost, floating downstream, towards the next bend in the river.

For a terrifying moment we thought the marauders would attempt the crossing, but they thought better of it, satisfying themselves with crude yells and gestures. Then they rode off.

Gerda and I stared at each other, sobbing wildly. Then she collected herself and pushed me into action.

"We must leave here, lady. It is not safe. Let's go downstream a little. We may find the raft."

And we did. The eddies had swirled it across a bend in the river and beached it on a shallow bank of gravel. The bundles, though wet and partly spilled open, lay where Guthlac had thrown them. His spear lay on the logs, and the punt-pole.

We had a choice now, whether to load things onto the two horses and press on into the unknown paths of the forest, or attempt to reboard our craft and take the river, so fast-flowing. Crazy with fear and shock, we chose the second option. We dragged the horses to the water's edge, but they baulked and refused to step onto the flimsy raft.

"Perhaps," I said, "if we tie them to the boat, they will swim." Wulf had told me how he had done this once, ship-wrecked in a narrow channel, and he and his horse had survived, as he clung to the planks of his broken ship.

We laid hides across the raft, rolled the bundles up properly and tied them onto the rough spikes left at the edge of the clumsy platform. Then, using the spear and the pole, we held the raft at the edge of the current, walked the horses to one end and tied their reins to thongs, lashed at the rear corners. It took much pushing and pulling and we were soaked through, but the river did the rest. Once the horses were pulled to chest height, they seemed to yield, and surged through the water after us. Round the bend, the stream widened and the current was less powerful. After some toil, we learnt to keep the contraption more or less in the middle of the river. However, even horses could not withstand the cold for too long and when they seemed to flag with exhaustion, we turned into the north bank once more.

We had not eaten since dawn, and did not know what state our small store of food was in. We landed at a flat stretch of ground, rather too open, but at least we would see anyone approaching. Now we needed shelter. The skies grew louring as the afternoon sun waned. I spotted a fallen alder, its root base exposed, like some great hairy wall.

"Gerda! Help me!" We tethered the horses loosely to graze beside the tree trunk, dropped our bundles by the big bole and then fought and wrestled the raft up onto the slope.

It took all our strength, and the use of Guthlac's horse to heave it to the point where we could tilt it up until it fell against the root base. Once the sodden hides were flung over the gap on the north side, we had a shelter.

Our half-used sack of grain was now wet, but if we mixed it with a little of the precious honey Guthlac had brought, it could be palatable. Gerda eventually managed to kindle a fire, but her teeth were chattering in spite of the effort. I laid the cakes to cook at the fire and, filling the cups with water from the river, put them to warm a little, too. If our herbs were not ruined, they would give some flavour. Then we held up a blanket, as wet as our clothes, to dry them as best we could. The musty steam rose and as the sky grew black, we managed to get them to the point of being damp, rather than wet. It would have to do.

The horses, too, would have to take their chance tonight: we had no dry cloths to cover their backs. At least the great tree would give them some shelter. We hooked everything up to dry on the roots at one side of our makeshift cave. We could not even find dry, fallen leaves as this time of year, but there were a few usable fronds of bracken for the floor. Our hands were sore and we throbbed with fatigue as we sank onto the damp blankets, turned our faces to the fire and ate and drank our meagre supper. We put outside an oatcake and a bowl of wine for the gods of the place. We needed their protection.

We debated the wisdom of showing a fire, but fear of animals, night-spirits and dread of the increasing cold decided us. We stoked up the flames and banked the fire with turf slashed with the blunt knife and our last strength.

We lay down, clasping each other for warmth and hoped for rest. Guthlac's death came between us and sleep and we whispered in horror about the way he had been killed and now lay unburied, for the crows and foxes, or was swept downriver, lost forever. We did not know if the men were raiders from Mercia or local robbers. I had never seen a man die before. He would not be the last.

We begged whichever gods inhabited this place to keep us safe.

We uttered the names of Gurth and of Wulfgrim, too tired to speak again of our fears for them, our love for them. In my hand I cradled the treasured piece of amber. I knew that Gerda had a little carved figure of a deer, given her by Gurth, strung as a pendant on a narrow thong, and kept close at her breast. She held it now. Gradually we fell silent and our breathing eased.

Neither of us could face the water again next day. There was a bone-chilling drizzle falling, so we carefully rewrapped our possessions, trying to keep the driest items under cover. We filled our water-bottles, finished the last cakes and led the horses to drink, before loading them.

"Lady," said Gerda, "I cannot ride alone." I stared at her in dismay. Of course she couldn't. How should a bondwoman learn to ride a horse? But we needed to move along.

"I will lead the way – we need not go faster than a trot in any case, or the horses will tire." I tied a long strand to her bridle and helped her up onto my steady mare, passing some baggage rolls for her to fasten on.

Then I tied the rest to Guthlac's horse and looked round to see if we had left anything behind. His spear leant against the tilted punt, so I took it, used it to help me as I employed the tree-trunk as a mounting-block, and couched it under my right arm, as I had often seen the hunters do.

At first we made good headway, going first over grassland, then through the thin spread of trees, which had stretched beside us ever since we crossed the Ouse. We stopped when we were hungry and ate the last of our cheese and dried fruit, before moving on.

But I was becoming increasingly concerned about Gerda. She was quiet, hunched over her horse's neck, and when I helped her down to drink at a stream, she was hot and flushed. She sat with her head in her hands and when I asked her how she felt, she shook her head silently. Then she vomited helplessly.

I was terrified. We had only the shelter of some scrubby birch trees – the track ahead seemed to pass between reeds. A track! We must have reached fenland.

"Gerda, stay here. I will ride ahead a little way and see if there is any habitation. No – I will be careful. I shall not go far. Just wait." She sank down.

I did not have far to go. The track led over a rise in the ground to a junction, where it was crossed by a small hollow-way. Ahead lay a reed-edged mere. To the left there was a wisp of smoke from a small, round, thatched building. I pulled my horse round and cantered back to Gerda.

She roused herself as I returned and I helped her to rise, hoisted her onto the mare and begged her to hold on. Then I walked between the horses, leading both animals by the head, and so came to the door.

Obviously our movements were heard, even on this soft ground. The hide curtain at the outer door was jerked open, and a grey-haired man looked out. He swore in surprise and then moved to help me as I supported Gerda.

"Best get her inside out of this foul mist. Here – come back for your stuff." He began to drop the bundles to the ground. "I will see to the horses." He nodded towards a lean-to structure against a rough palisade.

Thankfully, I half-dragged my companion through the tiny entry and into the house. A fire burnt in the central hearth, there were bedding areas at one side, and an eating space.

"Rest, Gerda," I said and went to fetch our goods.

For now, we had found shelter and hospitality. The gods here were merciful, it seemed. I had not, even then, learnt to distrust the gods.

10

The householder's name, he said, was Hardric. I told him that we had escaped from bandits, describing how our escort had been murdered. Hardric, a scruffy, grey-haired man, lived alone, since his wife had died shortly before Yuletide.

He gruffly accepted a piece of gold, though I could not imagine what use he would make of it, unless he found a smith willing to barter something for it. He gave us some hot food and mead to drink, though Gerda lay, almost inert, swallowed a few mouthfuls and sank back.

Tired though I was, I stayed beside her that night, wiping her forehead with a damp cloth, helping her to sip a little water, but by dawn she was delirious, calling out incoherently and shuddering with fever. Hardric showed me where his wife had stored herbs in clay jars, and I tried to remember all I had ever learnt about making medicinal draughts. I snatched mouthfuls of cheese, meat and bread, which he passed silently to me from his stool by the hearth. I left Gerda's side only to visit the edge of the midden, a few yards from the house, and to check that the horses were dry, fed and watered. I saw that Hardric had groomed them, and thanked him for this when I re-entered.

When the day turned black and the shadows flickered around me as I moved, Gerda fell silent, though her breathing rasped. I hoped she was sleeping, and bent to pull a blanket closer. She opened her eyes, dull and sunken in her white face.

"Princess." Her voice was a whisper. " I am sorry."

"Oh, Gerda, you have nothing to be sorry for. Sleep now." "No!" In spite of her weakness she was urgent. "Tell Gurth – you will – I beg – tell Gurth, I –" She could not manage any more.

"I promise," I said. "I will find them both. I will tell him." I gripped her hand, trying to give her some strength. She lay still, eyes closed, but her face relaxed and I knew she trusted me to keep my word.

I sat watching as she heaved for breath. Late into the night I found myself slumped at her side, but the hand I clasped was icy cold. My brave and loyal friend was dead. I wept, helplessly, but tried to muffle my sobs as Hardric was sleeping on the other side of the hearth. I could not face the association of a stranger then, and a man at that.

I kept a silent vigil until dawn; then I arranged Gerda's body and wrapped her linen around it. I took from her the only possession she valued, a little amulet in the form of a deer, carved in horn, which Gurth had given her. Somehow, I vowed silently, I would find Gurth, if he was still alive, and return it to him. But I had no idea how I was going to fulfil my promise.

Hardric, taciturn as ever, nodded when I indicated the silent, shrouded figure of my companion. He took a mattock from its place at the wall, shrugged on a leather jerkin and hood, pulled on some boots and withdrew.

When he eventually returned, his head and shoulders were sprinkled with snow, and he stamped his feet at the entry. "Come," he said. I swathed myself in shawl and cloak, but my feet were too scantily shod for snow. He picked up a pair of beaver-skin boots from a dark, shadowy place near the curved wall – his wife's, he said. I accepted them and took a deep breath as he bent and lifted Gerda's body and carried it outside.

I followed him, stepping in his tracks as he plodded round the back of his house, past the lean-to, through a gap in his broken-down fence of woven reeds, onto a small footpath made of willow hurdles, running round the grey mere. He had dug a hole in the muddy grass of what seemed like a small paddock. Still bare of turf since his wife's burial some two months before, lay another grave, just a small pile sprinkled with snow.

Now he knelt and stretched out to lay Gerda, quite gently, into the ground. He lifted a little shovel to begin scraping the earth over her, but I stopped him with a cry.

"What are the gods of this place?" I asked him. "We must invoke their favour. Let me fetch something for her." He nodded, and I went back to the house, searched hastily in our packs and came up with her comb, a cup and the small knife with the antler handle. I filled the cup with mead, broke a corner of bread from the flat loaf by the fire, and took the knife.

I laid them on her body and, on my knees in the snow, listened as Hardric named the gods of the place, so strange to me. I begged my favourite goddesses, Nerthus (my namesake), Freya and Eostre, to take Gerda's spirit into their care, and sprinkled the first handful of wet earth onto the grave. I watched as Hardric began to fill the little hollow, and the shape blurred. Then I turned and went back into the house. I changed into drier, cleaner garments, putting the old ones aside to attend to later. Then I cast myself upon the bed and sank into an exhausted sleep, too far gone to weep more.

Hardric let me lie there for a good seven hours before nudging me awake and proffering a bowl of broth, and, to my surprise, a cup containing wine. Much restored, I thanked him. "However did you come by wine?" I asked him.

"Travellers," came the reply. The little track we had found was actually quite a useful route through the fens, leading from a hamlet beside the river, past the mere, and eventually curving from a westerly to a northerly direction. It was, he said, a good route for people wanting to avoid trouble.

"What do you mean?"

"It does not go too near any of the main strongholds, and is never that far from the sea. You can hide in the fens, if you know them."

I sat, supping the broth. How could I go on now? A woman rarely alone, and certainly never unattended, I realised suddenly how vulnerable I was.

"You'll be staying here awhile then," Hardric pronounced

I looked at him cautiously.

"The snow. It won't go yet. While it lies, there's more to come."

"I should be glad to shelter here till the ways are passable, " I said. "I am grateful."

"That girl," he grunted. "She called you princess...." His eyes watched me from under grey, bushy brows.

"That is her pet-name for me. Was. My name is - Eadwine."

"I wondered, see," he said. "You talk like a fine lady, but you don't look like one, for sure." I did not reply.

"Can you cook and clean?"

"I can. I can also sew and mend. I will make myself useful until I can leave here."

"That's all right, then."

I tidied the packs to one side, determining to wash my linen as soon as possible. I wiped the wooden trenchers and rinsed the cups in melted snow. I swept morsels from the floor and fed the fire from the logs Hardric stacked by the entrance. He tended the horses and the hens and goats he kept in a small pen. He handed me a lanthorn when I went outside, and when he left in his turn, I hastily changed my shift, wrapped my shawl tight and slid into the bed where Gerda had lain.

I gazed into the firelight, and then, when the householder re-entered, I turned away, covered my head and sank towards sleep. Several times I awoke, startled from dreams. Guthlac turned into Gurth; I felt Wulf's kisses, but woke, shivering at Raedwald's touch. Hardric snored and rustled on his creaking pallet

So I got through the days and nights of this existence until, after about three weeks, the snow disappeared, aconites clustered at the foot of the fence, and the earliest hazel-catkins showed beside the track. Willows at the edge of the mere pushed open buds of silver fur. The wind from the north dropped and we had a couple of still days with a few shafts of pale sunlight. Hardric worked doggedly outside, trying to clear slush and mud from the path to his door. One of the goats produced twin kids and he let me play with them as he tossed them hay, and gave me baskets of grain for the hens. I cooked. We ate well: fish from the mere, a hare, once, even some smoked venison, though this was rather tough.

He remained terse, usually silent. At night he sat, sometimes whittling some unidentifiable object, often just staring at the fire, hunched on his stool. I was thankful. I did not wish to encourage any close association. I felt sympathy for his bereavement, being bereft myself, but did not care to share my own unhappiness or fears.

I did find out that the mere was, not surprisingly, a holy place. No priest lived here, but they came to perform the appropriate seasonal rites, and Hardric was rewarded by gifts of food and timber for his unofficial role as guardian of the place. It was apparently well-known in the fens, and in the spring, the fen-dwellers would pause and make offerings to the gods. Into the water they let fall objects of personal value, or sometimes things of great worth. Some sought protection from harm, others revenge; they begged for relief from disease, or they cursed their enemies. No wonder the mere was so often covered with a miasma, yellowish in tinge, and pungent. The air was full of prayers already, and the next festival would soon come.

Spring. My heart lifted at the very thought. Perhaps I could make a move. If a group of people came through, maybe I could join them. The path, Hardric had said, did eventually lead to the north.

At last, early in the month of the goddess Eostre, the wind sprang up again, cold and dry from the east. I had led the two horses out to the paddock, in the corner of which Hardric's wife, Elsa, lay, with Gerda next to her. Primroses grew in a shallow ditch at the verge of the little open patch and after pegging the long reins, I gathered a bunch and scattered them over the graves.

As I stood there, I heard the sound of voices calling and the thud of hooves on the ground. I ran round to the front of the house and came up to the track where Hardric stood, staff in hand. There were about nine men, four on horseback, and the rest tugging at a string of sturdy ponies, loaded with baskets, sacks and bales.

They wished to know how far it was to the river, hoping, they said, to take boats to the harbour downstream. Faced with a further two or three hours' riding, they opted to pause here.

"Woman!" called Hardric. He usually addressed me thus, and I did not mind, content that it avoided the intimacy of using what he thought was my name. "Fetch out the jug of ale, and see if the dough is risen yet. Come in, my masters, and rest out of the wind."

The leader dismounted and the horsemen followed him inside, leaving the carls to mind the animals. I handed out the ale, set out the warm rolls of bread, cut meats and flat, honey biscuits. I left them passing news, and went outside with a jug and basket of food for the men, passing down the line of animals to the last one. This man squatted by the fence. I held out some food and he looked up.

It was Gurth.

71

11

I staggered.

"Princess!" He stared at me blankly, then rose to his feet. "No – be careful. Those men are from Mercia. They must not know who we are." Certainly, he was barely recognizable, dressed in rough clothing, and filthy dirty. No longer a proud thane, he was a fine example of a lowly horseman. "When we reach the river, I will find a way to escape upstream or into the trees over yonder. Wait here – is it possible?" I nodded. "When I come back I will tell you everything – and you can tell me – ssh!"

The troop was re-forming. I passed him the jug and more food and he gulped hastily.

"I will come at night, maybe tonight, maybe tomorrow. Wait for me." He plodded off, stick in hand, at the rear.

In a daze, my blood thudding, I set about the trivial household tasks. Hardric told me it would be as well to have extra food available now that the pathway was open again. Soon it would be the month of Eostre, and folk would come to make offerings at the mere.

In the end, it was the third night before Gurth came. I was not asleep, though Hardric was. The low flames on the hearth flickered in the sudden draught as the hide at the door entry was carefully pushed open. I started up and he gestured to me silently.

We crept outside and down the tiny track towards the mere, pushed ourselves into a space in the reeds, and sat out of sight and earshot. In low, eager tones, we poured out our tales. A sliver of moon cut the black sky above our heads and clouds scudded across.

I told him what little I knew of Wulgrim's capture. He described the false trails they had laid, and the lies they had told to put the hunters off the scent. For weeks they had moved on, hidden for a time, then moved again, with several narrow escapes.. He told me how he, by himself, had evaded the hunting party and then tracked them to the point where Wulf had been forced into a boat and trapped on a tiny islet, far to the north. When he realised that he could not reach his master, he set off on the long and dangerous journey south, hoping to find some support and help in a rescue attempt, if not from Raedwald, at least from the princes' father, King Tyttla. Only later would we find out that no help would come from there. Gurth had apparently pretended to be a swineherd, a shepherd and most recently a horseman, and to safeguard his disguise he was acting as a serf to the trader I had seen. If unsuccessful at his own court, he was planning to seek aid from my father.

Then I had to tell him my story and watch the incredulity, and sadness on his face as I did so. From round my neck I slid the narrow thong and pressed into his fingers the carved deer he had given to Gerda. He sat there, shook his head a little, and then passed the thong over his own neck and thrust it into the top of his tunic.

"Are you safe here?" he asked after a few minutes.

"I think so – but surely, now – Gurth, please, do not leave me!" My voice rose.

"Hush! Think, princess. I cannot take you to Raedwald or his family, nor can you go home." He thought. "I must go back north. It will take some time, but I think I may find friendly faces further north still, beyond the River Tweed. If I can persuade even a handful of men to follow me, I think I could rescue Prince Eni. I will bring you to him, as soon as I can. You must be patient, but we shall find him, I know it. He so often spoke of you, and with love."

We argued in whispers, but no pleas or tears would shake him. It was hard enough for him, trained hunter and hardy warrior to pass through hostile lands alone. With me, the risk would be redoubled. I would have to be patient and cling to what courage I had. I gave him some of the pieces of gold Gerda had managed to pack away for me before we left; it would help to pay his way. To my astonishment, he pulled me to his great chest and embraced me. As we had agreed, I silently showed him where Guthlac's horse was stabled and he led it quietly away into the darkness.

Hardric stirred as I came back inside and I pretended to have an ache in my belly.

I lay down. If I could only struggle through the days of this mean existence. Mean! Only now can I laugh, for I little knew then just how grim the struggles would be, nor how low I would be forced to sink.

But at least I had kept my word to Gerda, and now I had regained some hope.

I had to pretend that the horse had been stolen – perhaps that was what had roused me last night, I suggested.

Hardric was not convinced. Why would a thief not take both horses? He spent some time roaming to and fro but found no clear signs.

For several days I maintained the routine which kept me busy, pre-occupied against any further familiarity than the sharing of meals.

As the days warmed, in spite of the prevalent easterly breeze, the trackway outside grew busier. Often, if not daily, people trundled by, walking, or trailing their belongings and children in a rough, wooden cart, and I was glad to speak to another woman, even though she took it for granted that I was Hardric's wife. Late one afternoon, a trio of men drew up and very gladly accepted Hardric's offer of drink. They ended up staying the night, bedding down on the floor and calling ribald remarks when they noticed me moving to my place as far away from the rowdy group as I could.

"What, man? Has there been a quarrel, then? Never let a woman get the better of you!"

"She's too pretty a lass to let her go lonely to her bed!"

I waited for him to put them right but, to my surprise and relief, he did not. If they thought I was free for the taking, the gods knew what could happen.

They left in the morning, as vulgarly cheerful as before, heading for the river to seek their fortunes on the water. I had listened to their news, but among the folk they had encountered, I found no sign of Gurth. I sighed and bent my back to the linen-basket.

"Well, now," came the gruff voice. "Maybe there is something in this. Perhaps I've been blind – that's it – blind."

I went on wringing out the cold water and lifting one of his tunics onto the fence to dry. Then he grabbed my shoulder, twisted me round to face him and pinched my chin in his rough fingers. I squirmed.

"Let me go!"

"Well, now," he repeated. "That's the whole question, isn't it? Let you go? And just where will you go? And who is there to go with you?" He relaxed his grip, but blocked my way, as I stood with the fence behind me. "You and me, we get on just fine, I'd say. We do well together, and I've missed the company of a woman."

I clutched my shawl round me, crossing my arms, and glowered at him.

"Let me pass!"

"Oh, that I will. But let us see how we fare when we sit and chat at the fireside tonight. We can be more friendly-like." Chat? We had never chatted.

I collected my wits. It would not do to confront him – he was too big and strong and I dared not provoke him. I managed a slight nod and made shift to pass him, when he clutched me and brought his lips down onto mine. One arm held me to him, the other cupped my breast.

"Oh, yes, pretty lady, you will suit me well. I have hopes of making something of this place – maybe an inn, and get one of those priests to set up and make a proper shrine. Folk like to be given a warm welcome, and you cook a treat." He chuckled and forced another bristly kiss, hurting my mouth, and squeezed himself against my body. He went off, whistling, and paused only to collect some ash-poles and his mallet. I could hear him as he hammered and sang.

I had no option. I had to get away. I felt sick to the stomach at the thought of subjecting myself to this crude clod of a man. Better to brave the way, if you could give that name to the muddy bridlepath through the fen. At least I could hide in the reeds, I thought.

Now – it had to be now, while he was busy working out of sight. Indoors, I hastily rolled up my garments, my few treasures, including the box with the amber nugget, seized some food, bottles of mead, a flagon of water, a knife, a cup. I rolled up two bundles in blankets and pieces of hide. Then I stepped cautiously round to the lean-to shed. I harnessed my mare and tied the bundles to the saddle, as

Guthlac had done.

I was just in time. I could hear Hardric's discordant voice, less distant. I urged the mare up the footpath and turned her onto the trackway, just as he rounded the back of the house.

He let out a yell and dropped his hammer. My last glimpse was of waving fists and an angry, red face, but I was free of him and set off at a trot, lengthening my stride to a canter, as my courage grew.

EADWACER

After half a year of practising sword-skills and horse management, Eadwacer stood once again before the prince. This time he held his head high, his body was muscular and trim and his eyes shone eagerly, as Raedwald told him he was being sent as emissary to the court of his former master. Word had come that there was a new lord at Wedresfeld.

Eadwacer was to carry greetings from Rendilsham and ensure that the alliance held. It was obvious that Tyttla was failing, and Raedwald needed to strengthen his position. That was the public face of Eadwacer's mission.

It was Raedwald's intention, and Eadwacer's too, to find out what had happened to the king's daughter. All they knew was that she had 'gone'. Had she fled in pursuit of Wulf? Was she married to another? If so, this was unlawful, as Raedwald had rejected her but had not gone through a formal ceremony of divorcement. To Raedwald, she was unfinished business, to be dealt with. Eadwacer's feelings were ambivalent: he was torn between contempt for her fickleness and the pricking memory of her sweet young face, her sweet young body. All the girls he had taken to his bed were young and golden-haired, but none brought him ease.

"When you have done your business at the court," Raedwald told him, "then go and search for her. Do not let her see you. Find out what you can and bring me word yourself."

As both Raedwald and Eadwacer had expected, the queen ensured that the former hall-thane had a cool greeting. In the name of hospitality, he and his small group were welcomed in the hall, fed and listened to. Courteous messages were passed to King Tyttla and, of course, his son. The queen's brother, now King Aescgar, followed her lead, and the thanes, many of them Eadwacer's former companions, took care not to appear overly cordial.

Nevertheless, on his way to the guest-chamber that night, Eadwacer encountered Niartha's uncle, Edgar, and the door-thane of the hall. They moved quietly into his room and all three sat, closely huddled, to talk in low murmurs.

Eadwacer learnt of the death of his king, the casting out of the princess. The thanes told him of sending Guthlac and Gerda with her, and when he heard that the horse-carl had not returned, Eadwacer's hopes lifted of her safety. The older man described their arduous and dangerous search for Eni and Gurth, how he was captured and marooned on a tiny islet at the mouth of the river Cocket, far to the north. Gurth was free, but hardly presented a problem. He was probably in the hands of some hostile tribe, or dead.

In turn, he told them that Tyttla's weakness meant that Raedwald must soon inherit the Wuffing lands. When he was appointed king, they would meet at the great feast and could confer again. Neither man was content with his lot under the new regime and Eadwacer had hopes of bringing them, and whatever faction they gathered, under Raedwald's hand.

Next day he set off, with a barely ceremonial leave-taking, and was escorted to the boundary of the land. He rode east until they could see him and his troop no more.

Pretending that he had a relative to visit nearby, he sent his retinue back to the Wuffing court, keeping only one lad to mind his horse.

He wheeled round to return to the shrine at the crossroads and took the trade path toward the Granta crossing. In due course he arrived at the charcoal-burner's house. The wife was very pleased to help, and willingly directed him. Eadwacer hastened on.

At the great river he paused and hunted up and down. In spite of all the time that had passed, he found telltale signs of a fire, but only when he walked along the river-bank downstream did he find the gruesome remains of a man, beached on a bend in the river, under the overhanging bank. It was unidentifiable, of course, bones, cloth, skin in parts, and beneath the hood some hair, all sodden and muddied. In frustration he kicked at it, and then he saw the belt. The simple buckle had a horse scratched on it. Such a one Guthlac wore. It had to be him. Eadwacer gazed at the corpse and frowned. Then he drew his knife and called the boy to help him. They cut turfs from the grass margin and after scooping up as much mud as they could to cover Guthlac, they laid the turfs over him so that the earth-mother or the river-god could take him. Only then did he realize that Guthlac must have died in defence of Niartha and her woman.

There was no way, he thought, that the women could have crossed the swift-flowing river. To go east would have brought them too near the lands of her kin, or of Raedwald's. They must have gone south; always supposing they had not been drowned, or taken as slaves by whoever had killed the horse-carl. He would travel south for some days, before returning to the prince with such news as he had.

12

Only when twilight deepened did I stop. I led the mare to a small birch copse away to one side of the track, stepping carefully over the marshy ground, glad to find it dry and firm among the trees. I let her drink at a little pool and pulled some grass for her, encouraging her to crop for herself, tethered to a slender alder trunk. I pulled undergrowth into a sort of mat and laid one of my hides upon it. I dared not make a fire, not sure how safely I was hidden from anyone on the marsh path, though I had seen no-one the whole afternoon. I was afraid Hardric might have raised a pursuit, but guessed he was frustrated in his isolated hut.

I was hungry, and stuffed meat into my mouth and swallowed gulps of water. It tasted clean, but I did not know how long it would stay sweet. I kept the mead for later. Then I lay down, pulling blankets and the other hide over me and hoped it would not rain.

I lay, gazing at the moon, glad of its light. Darkness would have been terrifying in such a place. Tales of marsh-monsters had always sent me quaking to my bed. I wondered if Gurth had ridden far enough yet to reach what might be friendly territory. I had no idea how many days or nights it could take him to ride there, evading capture, finding new allies. Then, with a shock, I wondered how he would ever find me.

At last I let myself think of Wulf. I pictured him, not on some lonely, frozen crag in a wilderness of sea, but cradling me, warm in the sweet-smelling hay, or in the thick fur of our bed. I ached for him, and at first I cried. Then I flung myself on my back. If I gave in to self-pity and weakness, how could I hope to survive, find him again? I had to be strong, if I was to face up to the dangers of my lonely road. I had never actually been alone before, although loneliness I had certainly known.

I did sleep, but as soon as the sky lightened, I packed up and left. Twice that day I heard voices and left the track, standing deep in the reeds, hoping that the mare would make no sound. One group was walking from the west and I let them pass before moving on. I only just managed to hide behind a bank where the path had been cut deep, as two men galloped up from the east, behind me. I dared not ride too fast, as I feared to come upon trouble round the bends in the path. This, itself, was invisible in places, and the track, often water-logged, was treacherous. I let the horse have its head, trusting it to find safe footing. Not long after that I stopped again for the night.

Soon I would need more food, clean water, shelter from the showers, which I could see slanting from the clouds around me. The hides protected me from the worst of the rain that night, but it was not comfortable to ride, relatively unprotected, except for my cloak. At about mid-day on the third day of my ride, after crossing a river with some trepidation, I drew to a halt. On a wide knoll, I saw a cluster of thatched houses, surrounded by a palisade, much like the homestead of my people, but smaller and possessing no great hall.

I took a deep breath, flicked the reins and walked the mare toward the gate. A few small boys ran into the compound, shouting, and some people came out of their houses and moved towards me. They did not seem to be hostile – rather, wary.

I greeted them and slid to the ground. I managed a smile.

"May I ask for shelter and some food? I have journeyed many miles."

"Tell us who you are." A gruff-voiced woman. I had thought up a credible tale, I hoped.

"My husband has died. He was drowned in the river. Not this one, nearby – the Ouse. I must return to my father's home. That lies to the west."

"Then you have been this way before." Still suspicious.

"No," I said confidently. "My husband brought me by the great stone-way to the west, beyond those hills." Thank the gods I had listened to the wayside chatter at Hardric's house. "My name," I stated, "is Eadwine."

"Come then." The crowd parted and let me through. A man took the horse and tied her to a post beside a wooden trough of water. He unhooked a net of hay and dropped it at her feet. I thanked him and followed his wife inside.

It was good to sit and eat. She was hospitable enough in her dour way, and when I offered her a little shell necklace to barter for food, she accepted. I was allowed to spend a quiet, cosy night at their hearth, watching the children playing. People came in and out, making various excuses to meet this stranger.

"Why are you not attended? No man, no girl to ride with you?" I told them the manservant had been murdered. For all she knew, I was a bondwoman myself, though she had seen me on horseback. She never dreamed that I came from the great court of her people's enemy.

"Is anyone likely to be travelling to the west from here?" I asked. They glanced one to another, but shook their heads.

"We expect the holy man to return from the mere to the east soon," said one man. I remembered the group moving east, from whom I had first hidden.

Even if they stayed beside the mere for two nights, they could be here in no more than four days, and would have listened to Hardric's tale of a runaway wife, I had no doubt. I had to leave the next morning. But I said no more. I did not want to meet up with this priest. Such a man would be too knowing.

I did not sleep well, but had learnt enough to know that a crossroads lay ahead, and that one arm drove towards the north.

The gruff woman honoured her agreement, and I set off, fortified by a good meal of eggs and ham, and with a flat basket stuffed with provisions, and clear spring water in a large bladder, bouncing at my knee. I thanked them warmly, and resisted all pressure to wait for the company, who would travel west with me, for sure, they said. Who knew what perils lay ahead?

I felt sure that I would have to face even more dangers than they could imagine, but left them, standing in their little family settlement, still amazed that any woman should journey alone, however pressing her needs.

I realised, with growing fear, that I would be the talk there for many days. I hoped they would not be spurred into pursuing me on Hardric's behalf, or to satisfy the curiosity of the priest.

The land was far less marshy, rising gradually, and covered with sparse scrub and gorse. I could make good going and the mare was fresh and strong. I stopped only when necessary to see to my bodily needs, and trotted eagerly onward, only looking around me, before and behind, in case of any encounters.

When I reached the crossroad, I checked the horse and looked to and fro. One way led to the westering sunset, and the track I had just ridden trailed away south, curving steadily. Beside me, a smaller path headed east, toward more fenland. I took the reed-path to the north, as the light faded and the stars glimmered with increasing brightness. With the moon growing fuller, there was still enough light to see, so I pressed on for as long as it was safe to do so. Any men following me expected me to turn to the west. I must have bought myself some time.

I forgot that I needed to take as much care of what lay ahead, as of what might come from behind.

I had sheltered by a thicket of willow-scrub and hawthorn and slept deeply. I woke suddenly to early morning light and then realised that I was in full view of the path. I had been roused by voices. Towards me, backs to the north, came three men. It was too late to run. I could only stand and face them. I was terrified. First they circled my little camp, horse, bushes, baggage and all. Then they drew in. One trapped me between his horse and the spiky bush, spear at the ready. If only I had remembered to snatch Guthlac's spear in my hasty flight from Hardric! The other two tossed the bundles so that they unrolled. They seized what took their fancy – their shouts and laughter in contrast to the silent menace of my custodian. I saw what they did not: my precious box rolled under a dark root and they did not take it.

I thought they would rape me, but as I sank weakly to the ground, groping blindly for my knife, a stone, anything with which to defend myself, they swerved aside. As the two robbers leapt to horseback, the silent one swung his sword, severed the tie attaching my mare to a branch, and seized her rein. Again he swung his weapon and I fell flat, certain of death. But their noise receded and I was left in sudden silence, only my breath gasping.

When I could bring myself to look up, I was reduced to helpless, furious tears. My cloak was torn. I collected what I could of the debris. The bladder of water was split and emptying. One stone bottle was intact. I found my knife, too late. One blanket lay where it had slipped from the robber's hold. A cloth in which oatcakes were wrapped was still lying folded; though its contents were broken they would be edible. I grabbed my box and hugged it to my breast.

I stumbled off, my pitiful bundle of goods slung over my shoulder. I was bruised and trembling, but I was alive. My horse was far more valuable to those bandits than was my body, though I feared that they could yet return.

If I walked alongside the path, not on it, I might have time to hide if anyone came by. I blamed myself for my stupidity. I had wept before, for the loss of my friends. Now I cried for my mare, but still I walked on, the east wind driving a light sudden shower of hail against my side. I shifted the makeshift bag to my shoulder, for more protection, tucked the hood of my cloak round my tangled hair and trudged amidst the endless, hateful reeds.

13

For three days I had to follow the track as it curved westwards, around a huge, deep, open fen, before turning north again. I had heard of the fenlands, of course, from traders, and our own foragers, hunters and warriors had all contended with the problems they posed. Think of a water meadow, but then imagine it covering a swamp. You dare not step heedlessly from the track for fear of sinking into a black morass. The track itself is narrow, winding between high reeds or opening onto clear stretches of water. The fen-folk (who do not, I found, have webbed feet) make their living from eeling, fishing, fowling and trapping creatures for their fur. If land lifts above the level of the water it is green and lush enough for sheep, so that wool and meat can be traded. In some parts the waterways were blocked by reed-beds, or silted up; in others some efforts had been made to cut channels and open up some sort of route for such trade as there was.

This meant that the apparently sodden and vast tract of fen was not unpeopled, but I was fortunate enough not to meet with anyone else on this remote and ill-marked way. I saw men working in the reeds, collecting osiers for basket-making, or lifting fish-traps. Once a man was poling a punt over a shallow pool, but I crouched for a while in the damp sedges, and waited till dusk before moving on. I had to sleep outside, covering myself with reeds, and finding some hollow for my head. I barely closed my eyes, jerking awake with terror at every rustle in the reeds: what evil spirits might lurk near, I dared not think.

I do not know how far I trudged, sometimes less than ten miles a day. I had never walked any distance before. After the first day, I tore strips from my cloak and bound them round my slippered feet. These were rubbed sore, and the soles of my shoes were disintegrating, but my makeshift efforts helped. I ate the crumbled oatcakes sparingly, and sipped some mead, but I needed new supplies. At least the sun was warmer now and my clothes dried quickly after the damp of the night.

One day I approached a small dwelling where a woman was milking her goat. She stared at me in amazement, but I gave her much the same story that I had used before. She let me sit and gave me milk to drink, filled my bottle from the spring, pressed some bread into my hands and some cheese.

"I have nothing to give you in return," I said, overwhelmed by her willing generosity. She smiled and shook her head.

"You are my guest." The laws of hospitality were strong. A guest, I well knew, was to be honoured. It was only on the road that one fell prey to robbers – I told her of the attack on me. To my astonishment she insisted that I stay to rest that night. Her husband had gone to the monthly market, held at a burgh some miles away. He had taken peat, two young kids, dried fish and some ducks' eggs, and would return with meat, wool and grain. Her name was Hilda.

Gladly I accepted her offer. It was bliss to wash myself and my clothing and comb my hair. When Hilda saw that I had no other gown, under-dress or kirtle, and that my shoes had fallen apart, she rummaged in a wooden chest and pulled out a rust-coloured gown, with a cream under-dress and kirtle and some shoes with stout soles and ankle-high uppers. My eyes filled with tears; I could not remember when I last met with such kindness.

We talked as we worked together, feeding her chickens, gathering in the washing, setting out some food for our supper. She gave me some yarn and watched as I sewed my torn robe and cloak.

"That is fine work. You have been well taught. Your mother?"

I gazed at her. Then I told her the truth. I wondered how she would react to my father's name, but she took no interest in the remote skirmishes in which her folk and mine had fought. I gave her my real name – Niartha – but begged her to keep my secret in case I was followed. I even told her how Gurth had found me, and how he was going to return to take me to the man I loved, though I did not give Wulf's name, nor spoke of his exile. Suddenly it dawned on me that Gurth would not find me at Hardric's place. I shot up, spilling my mending to the floor.

"What shall I do?" I cried, and explained my outcry.

"Did he come this way?" Hilda asked. I did not know.

"He was on horseback," I said. He left me at the end of the month of Hretha. "Riding, it could not have taken him more than, what? Two days?"

"Perhaps he passed here," she said, thoughtfully. "We see most passers-by, though not all stop to talk. He may have come through by night." She told me the walkway became firmer after it crossed a ford, then went straight along an ancient stoneway to a large settlement by the River Witham. "He could travel fast," she said. "You might do well to wait here for a while. You are safe here, and my husband and I can hide you if you are being followed. If your Gurth comes on this road, he will find you."

I considered this idea. I longed to get nearer to Wulfgrim, but had no real idea of where he actually was. I had to rely on Gurth, and I needed rest and a place to hide.

"Hilda," I said, quietly, "I will find a way to thank you. One day."

I stayed there for a month. On his return, Hilda's husband, Hubert, greeted me civilly, though with surprise. Hilda told him my tale of a dead husband and said I was waiting for a relative to pass this way. If he did not come, she said, then Hubert could take me in the cart with him to the market in a month's time. She was not sure that he would accept me as an outcast from a hostile tribe. What he didn't know, he did not need to know, even though he was a kindly person. He heard her words, nodded and went off to see to his plot of ground.

I learnt to relax, to let the warm days soothe my tired body. I gladly helped with the work of the house and in the meadow. I showed Hilda some ways to use the herbs we found. It was always a habit of mine to gather useful plants, storing them in small bags or pots, once dried. She showed me some of the many ways she used reeds. I walked up the bridleway quite often, before turning back, partly to maintain the new strength in my body, partly to look out for Gurth.

Still he did not come. One evening I heard Hubert telling Hilda that he would be setting up the goods for the market in a couple of days. We had made cheeses from the goat's milk and wrapped them in fine linen, coated with beeswax. Now she made flat loaves and stacked them in baskets. We had spun yarn and I had helped her to dye lengths in wooden vats filled with various herbal concoctions that produced good, strong colours, browns, greens, rusty red or yellow. Once dried, the yarn was folded into hanks and tied off. This would trade, certainly. So would the duck eggs, dried eels and reed baskets. They wanted to exchange goods for a sheep or two, or even a cow.

My time here was coming to an end. I must move on, and was glad to have Hubert's strong, quiet presence on the way. Hilda and I embraced.

"One day," I vowed, "I will come back." I tried to thank her for her friendship, but my voice was breaking up.

"I will watch for Gurth," Hilda said. "When you find him, try to let me know somehow. Now the travelling months are here, there will be folk willing to pass on a message. Call yourself Eadwine." I promised, but never did tell her if I found Gurth again. Too many miles, and too much time lay between.

She waved to us as we set off early next morning. The cart was loaded with goods for me, as well as for the market, and I rocked precariously on the wooden seat as we jolted along behind the small, sturdy pony.

We stopped at a fair-sized settlement, at the bourne of this region. I was anxious not to get involved in the market; the suspicious people from the hamlet I had visited might come this far now that summer was here.

I thanked Hubert warmly for his generous hospitality, and praised his sweet wife. He helped me to offload my basket and the leather sack, which Hilda had given me, as full of useful things as I could manage to carry. It might be best, he suggested, if we stopped at the hostelry to hear the news of the highways, to watch out for Gurth, and even to see if any group was willing to let me join them.

This was good sense. I sat on a bench in the sun while Hubert refreshed himself, coming back a while later to say that the traders reported no trouble. He had also found a family who would be heading for the wolds beyond the River Witham, taking their daughter to be married. She needed a servant. He watched me.

"I said – I thought – " he hesitated.

"That is good," I said. "Thank you, Hubert."

"No-one has heard of a stranger called Gurth," he said." If he comes, we will tell him what has happened."

He took himself off to the open space where the market was set up, and I turned towards the little family group. Heartened as I was by the warmth of the hospitality I had found with Hilda and her husband, I should have done well to be more chary. It was good, I thought, not be alone.

RAEDWALD

When Eadwacer had returned from his fruitless journey to search for the girl who was still Raedwald's wife, the prince surprised his messenger at the way he received the information. While Eadwacer seemed certain the women must be dead, or taken thrall, Raedwald was not convinced. Nevertheless there was no point in going on with the search, and in any case, King Tyttla's health was deteriorating and there were more pressing needs. The issue of the girl, Niartha, and the fate of Raedwald's brother could, for the time being, be set aside.

Indeed, in the early summer of that year, old King Tyttla died and was interred, like his father and grandfathers before him, beneath a colossal mound on the ridge four miles from his hall. Without a queen to help him, Raedwald was glad to use Eadwacer's experience as hall-thane in the organization of the days of feasting and the lodging of so many revered guests. Many flocked to honour the respected leader of the Wuffings, and to lay treasures beside him so that he would arrive proudly in Valhalla, like his forebears.

Perhaps Raedwald felt some nostalgia for the carefree life he had so far led, taking his pleasures where he would: hunting in the forests; riding where he chose; bedding any girl he chose. He had enjoyed the licence of the younger son: it was Eni who held the weight of being the nominated heir. Now he would have to prove himself.

After the funeral came the throning. The hall was arranged to accommodate the guests. All but the most elderly and the most important had to stand. The fires were doused in the hearths, which were obliterated, and tables removed. Fresh rushes, spread with the meadow flowers of early summer, covered the floor. At the end of the hall furthest from the doors was placed the king's dais on which stood the carved and gilded stool, its curves polished and shining. Behind, hung beautifully woven cloths, glowing with colour. To each side the priests of Woden stood. One, clad in deerskin, high antlers on his brow, held a board of polished alder. On it lay squared slips of wood from a yew tree, marked with runes. A second priest averted his eyes, put out his hand and selected three of the pieces. He handed them to a third, the chief priest, who scrutinized them, murmuring as he did so. The hall hushed to hear his response, "It is favourable! Proceed!" Voices buzzed in anticipation.

A horn sounded from the yard and the hall fell silent. The door-thane closed the doors and, the sunlight gone, men waited in torchlight for the ceremony to begin. There came three loud knocks on the door, as Raedwald beat on it with his newly-crafted spear.

"Shall this man be admitted?" asked the priests in unison.

"Let him come in!" replied the assembly, male voices resounding. Light burst in as the doors were flung open.

Raedwald moved up the hall as the throng parted. He wore a white tunic with fine embroidery at the neck and hem. His shoes were of fine, soft leather. He wore gold armbands, a gold collar, and the cloth at his legs was laced with gold, red and blue braid. At his waist was strapped a strong belt with a great gold buckle, a gift from his kinsmen of Helmingham. His face was stern, though his eyes shone. He stood, facing the hall, in front of the throne-stool, priests on each side.

The chief of these, wolf-head hooding his bony skull, stepped forward. He was blinded in one eye, like his god, and wore a black scarf across the dead socket. He carried a staff, marked with runes and tipped with the tusk of some fearful sea-beast. His cloak was stitched with symbols of the gods and round his neck he bore a gold disc-shaped pendant, engraved with the sign against the evil eye. His name was Garmund.

"I name this man to you. He is Raedwald, son of Tyttla, grandson of Wuffa. His father nominated him heir to this kingdom. I ask you now. Shall he be our king? Speak now or else hereafter forever hold your peace."

Silence. There was no man here who did not know the story of the elder brother's disgrace about eight months before. They knew of Raedwald's wild youth, and for the most part approved of it. He was young, strong and decisive. Wisdom would come with age.

"Does this man have your voice?"

Again and again they shouted, "Raedwald!" Each man raised his right arm and punched the air.

"Kneel!" commanded the priest and the prince obeyed. A second priest stepped forward, bearing a gold dish on which sat a large candle. Garmund extinguished the flame with his hand and used the soot from the blackened wick to draw a sign on Raedwald's forehead. This was the sign, the *fylfot*, a mark of protection against harm. Each man present copied the action on his own brow.

The priests, each in turn, invoked blessings on the young man, that he might bring riches to his people, preserve them from famine, disease and war. They begged a fruitful marriage, conveniently forgetting the wife he had cast off.

Garmund took from a third priest a simple, broad and shining golden coronet, hitherto covered with a white cloth. He stood behind the throne and, lifting it above Raedwald's head, he proclaimed,

"Behold your king!" He laid the gold on the king's head. Into his hand he placed the ivory wand, with which Tyttla had proclaimed Raedwald his heir.

"The king! The king!" came the eager cries, and shriller voices echoed the call from outside the hall.

The chief thane approached and raised Raedwald to his feet. He set the king on the throne-stool and signalled to another, who brought Raedwald's sword – Beorhtfyr - to him, the only weapon in the hall. He laid it over the king's knees. Raedwald spoke.

"With the help of the gods, and by the power of this sword, I swear to do all that I may to fulfil the trust you place in me. I will do all I may to see you fed, offer you protection, and reward good service. By Woden and Thunor, this I swear!"

Then the oldest of the thanes recited the names of the lands held by the king and the names of those who held them for him. He recounted those in alliance, some of whom were not present on that day. As each name was spoken, the bearer of it came forward and laid his hand lightly on the sword Beorhtfyr to swear loyalty and service to the king.

When it was over, the king, priests and thanes left the hall to be greeted by the men, women and children pressing eagerly outside. That night came the last of the great feasts, before the guests departed.

Very late that night Eadwacer spoke with Niartha's uncle, Edgar. No news had come to them of the outcast girl, or her companions. No sighting of Gurth was known. The queen ruled in all but name, and her ways were alien. Edgar would be willing to throw in his lot with the newly-crowned king. Eadwacer nodded. Raedwald would know of it as soon as there was time to think.

14

The father of the family was a large man, rough in body and manner, his wife waspish and complaining. The girl, Ulrica, was, I thought, sullen or possibly cowed. Her brothers were downright bullies. They were accompanied by two men to see to the horses and act as guards on the road. Apparently the maidservant brought with them had suffered a miscarriage and had been left in one of the nearby houses to wait for their return.

I set myself to be pleasant and useful to the whining woman and the bride-to-be. At least we had a couple of sturdy ponies to carry the baggage, and there were enough of us to deter robbers. Hilda had been right about the stoneway, which proved to be wider and firmer underfoot, and headed straight towards the north. In fact I did not have to walk, being permitted to ride on one of the ponies, packed round with various bundles.

We rode about ten miles or so, and stopped for the night at a small settlement spanning a ford near an important crossroads. The families offered a largish-sized house for guests. Now I discovered just what a lowly position I held. I helped to move luggage inside and to see to it that Ulrica and her mother had everything they needed. At this point they took the goods I had been given by Hilda. Only after food was served and beds made up was I free to sit and eat, and then to find a corner to lie down in. I did not care overmuch – I was under cover from the night, and was advancing on my journey. Every step toward the north brought me nearer to finding Eni Wulfgrim.

Next day started badly. Taking a pottery bowl to wipe it clean before wrapping it for the journey, I was jostled roughly, as one of Ulrica's brothers pushed past. I dropped the bowl, which shattered. He swung round, and I thought he would ask my pardon. Instead he swore harshly and raised his arm to strike me hard across my upper arm. I cried out and clasped the hurt.

"Be silent, girl." He slapped my face. "Clumsy fool. Clear up this mess." He stomped off and, shocked into tears, I bent down to pick up the shards. The two women watched, saying not a word, though they had seen what happened.

Eventually we set off and made good headway till a thunderstorm threatened. We had covered rolling ground and we now paused on a heath top, looking down into a wide, watery valley, with a large settlement on a steep hillside, some three miles away, beyond a river wide and deep enough for ships.

`It began to rain and the men urged the party forward to the shelter of a barn. A few sheep fled before us, and the place was dirty. The roof leaked, but we were safe from the angry blasts from overhead and the lightning, which knifed from the clouds to cleave the earth.

Once the storm passed towards the north, the two carls were sent down towards the town to seek accommodation for the night. Ulrica's brothers tethered the horses and I was left to unpack the bags, so that hides could be laid over piles of filthy straw to form seats. I found drink and food, hastily gulping some mouthfuls myself before tidying up the left-overs.

Darkness threatened, but there was still no sign of the grooms. At moonrise I had to begin preparing more food, but could not get a fire going quickly enough to satisfy my master.

"Useless girl," he snarled as I fumbled to make a spark with firestone and damp straw. He smacked me across the head so that I sprawled in the mire.

Trembling, I crouched over the makeshift hearth and tried again. At last a spark took hold and I fed it carefully. Under the scornful eyes of the group, I mixed some oatmeal and water into a porridge and set the pot to warm while I found some bowls and ladles.

I had just served this mess to the family when we heard horses' hooves and the grooms returned. One of them was sober enough, the other, helpless, was tied across the horse's back, head lolling. They had found an inn, and we were expected – but the fool was so drunk he could barely sit straight.

The men were soon taught a lesson. The one who could stand was dunked in a scummy trough at the door of the barn and shaken till his few wits returned. The senseless one was flung on the ground and kicked viciously. A flying boot left him totally insensible. The family mounted and rode off, leaving me with the incapable sots. I wiped and packed the bowls we had used, kicked earth over the pathetic fire, rolled up the hides and tied them to the pack animals. I looked at the two men. Then I pushed the inert one onto his side so that he did not choke on his own vomit. The other sat on the floor groaning with his head in his hands.

"Can you hear me?" I demanded. He nodded, then winced. "I am going to this inn," I said. "Find us there in the morning, and bring that drunken oaf with you, fit or not." He did not argue.

Needless to say, I found no comfortable welcome, but fell onto some hay in the stable of the inn at Lindon, and shared the warmth of the two ponies, as well as their blankets. Needless to say, we did not make an early start next day.

So began my life as a servant, working obediently in fear of physical punishment and subjected to verbal abuse. I preferred it when I was ignored. I wondered what life would be like when we arrived at our new home. Presumably I would be spared from the company of Ulrica's family – I could only hope that her husband was a different type of man, and that his household was better run. Our journey took us two more, slow-moving days, with nights spent at a farmstead called Nettleham (well named) and in another small market place beyond that. Then we found the track that led alongside a stream in a valley folded in the gently-rolling wolds to our right.

All the time I was hoping that, just as he had so unexpectedly done before, Gurth would find me – bring me the words I longed for. At each halt, I listened for any news, scanned the faces of the few wayfarers who overtook us. Nothing. When we turned off the comparatively well-worn road onto the little greenway my heart sank. Gurth would never dream of looking for me in such a remote spot.

In a state of misery I climbed down from the pony and stood while the family were greeted. A group of some half-dozen houses stood by the stream, and from these came a small crowd of people, children eagerly jostling about or peeping shyly from their mothers' skirts. Men put down their tools as they left the near-by fields, and from the largest house came a broad, fair-haired man and an old woman, white-haired and using a stick to aid her as she hobbled towards us.

I had never seen Ulrica's father so affable. He pushed her and her mother forward as greetings were exchanged. Hands were clasped, there was laughter and a flurry of activity as our little party was drawn in and the ceremony of welcome was made.

The next few days reminded me of the time before my own marriage to Raedwald, eighteen months before. So much had to be done, and I was at beck and call from dawn until the lamps guttered and went black.

I stood with other serfs on a little knoll close by a spring sacred, appropriately, to Freya, the goddess of love. My eyes were watching the actions of the priest as he tied the couple hand-fast. He called Freya's blessing on their union, that it might be fruitful.

I had heard the same sort of words used as I stood beside Raedwald, but it was Wulfgrim I thought of now. I begged the goddess to preserve our love. I called silently to Rana, goddess of the sea, to keep him safely in her care, for he had served her well. I swallowed back tears and turned my attention to my duties.

I could not have guessed how long I would stay in this hamlet. After Ulrica's family left, she began to look to me, as if our brief familiarity was some comfort to her. Though fourteen years old, she found it hard to adjust to married life. Oswald was not rough with her, but he was demanding in every way. Her mother had not taught her well, and her management of the house was inexpert. Her husband's mother was quick to find fault and seemed always to be watching. I tried to cover up for Ulrica as often as I could and saw to it that the daily tasks were performed by me or one of the other women.

She lacked any confidence in herself, which was not surprising when one considered how she had been reared and dominated. Over-anxious to please, she could be very irritating, and chattered nervously, when a wiser woman would have held her peace. Nor did she enjoy the act of sex, complaining to me of pain, and only too obviously quailing when Oswald took her to their quarters.

The hamlet was not fenced in; there was no need, with the stream curving round it and the hill behind. If I walked too far, someone would call out. No servant was given the opportunity to roam out of sight, and hardly ever to rest, except at night. So I was caught. I was torn between the desire to move on and a lingering hope that somehow Gurth might find me. Moving on meant running away, alone, and I had to find out about the area before I tried to escape. So I befriended some of the other women, learning how close we were to a great river near to the coast. Somehow I would have to find a way to cross this river. But now the summer had turned and we were heading towards harvest. If I did not go soon, I would have to brave the winter months. How could I survive?

Then Ulrica became pregnant. She was, of course, hopelessly sick, constantly feeling faint. The old woman was thrilled: her splendid son was making her a grandmother. She was constantly mixing herbal drinks, sure to produce a boy, she said. I poured most of them unobtrusively away, while prompting Ulrica to express fulsome thanks. She basked in the attention.

As the year waned, the little community performed the annual rituals. Bonfires were lit, when sheep were slaughtered, skinned, the fat stored in jars, the wool put to good use.

Yule-tide and the Mothers' Night came and went with the usual celebrations. I was kept busy gathering first berries and later hazelnuts. Fish were dried and grain was pounded. We made the pancakes of late winter, and we huddled round the fires against the frost and the rain.

It must be nearly a year, I thought, since my father had died. A year since I had set out with Gerda and Guthlac. I remembered silently my brave and loyal companions. I thought of Hilda, so bright and generous, and I took some heart.

When Ulrica was more than six months into her pregnancy, the old woman forbade Oswald to sleep with her. His activity, she said, could harm the child and risk causing an early birth. He did not like this, but complied. A month later it was fairly widely-known that he was visiting a woman in one of the little houses. Her husband was out on the wolds, rounding up the sheep and bringing them close for the later lambing. In the month of Eostre, this man returned.

Oswald turned his attentions to me. At first it was easy to turn him away, by pleading the woman's monthly gift, but he was growing insistent. I begged Ulrica to warn him off, but she was only too relieved to be spared, herself. What did it matter?

That night I pleaded frantically with all the gods I knew. Then I knew, for sure, that all help had gone. Gurth had not come. He was lost to me – or dead. I would never see Wulf again. I lay, sobbing quietly, and so Oswald found me. He ripped off my shift and flung me back on my straw bed. I struggled but he pinned me down with one arm while he fumbled to loosen the tie of his breeches. His purple, engorged member swung free and he fell on me, forcing my legs to part, and rammed into me, lunging again and again. I turned my head away from his foul breath and wept. He gave a groan and collapsed, sprawling over me. I squirmed, desperate to be free of his body. I felt like an animal, bestially abused. He roused himself enough to make his way off to his own bed, without saying a word.

Shuddering, I left the house, stumbled down to the little river and waded into the chill water. I rinsed my body as clean as I could, praying to the goddess that his seed would not grow within me, then went back to the fireside. Huddled inside a blanket, I stared at the embers and thought desperately. If I could find in the old woman's store something to end a pregnancy... what was it? A strong dose of tansy should do it! Then Oswald could not ruin my life when he came to me again. I could hold on until Ulrica's baby was born. Perhaps in the ensuing commotion I could slip away.

In the hillside close behind the hamlet I created a cache between rocks, where grass grew tall and thick. I stowed some clothes, shoes, a rug and a hide, the old cup, bottle and knife in the leather bag Hilda had given me. I would add dried food later, as the time drew near. I always kept Wulf's present to me in the purse hanging at my waist, between my over-dress and my kirtle. At night it was hidden, rolled in the same clothes. As I had dreaded, Oswald returned, but only three more odious times. On each occasion I drank a concoction of tansy, and greeted the sign of that month's blood with secret joy.

I expected to wait four weeks, but it was only two when Ulrica woke us before daylight, shrieking. The midwife heard her three houses away. The house was cleared of men, cloths were brought out, and water warmed for washing the baby. It took nine hours of encouragement, reassurance and urging for Ulrica to give birth. Luckily for her (and for me) it was a boy.

A girl would have been tolerated, and clucked over by the women. A boy was given to the father to show off to the people and a feast was hastily prepared.

I took my chance, together with some food and drink. As the party assembled in the open ground at the heart of the settlement, meat skewered on sticks held to a great woodfire, and dark shadows flickering, I left Ulrica sleeping after a narcotic draught. I gathered my stuff from the rocky hideaway and walked off quietly into the night.

In the paddock at the turn of the river grazed the horses. I 'borrowed' one of them. If I could ride it now until it was exhausted, I might turn it free for the pursuers to find. If they bothered. It would be the horse they wanted to reclaim. I would decide, later.

The moon was just past its full size, so I picked my way fairly steadily down the greenway to the track and turned right. Now we moved faster and, although I dared not put the horse to more than a trot, it was still dark when the way was crossed by another track. Ahead was a low bank of darkness with a strange, glimmering light beyond. I would have to turn left or right. I stopped and tied the beast loosely to a tree. I climbed the bank and gasped.

Before me, black and glinting in the shining moonlight was a vast river, flowing powerfully to the east. As I gazed, the sky lightened. Now I could see the dark shape of the land rising on the opposite bank. To my right must be the coast. To cross this water I had to turn west and move upstream, until I could find a suitable place. Then I could once again set my face to the north.

I climbed down and debated with myself for a moment. Perhaps I could put any pursuit off the scent. I pulled a shawl and a gown from the bag and then tugged the reins so that the horse struggled up the bank, with me heaving at its head. I threw the shawl onto the ground and pushed the gown so that it lay at the edge of the water. Then I persuaded the animal to slither down again – the mess it made, tearing the grass as its hooves slipped, would surely attract attention. For good measure I sacrificed one of the shoes I had packed and dropped it by the muddy slide. Please, I begged the gods, who had not always helped me, please let them think I have drowned myself.

Then I remounted and rode on, the rising sun behind me.

An easterly wind sprang up and flung my cloak about my face. I tossed back the hood, shook my hair and set the horse to a canter. I rejected any thought of returning the animal. Oswald owed me something. No longer Eadwine, the servant, I felt renewed in my freedom. I was Niartha again.

15

Once again I feared pursuit. However, Ulrica was weak and probably too preoccupied to bother about me; and Oswald too happy with his new son, I hoped. In any case, how could they know that I would head north, as I had never spoken of my intention to them? Unless Hubert had mentioned this when he arranged for me to become servant to Ulrica.

At all events I often looked over my shoulder, and at about midday, beyond a curve behind me, I saw movement. I had to hide – but where? Ahead, what appeared to be a sort of cleft lay to the left of the way. I galloped towards it and swung the horse onto a narrow path beside a river that was forging its way towards the fast flood I had ridden beside all this time. We raced up the path, but I found no tree or bank to hide me. I kept going as far as I could from the highway and then stopped and slipped to the ground. Desperately, I knelt and tugged on the reins to force the horse to its knees, until it sank down. If only we had not been seen, or heard. I waited, trying to control my breath so that I could listen. I could hear nothing, but kept still until I was sure that whoever it was had attempted to cross this torrent, or had not followed my route. Now I had to decide how to cross this river, myself.

In the end I walked on up the path, leading the horse until we came to a low, half-ruined barton on the shallow bank of the stream. Thankfully, I urged the horse inside and sought what comfort I could. Only then did I realise what I had forgotten to bring with me – a firestone. I could not make a fire.

I spent two chilly nights, moving about vigorously to keep warm, sleeping fitfully. Early on the second morning I set off again, keeping beside the water until it narrowed and became smooth enough, for me to swim the horse across. I rode back, down beside the stream, until I found the mighty, wide river again. I turned west alongside it.

Resolutely I pressed on into a cold drizzle. I felt chilled to the bone. After some hours, I came to a few dwellings. To my joy I saw that they stood beside the river and, best of all, they marked the head of a low, wooden bridge. The river ran fast, but it had narrowed here. I had found my road to the north. The mirky weather must have kept people inside. Only when my horse's hooves clattered on the timbers of the bridge did three or four men appear. They called out something but I did not stay to hear if it was a greeting or a warning. At the far end of the bridge a man ran from his house and waved an arm at me. I waved back and wished him 'good cheer' as we passed. We galloped on.

Soon my elation faded. I was feeling ill, my head hurt, the movement of the horse jolted me and I felt now hot, now cold. I remembered how quickly Gerda had succumbed. I had to find a warm place. We came to a spot where five ways met. Perhaps I should have taken the road straight on, but it looked barren and empty. If I turned down one of the others, maybe I would find some habitation?

At random, too tired to think, I turned left. The horse carried me across one stream, but a mile or two further on it stopped. Before us was a slightly wider river, and on the bankside was a small inn, surrounded by whin bushes.

Suddenly a dog rushed at us, barking, and I heard a man's shout. My horse reared in fright, neighing, and I fell.

I awoke in a warm, smoky room, lit by a guttering lamp. Someone was holding a cup to my lips – it tasted sweet and spicy, and I coughed. My head hurt, but worse was the pain in my arm.

"Be still," said a hoarse voice. "Drink this now and sleep." I felt too sick and faint for any further effort. I drank and slid into oblivion.

I was ill for several days, and was kept quiet with potions, fed with thin soup and offered mead or cold spring water to drink. When my head cleared and I could be propped on a pillow, I found that I was being nursed by an elderly couple. I was very weak and was glad to rest and regain my strength.

We talked. I told them I was going north to find my husband, but feared he must be dead. Indeed, by now I believed I would never find my love. Could he have survived two winters, marooned on a cold, northern crag? My broken arm took weeks to mend, and I could do at first only a few light tasks around the place. To ride on was impossible,

It was probably not even necessary. By sheer chance I had been brought to a halt at a place where a marsh-path crossed the River Derwent, one way leading back to the Humber, where I had crossed the bridge. The other way led to a large township. Anyone coming from the north and wishing to avoid the hard moorland paths might pass this way.

I asked after Gurth, but they shook their heads. Too many people stopped here for them to remember.

"You are welcome to stay here," said the old woman. I thanked her.

"I have nothing to give you towards my keep – except my horse. You may use that if you wish." The old man was satisfied with this.

I thought they owned the inn, but the place belonged to their son, Edmund. His wife had died and he had kept the place on. Every few weeks he rode to market where he could barter river fish and honey for grain and meat. In a small hut next to the inn he made his brew, fermenting his honey and storing it in pottery jars.

I stayed there, healing steadily. I learnt to be less nervous of the wayfarers who passed through, and listened with interest to what news they brought. Sometimes a family would halt for the night, maybe on a wedding journey, such as that which took Ulrica to Oswald. Men from the little settlements like nearby Wressle, passed noisy evenings, singing songs and reliving the adventures of their youth.

I did what I was good at, preparing food, serving it, cleaning and washing. This was my new life. Until I knew where to start looking for the island where Wulfgrim was exiled, I could only wander aimlessly. I was not happy, but I accepted the need to pause.

Edmund tolerated my presence, finding that I was useful. I kept close to his old parents, wary of a repeat of my experience with

Hardric, or, worse, with Oswald. I did not like him. Edmund drank too much and he was uncouth. He did not respect his parents and sometimes was barely civil to his guests. I stayed as far from him as I could.

I had little enough time to myself. Sometimes I would wander beside the river, usually content to have a moment's solitude. But there were times when I was overwhelmed with a sense of isolation, devastated by loneliness, fear and loss.

It was at such a time, after harvest, almost six months since I arrived at Barmby, when I stood in a dark reverie on the riverbank. Once again, as it had swept over me before, came the black certainty that I was never going to find the man I loved.

Sunk in angry misery, I did not pay heed to the quiet arrival of a flimsy riverboat. The familiar sounds of greeting faded. Soon I would have to go back inside. I sighed and turned. He took me completely unawares, stepping towards me, as amazed as I.

"By all the gods! No – is it – yes, can it be you, princess?"

Eadwacer stood there before me. I looked at him, then wildly beyond him towards the inn.

"Is he, is Raedwald - ?"

"He is not here, lady. I have come at his bidding. He has sent me with a message and this token. Here!" He pulled something from his purse.

I did not wish to meet his eyes, so bent my head to receive the small packet wrapped in cloth…

***

"So now you know it all, Eadwacer. Now tell me I shall find welcome in my husband's hall. Who would find it in his heart to take me now?" I lifted Raedwald's brooch and, before he could stop me, I hurled it into the river, gold, dragon, flower and all.

16

Eadwacer stares at me, his green eyes steady, but full of warmth, not shocked or contemptuous, as I expect.

"Oh, princess," he says, "if you only knew how much I regretted what I did." I turn away but he pulls me firmly back.

"If I had done nothing, Prince Raedwald would have taken you away, and none of this would have happened."

"And what of Prince Eni? Do you think that Wulf and I would have been so easily parted?"

"Niartha, surely –"

"The only sure thing, Eadwacer, is that we loved – we love each other."

"But you were wedded to Raedwald. You still are."

"Oh, yes, and we know why! It was convenient, to reinforce the alliance between our two kin. Raedwald only wanted me because I was useful to him – he never loved me."

"Lady, he says he knows you were both younger then. At the time he could have killed you for your betrayal. Now –"

"Now it is too late. Now I can be of no use to him at all. And I have lost everything. I do not know if my love is still alive, or where he is," I sob helplessly. Suddenly I find his arms round me in the way he used to do when I was small.

"Eadwacer, I –"

"Hush, princess. All is well. I am here."

All the pent-up months of fear, loneliness and anxiety surge up and I cling to him, familiar and warm as he always used to be. He kisses my hair, wipes my wet cheek with his finger, gazes at me and gently strokes my face, my neck, my arms.

It is so long since I was clasped like this, or shown tenderness, that I relax into his embrace. Yearning for solace, I accept his kiss, first a mere brush of the lips, then compelling, urgent. I begin to recoil from him but I do not want to. What begins as an attempt to repel him turns into an embrace pf my own. We sink to the leafy ground in the shelter of group of alders. I do not know whose desire is the more avid. Mouths, hands, breasts, bodies move together until our lust is sated. The cool air rouses me from languor and I clutch my clothing to myself in sudden shock. What have I done?

As I scramble up, Eadwacer catches me by the hand.

"Lady-"

"Do not speak! I should never have —" I stop and gape at him, appalled.

"Niartha." But he cannot find words. He kisses my fingers. I snatch them away -"

"Eadwacer, I should never have let you —"

"I know it. But I can never regret this. You are so lovely."

"You must leave. Tell Raedwald that I cannot come to him. Tell him —" I falter, aware of just how much Eadwacer might reveal. "Tell him that I am not fit to be his wife."

"Niartha, you could be a queen. Indeed if you return with me, that is what you will become. Tyttla is dead and Raedwald is now king."

"And Wulfgrim?"

"Prince Eni is far beyond your reach. On an island beyond the great moorlands to the north – he can hardly have survived." I shudder. "I have to tell you, lady, that if you refuse to return, Raedwald will declare your divorcement. There are kings to the south and across the sea, who are eager to give their daughters to the Wuffings' king."

"Then let them!" I cry. "I beg you, Eadwacer. You must go! I should never have let myself do this. Please, leave me now." By now I am hurrying, anxious to be free of him, to return to the refuge of the inn.

His stride lengthens and he grips my elbow. "Niartha, you are not to blame. I will always remember your beauty." I am burning with shame at my weakness, full of self-recrimination.

"Promise me one thing, Eadwacer."

"Name it."

"Do not tell Raedwald where I am." I know this will be hard. He has spent months seeking me. He makes one last attempt on behalf of his lord. Raedwald, he says, will fulfill the vows he made at our wedding; he will give me all he has – and he has plenty to give. Eadwacer repeats the enticements: a growing hoard of wealth, horses, new land and a great hearth of his own with the people amongst whom he has chosen to live. I will be the greatest jewel in the king's possession.

"I do not want to be possessed. I have given my love elsewhere. I can never be his companion, his help-meet. Promise me, do not say where he can find me."

"I will not tell him. But remember, Niartha, that I do know where you are, and that I know your need." He leaves me. Can I trust him? What do these last words mean? Is it a threat, or meant to be reassuring?

It is too late to ask him more. I become caught up with the provision of food and drink, and we do not wish to speak, with others nearby. I watch the boat slipping as silently downstream as it has come, moving in gathering dusk toward the river's larger sister and onward to the sea. Eadwacer, Raedwald's emissary, must take my cold message back to him, over the equally chilly waves. As I go back into the inn, I see Edmund's eyes on me, with a curious look. I wonder if he has seen me talking with the stranger, but he says nothing and follows me inside.

It was at about the shortest day of the year when I became certain that I was with child. I felt dismayed – no – shocked, outraged, at my own reckless act and the way Eadwacer had taken advantage of my weakness. He had betrayed his king, in the same way that Wulf had, the man he had exposed. Filled with disgust and loathing, I struggled against nausea and lethargy, and concealed my growing size from the old woman, with a large apron and my shawl. Of course, in the new year, the discovery became inevitable, but what was so unexpected was the violent anger and rejection by the family. She accused me of sleeping with her son, then with her husband, when Edmund denied any such deed. If I would not, or could not name the father, I had no man to house me and the child. I was no longer welcome in the community.

I begged to be allowed to stay until the baby was born, but they became adamant. Obviously I was going to be of no use to them and they did not want to feed another mouth. I wondered why their attitude had changed so much. I had offended the laws of hospitality, apparently, and would now pay the price. I was again an outcast.

EADWACER

The small boat wound its way between the riverbanks, sometimes studded with alder or aspen, sometimes thickly wooded, or open as leas for cattle. Eadwacer sat hunched in the stern as the boatman bent to the oars, occasionally using one as a pole. As the stream grew wide and deep, strengthened by sister brooks, the man pulled in to a small wharf, just short of the confluence with the great river.

"I'll thank you for the payment now, master," he said. "I can go no further."

"The deal was to get me to my ship," Eadwacer objected.

"See now," said the man gruffly, pointing to the mighty, flowing river ahead. "Tide is in full flow and this skiff is too light. I'll send my boy down the bank this side and he can signal them when he spots your ship."

Eadwacer had to concede, and clambered ashore. "It's growing dark," he grumbled. "How will the boy see anything?"

"There'll be lights, master – or a fire. At all events nobody can find you till tide turns and daylight comes."

"I need shelter then," said Eadwacer. "I can offer you more, when the ship comes for me."

The price was cheap enough. In return for the promise of an extra box of tallow and some cord for snares or fishing, the king's messenger was given a grubby pile of sacking stuffed with bracken for a bed, and a dish of smoked fish with rye bread. The water tasted brackish, but Eadwacer lay down satisfied enough and tried to sleep. The memory of his coupling with Niartha had him tossing in agitated arousal. He had longed, since she had reached womanhood, to possess her, and she had met his embrace with eagerness and animal need, of that he was sure. But her reaction had hurt him. If she had felt so strongly that her body shook as it came to bliss, as indeed it had, then why the strong renunciation, why the loathing?

Raedwald, for sure, must never know: he would be rightly outraged. It was true, what Eadwacer had told Niartha. Raedwald had sent the message. When the king considered what token he might offer as proof of the authenticity of his offer, Eadwacer mentioned the love-token, the brooch he had picked up from the floor of the hall, where Raedwald had dashed it from her hand in rejection. He had had it in his possession ever since, and he had often fingered it, though now he told the king he had suddenly remembered it. Raedwald had looked at the jewel as it lay in his palm. His face was inscrutable, though he closed his eyes for a moment as if calling something to mind. Then he handed it back to his messenger.

"Search for her to the north this time. Take a ship. The Seawitch will do. There are rivers to search, and to cross. Take a crew to sail her and to act as fighters, if need be."

Then he paused and stared across the valley from the ridge-path on which they stood. He spoke the words Eadwacer had repeated to Niartha.

"If she will not come, then leave her wherever she is. I will deal with her myself, though you need not tell her this. Whatever the outcome, you are to bring me the news that she is dead or alive, and how she replies to my message. Do not delay. Bring me word yourself."

That was next to do. The girl's fate would rest with Raedwald. If Raedwald divorced himself from her, then he, Eadwacer, would find a place to keep her. At length Eadwacer slept.

Next day broke with a storm. Eventually the boatman's boy returned, soaking wet, to say that he could not light his torch to signal the ship. It was lying at the far bank some miles downstream, but, again, the tide was running out. Perhaps, said the man, the two of them could row their reluctant guest across, at slack water. Perhaps they could then borrow a pony, or start to walk. The boy would tag along to make sure of the goods they had bartered in exchange for the use of their boat.

Cursing in frustration, Eadwacer had to agree. So it was, when the storm abated, and a day after leaving Niartha, he crossed the Humber and turned east, on foot.

When he saw a small group of men riding towards him, he paused. It could be his men, come to seek him. If they were locals, he would have to come up with one of his plausible tales to fend off suspicion. He had a sword and a knife, but no horse. Words would have to do, so he stood his ground. The riders slowed to a walk and surrounded him. One startled him by dismounting, signalling to two others to do the same. These two stood at his shoulders and he looked the leader in the face. It was Gurth.

Neither man was prepared for this. Neither had any personal animosity against the other, but each was bound by loyalty to his lord, one to Eni, one to Raedwald. On his travels, Gurth had heard of Raedwald's crowning. He was suspicious when Eadwacer asked if he knew anything of the princess, so he denied all knowledge of her, though he had, in fact tracked her from the fens to the wolds. He did not believe Eadwacer would seek her for her good. Eadwacer, of course, said nothing of his encounter with Niartha.

Nor did Gurth rise to the bait when Eadwacer told him he was to seek out Wulfgrim. Gurth pretended that he was leader of this band of outlaws, ready to fight for whoever would reward them. He lent Eadwacer a horse, so that he could reach the great ship their troop had passed a few miles downstream. One of his men, Eric, would ride behind, and return with the horse quickly enough.

"And our payment," growled the boatman's son. While they waited, Gurth gave the lad food and drink. It was easy to find out what had happened with Eadwacer. Much later, Gurth would regret not having killed the man while he had the chance. Eadwacer's next mission, he would learn when he eventually reported to Raedwald, was to ensure that Wulf was dead.

Once Eric returned, Gurth and his followers rode on, to the wooden bridge Niartha had crossed so many months before. They did not find the inn at Barmby, and heard no word of the girl. Gurth headed north, sure that Niartha was trying to reach Wulf.

They set off, taking the most likely track, towards the ruined city of Eofric.

This was a place of terrors: the fearsome Romans had taken huge stones, as they did wherever they went; an unnatural act to use the strength of the earth to make towers and palaces and employ them in the destruction of honest folk. The practice of dwelling in timber houses and halls meant that, if they were destroyed, or if a man, or a people, died out, then all returned to the mother-goddess who had provided them. The great stone walls were left untouched: works of wicked wights. Desperate or bold, some folk sheltered within, but most followed the traditional ways and lived near land that could be tilled, or woods, outside. Still, Eofric made a meeting-place for market-days. It was the most likely place to pick up the lonely woman's trail. Gurth headed northwest

17

At least I had found a boatman willing to take me as far upstream as he could travel, to his home and his wife gave me a night's shelter. Next day she turned me out, and I began the longest, hardest walk of my life. As far as possible, I held to the river as it wound its way ever northward towards its source. Where the ground became dangerously marshy, I had to detour to rising ground, but at least I had water.

I met an old cowherd on the second day. I had slept the night in a crazy byre he had built for his little herd. He gave me some milk and cheese and was civil enough, even though he eyed me curiously. He warned me not to stray to the west – there was a settlement there in the ruins of a great city, haunted, he said, and the folk were not friendly. Later, I was to discover, if only I had known he spoke of Eofric, I might have had word of Gurth! As it was, grateful, I plodded on. At first, as the weather remained dry, though cold, I made reasonable progress. I was covering about eight or nine miles a day, even over the difficult ground, and in spite of stopping often to rest.

I found a pen, fold or barn to sleep in here and there, or made myself a shelter in the roots and bole of a gnarled tree, as I had done before. I avoided people where I saw the occasional house or hamlet. I even waited for nightfall before, on the sixth day, I crossed the river at a precarious and ancient bridge of mouldering planks, invoking the god of the stream. I sheltered in the lee of the bridge till early light and moved away before I set dogs barking.

By now, I needed to find food. Milk I could take from the sheep or cows, if the little fields were not too near a homestead, but I needed bread and meat. I picked up courage as the riverside path passed a lonely house, and a woman looked out and called a greeting. I told her I was walking to the next village – luckily she did not ask its name – and she gave me some bread and honey and a cup of mead and told me to rest, her eyes on my swelling belly. Was I going to my mother's? she asked. I told her my mother was dead, but her sister would look after me. My husband, I said, was at sea.

"How lucky you are," she sighed. She longed for a baby. I stared at her, heavy-eyed. I loathed this stranger, struggling within me. I could feel slight ripples of movement by now, and cared not if my wearisome journey caused me to miscarry.

It felt as though mere habit was driving me northward. Like some migrating bird, I held to my course, though I did not know where I would find my ground.

I thanked the woman and moved on. About some seven miles further on my route was crossed by a pathway running east to west. I had nothing to offer the god of the crossing, but laid my hand on the small, roughly-carved figure in the shrine, in supplication. I lifted my head and saw, as if in answer, a house, whose timbers clung to the stones of the moorland, rising steeply behind it. The heights were white with snow, and the clouds above were dark and threatening. I was too tired to drag myself further that night. I would have to beg for food and shelter. A girl came in answer to my beating at her door and called to someone inside. The householder came out, leaned on the doorpost and peered at me suspiciously, looking round to see if I were alone.

He took me for a runaway serf and, though he could see the state I was in, he shook his head, gesturing angrily and told me to be off.

As she closed the door, the girl jerked her head and her finger pointed. I heard the wooden bar slam down inside. Beside the house was a small hut, its door ajar. I peered in, cautiously, afraid of rousing a dog or frightening a horse, but I found it to be a little storehouse. Logs were piled along one wall, and on shelves were pots of grain, honey and dried fruit. I seized my bowl from my bag and simply mixed the foodstuffs together, uncooked and cold. It tasted gritty but delicious. I drank water from my flagon and stretched out, laying my blanket on the dirt floor.

It was hard to sleep. The creature inside me shifted, and I could not get comfortable. Then, as I twisted awkwardly, it came to me abruptly that I was taking another man's child on a journey to find my lover. I felt my stomach heave with dread and lurched outside, overtaken by uncontrollable nausea. I crept back to my blanket, my hair damp with falling snow. Eventually I slept.

I was startled awake by the stamping of feet and the screech of the hut door, and sat up. It was the girl. She put her finger to her lips and whispered.

"You must go, quickly. He is coming to get wood." While I scrambled my belongings together, she scooped grain and fruit into a bowl and shoved it into my pack. She peered round the side of the hut and froze. I heard the man approach and flung myself behind the open door.

"Have you got the grain for grinding?" he demanded.

"It's here," she replied, pushing some into another bowl. "I need a little extra. We are making some griddlecakes to welcome the new month."

"Then make haste. The fire will be hot soon." He took his basket of logs and disappeared.

"Go now," she hissed. "That way – you won't be seen. Here, take this." She seized a jar of honey from the shelf and pressed it into my hands. "Coming!" she shouted in answer to a shout from the house.

"I thank you," I said. She smiled and left me.

I waited for a moment, looking at the swirling flakes outside. The ground was whitening rapidly and my feet were already cold. It was against all the principles of hospitality, but I was hardly a guest here. I pulled a sheepskin from a wooden peg on the wall, held it over my head so that it lay across the bundle at my back, and fled.

A few minutes later I felt sure I was not being followed and my prints were filling up, almost as I moved. I leaned on a rock, took out my knife and, as I had done so many months before, I bound up my feet, with strips of skin, woolside inward.

It was bliss to walk on, so protected.

I did not feel so happy for long. As far as I could see, the track stretched ahead, curving round the sides of the lower moorland. Unless I found some shelter, I would perish of cold. Somehow I kept going, grateful for the food I had been given. I passed one beck surging down the hillside and refilled my flagon, my hands quickly turning blue as I fumbled with the stopper. I drank some of the icy water, and pushed on; it was warmer to keep moving.

That night at Hardric's, Gurth had told me of the great mountains, the blizzards and the icy ways that lay between the fenland I knew and the remote coast where Wulf must spend his exile. I blundered on. Even if Wulf were alive, even if I could find a way to get to him, what welcome could I expect to have? Burdened by the child I had so rashly conceived, and the father of whom was the man who had caused Wulf's banishment, how could the prince feel anything for me but loathing and disgust?

Blinded as much by tears as by snow, I staggered into the northwest wind until my feet slipped and I almost fell headlong into a ghyll, which carved a gulf across the road. It came down a cleft to my right, and I could see a huge rock on a spit of stones where the water separated to form a tiny islet. Growing on the rock was an ancient, twisted yew tree, its roots snaking down into the earth like the warped fingers of an old woman. The rocky sides of the little gorge were tufted with thorn bushes and brambles, black now against the snow.

It was growing darker now. I flung my bundle over the stream onto the eyot, then I stepped from rock to rock as the torrent swept past, fast-flowing, if not very deep.

Nevertheless I slipped and was wet to the knees when I scrambled onto the ground and leant, gasping, against the rock. It was like a cave, arching out above my head, and held by the roots of the great green tree that curtained it from the wind and snow. Normally I would have shrunk from such a tree. The yew is sacred and dangerous, not to be abused, but I no longer feared its spirit. Compared to the wildness of the storm, it held no terror for me

Hastily, though clumsy with cold and fatigue, I unwrapped my store, reaching for the precious flints to make a fire. I coaxed the sparks to life with a pull of wool from my stolen fleece and fed it with hairlike roots and then bigger twigs. I braved the curve of the rock and gathered fallen wood from the great, sheltering tree, wearily lugging it back to dry by the fire, feeding it until it was giving out a blaze of heat. I was tired to my core, but found myself impelled by the need to keep alive.

I warmed water and found a flattish rock on which to pound grain. I mixed the rough flour into a paste with water, honey and some fruit. I drank warm water. I tied my piece of hide to some hanging roots to give extra shelter from the wind, put my sheepskin onto some leaves and gathered my shawl, cloak and blanket round me. I lay, spent, for a while, gazing at the flames, rousing myself to bank the fire with more wood, some damp moss and earth. I placed some flat pieces of rock around it and huddled down again.

I wondered why I had bothered. Would it not be better for me to go on into the dark snow until, exhausted, I died in the cold? I did not care whether I lived or not, and I longed for the time when I could be rid of the whelp that Eadwacer had left in my womb. If I lived, I vowed, if it was born alive, it would not live for Wulf to see. This night, I prayed to no gods. None had given me aid. I did not fear death now, however it might come. As for Wulf, I was so exhausted that I could not summon the energy to think of him. My desperate plight left me no room for hope. Its promises were like a disease, tearing at my heart – too painful to be endured. I closed my mind and slept.

In the morning the water drops were frozen into icicles. Only the turbulent stream had sufficient energy to flow, and the snow continued to fall. I stayed where I was. I could not go on, even without the encumbrance of the thing I bore so unwillingly. But I was still alive.

WULF

My happiness has died, totally. I exist, working merely to keep alive. I pile stones at the broken walls and hew timber, such as I can find: a little, low-growing scrub of willow and birch. Sometimes I find driftwood on the rocks and shingle, and lift it out to dry. There is grass and moss to make a fire and a torch to guide my steps in the treacherous darkness.

I have taken a young peregrine from its nest on the ruined tower and will train it to fly from my fist and to go hunting for me.

I thought I knew loneliness before, that the voyages into the dark waters and the long treks overland were the worst that fate could bring. Now the yearning once again to cross the waves, to return to the life I knew, overshadows all that I do, all that I see. The land lies so close, yet is impossible to reach: the waves are too strong.

Instead of the bright voices calling in the hall, and the ribald shouts of men in the ships, I hear the whoop of the early swan, the sad cry of the cuckoo, the cold scream of the eagle. When the graceful fulmar spreads her wings, I see the white arms of my beloved. My mind wanders over the expanses of the ocean, carrying me in a powerful, sweeping tide, where memories and dreams swirl together.

This is the place where all winds blow. I have survived the biting grip of the north blast, and turned my face to the warm breath of the south. It is the east wind that sets my blood singing.

The easterly will carry me towards the land. This is the wind that makes me feel alive. Somehow, some day, I will follow it, or feel its power guiding me towards the distant hills over the cruel, narrow strait. This chill wind will rouse my dull spirit and urge it across the water.

18

As the days passed, I gradually built up the sides of my little cave with rocks. Wrapping my hands against thorns, I used the bushes for tinder and for extra roofing, weaving strands among the roots and branches of the cavernous yew tree and packing them with the sparse earth I could scratch with my torn fingers.

I eked out the food I had, making small cakes, taking small handfuls of nuts and fruit, and using sparingly the dried meat I had been given by the childless woman I had met. Even so, I had to find more than this. When the blizzards stopped and the occasional thaw started, I began to seek round. I dug for herbs in the snow, finding withered bilberries and a few bitter, frozen blackberries left over from autumn.

Then I remembered watching Guthlac fashioning a snare. I cut a thin string of hide and placed the noose where I had seen animal prints. In the morning I found it had been torn from the sprig where I had attempted to fasten it. I tried again, several times. One night I caught something, but it had been killed and gnawed at, presumably by a fox. The next night I was successful – a white hare lay there, cold and stiff.

Again, I remembered the work I had watched as a child, Gerda's hands skinning, gutting, cleaning, spitting the meat on a wooden skewer. I clutched my knife and began to hack, slash and pull. In the end I looked with a kind of horror at the skinny creature, so like a baby. Then I rigged it over the fire and made shift to spit roast it, the smell mouthwatering. I caught the little juice and fat there was in a

127

bowl. Mixed with the creature's brain, liver and heart, chopped into some grain, I would have at least two or three more meals. The cold weather would help to keep it, too.

I was so hungry I devoured the meat from the legs, picking at the skinny body and pulling the bones apart. I flung the remnants into the little midden I created downstream, across the roadway and well away from my dwelling. So I kept myself alive.

Another woman would have taken solace in her unborn child, might have talked to it and felt less lonely; but I tried to ignore its insistent stirrings, utterly rejecting it as a source of comfort or companionship. I was desperately lonely, imagining telling Gurth, or even (when I dared to hope) Wulf of my journey, of my persistent urge to survive. I should, perhaps have felt thankful to whatever goddess was protecting me, but I gave no thought to the gods. I felt they had abandoned me.

In the spring I found that sheep were let to roam over the lower slopes, and I took milk – I had no means of turning it into cheese, but it felt nourishing. Once, desperate for food in a week when it rained non-stop, I took a tiny newborn lamb from its mother, leaving her with its twin. I had to kill it in spite of its wide eyes and frantic bleating. It lasted me for days.

All the time I grew in bulk, my body ungainly and awkward to move. The kicking from within felt ever more invasive, repellent. I could not wait to be rid of this thing.

I thought of Ulrica and how she had shrieked with her pains for a whole day. I needed help, but I could not go back to the place where the girl had hidden me. I repacked and, burdened before and behind, I walked slowly down the road.

It took all of that spring day, but eventually I came to a group of houses in the shade of three large holmoaks. I was fortunate. The headwoman of the family took one look at me and hustled me indoors.

She silenced her husband with a look that would have stunned a pig, and I was bathed in warm water, my hair was combed and my filthy robe replaced with a clean one. I was fed a nourishing broth with lamb and barley, flavoured with rosemary.

I told them I had lost my husband and had trudged too far in the wrong direction. I repeated the tale of finding my mother's sister, though I was sorry not to reveal the truth. The wife, Steinunn, took it for granted that I was concerned for my baby. She made me up a deep, warm bed and laid me on it. I slept almost before I could utter words of thanks.

In the morning I broke my fast with the family, gulping good, rich milk and nibbling cheese and hot oatcakes, while three children watched me, goggle-eyed.

"How far is it to the next village?" I asked.

"Why? You are never thinking of leaving!" Steinunn would have none of it. Indeed, I felt so tired from the hardships I had endured on my little island that I did not care to argue.

That day I met the other women and girls from the hamlet. I was pressed to give them details of my journey. I mentioned a market-town, a lift with a carter. I spoke of finding work at an inn. I told them nothing of the last four months. They did not even know which direction I had come from. They wondered how my husband would find me, here at Keldholme – he had a long way to come from the sea! I told them his name was Gurth. If ever, against all hope, he passed this way, they could pass on my name. Again, I called myself Eadwine.

At last I felt safe. Here I would give birth. When I was strong enough, I could move on.

One morning, shortly after Midsummer Day, as I was laundering clothes, I bent to pick up a wet tunic from the grass and was gripped by a sudden backache that made me gasp. I sat down on a bench by the door and let the pain pass before going back to the washing. Only when the third pang seized me did I realize what was happening. At the same moment my waters broke and I stood, my skirt sodden. I cried out for Steinunn, who sent her boy running for the other women.

They spread a thin cloth over the bed and laid me down. The menfolk were dismissed to the neighbouring house, and the inexorable business of birth began.

19

I fought it all the way. They inspected my body, and then for hours made me walk up and down, sometimes letting me rest to sip water, wiping my sweat away, until I felt a tearing, wrenching urge to bear down. They laid me on the bed, and two stood at each side, bending up my knees so that my feet were pushed against two sturdy hips. They gripped my arms and shoulders and after three or four straining, ripping pains, Steinunn cried,

"It's coming. The head is here – just pant, now, Eadwine."

I heaved breaths in and out, and then there came one last, explosive thrust and I felt the baby leave my body. I lay back, one woman stroking my stomach, while the other two exclaimed in excitement.

"Look, Eadwine, look! You have a fine son. He is perfect!"

Then came another convulsive pain, and some warm, slippery substance slipped from inside me. I was quickly cleaned, staunched with cloths and propped on a pillow stuffed with wool, a clean shift slipped over my head. I craved water and shook with exhaustion.

Steinunn brought the baby to me, after washing him. She held him out, his reddish hair dark with moisture and his sex bulging between fat little thighs.

"See! He is bonny – listen to his yelling. Here, let me wrap him."
She padded him with wool wrapped in thin cloth, and wound him in a small woven blanket. Then she handed him to me.

I did not want to take him. I loathed the act of his conception. I had hoped for his death in the womb. All I wanted through the

131

long hours of labour was that he or I would not survive the ordeal. The three women waited, with eager anticipation, their eyes fixed on me. I raised my arms and took the child. I was awkward – someone nestled the little round head into the crook of my elbow.

He stopped crying, opened his eyes, and gazed at me blankly. His eyes were as blue as mine, his hair beginning to glint with the same red-gold as it dried. He screwed up his face, opened his red mouth and squawked.

"May the gods bless him," said Steinunn. "He's hungry already."

Simply, in spite of my swelling and painful breasts, I had not truly realised this – I would have to feed him. I felt weak at the thought, but they were pushing me upright with more cushions, and pulled open the front of my shift. The child searched, latched onto my breast and suckled. I felt a deep, responsive stirring within me, and a confusion of emotions, part revulsion, part thrill. I was weeping and the women uttered little, sympathetic cries. They assumed I was overjoyed.

I did not feel joy, but as I sat there with the small, living creature drinking contentedly, I was amazed to feel a sense of achievement. They showed me how to lift him, pat him to bring up wind, and turn him to the other nipple. For a short time I was left to the task while they tidied up the debris of this day's work.

I leant back a little, the child's weight solid against me and watched him. One small arm had struggled from his wrapping and he waved it aimlessly for a few minutes. Then, sated, he fell still, his eyes closed, swelling under blue-veined lids, and his mouth relaxed.

I was not overwhelmed with a sudden, fervent love for him, but rather a realisation that he was innocent, trusting and vulnerable. It was at least partly my fault that he was conceived. I had not wanted him, but he was mine.

He was mine! I had lost all I had loved, and here was a tiny, warm, vital being, who depended on me for life. I cuddled him closer and rested my cheek on his soft head.

"What name will you give him?"

A name! My mind was blank. They tried one and another, laughing happily as I looked down at my son. Suddenly I wanted to find something that was especially his, not to name him after any man I knew. He would never know his father, and my father and grandfather were nothing to him.

"Ricberht," I said. "He is Ricberht."

"A good name!" cried Steinunn. "One for a strong-minded man, a shining warrior! Now let me take him. You must rest. There will be time for celebrations tomorrow."

I thanked them warmly, these good, able women. The child was laid in a borrowed cradle and I sank into a quiet sleep.

Anyone who has had children knows what happens next. Nights are broken, daily tasks seem to revolve around feeding, cleaning, laundering. I was very anxious not to disturb the family too much, especially as Steinunn's husband was a hard-working farmer. They insisted that one more child made no difference – they were used to upheaval. I was grateful for their support, and needed the kindly advice and guidance of the women in this little family group.

They never put any constraint on me to account for my husband's absence, my reluctance to contact my spurious aunt, let alone to say where I had come from. I knew enough of a seafarer's life from Wulfgrim's tales to keep the children's eyes wide with awe. We also shared tales of the great heroes, such as are sung in every hall. The wives chuckled with sympathetic humour as I told of the boisterous behaviour of customers at the inn where I had worked.

As my strength returned and the child settled into a routine, I began to help with the household tasks. We shared the work and I enjoyed the companionship and collaboration I had never had before, except with Hilda. Harvest was a time of great joy and I felt the warmth of the occasion amidst these happy people.

Yet I knew that before the year turned toward winter I must move onward again. I had to climb and cross the moorlands that stretched above and beyond the settlement. I dared not risk the rain and winds of autumn, let alone the treacherous mists, frost or snow of these northern hills. I planned to walk to the nearest market, hoping to barter for a pony – searching my possessions, I realised with a dreadful pang that the only valuable thing I owned was my piece of amber. How could I give away the only thing Wulf had ever given me? But I could not make this journey safely on foot, carrying my baggage and my child.

Steinunn found me crying quietly. I told her I was feeling useless and helpless. I begged her to let me go out to gather flax to make linen. If I could sell some cloth, I could perhaps save my beloved token, I thought. Before I left, I would tell Steinunn the truth – I owed her that, and she would otherwise not understand my desire to leave.

I was out on the strip of field, pulling at the tough, withering stems and stuffing them into a straw basket, one warm afternoon, when I heard Steinunn shouting for me. I turned, shading my eyes, and saw that she stood at the door, her husband beside her, and he was not alone. He held the bridle of a horse whose rider was dismounting, swinging down with his back to me. Several other riders held their mounts a few paces beyond him. Steinunn rushed towards me, smiling broadly.

"Oh, Eadwine, my dear girl, it is your husband! It is Gurth! Look!"

Gurth spun round, amazed, he said later, at being called my husband. He was just in time to catch me as I fainted.

When I came to, I was on my bed, Gurth standing over me and Steinunn wiping my face with a damp cloth. She made me sip some mead, but once she saw I had recovered, she patted my hand, smiled at me and left.

Outside I heard the voices of the children and the men's in reply. I sat up. It was really him, after all these months. He was the same robust, man Gerda had come to love and I to trust. I began to speak.

"Hush, now, princess. All is well. I thank the gods I have found you at long last."

We talked, quietly but urgently. He knew, or guessed, most of what had happened to me. He had followed my trail to Hilda, who had told him what had happened to me after I had left Hardric, and how her husband had left me with Ulrica's family. He had managed to pick up my trail, and had even found Edmund's riverside hostelry, after his encounter with Eadwacer at the Humber river.

Then he had lost me. He had tried one road and another, to west, north, east, even once reaching the coast, before turning back to where people dwelt below the edge of these moorlands. Not all the people he encountered were friendly: there had been one or two fights. Bad weather had them holed up for some weeks last winter, he said. They had crossed the moors more than once, but at last he had found me, by sheer chance, when he gave his name to the farmer in his field.

Then the baby cried. I lifted him up, cleaned him and raised him to my breast – then saw Gurth's expression of astonishment. I felt my cheeks redden, but folded Ricberht protectively to me.

"He is mine," I said quietly.

"Yours – and – whose?"

"It was Eadwacer. He – I did not want it to happen, but-"

"I will kill him. How dared he force himself - ?"

"It was my fault, too. I thought you were dead. I thought Prince Eni must be dead as well. Eadwacer was someone I knew, a familiar face. He was kind to me once."

"He betrayed you – and Wulf." He was shocked and accusing, on his lord's behalf.

"I know it. That is why I left, why I kept on travelling. I did not want him to find me again."

"I found you. So can he."

"Yes." That was one source of dread for me.

"And Wulf? What of him? Will you take this other man's child to him?"

"I did not intend to. I wished it dead. But, see, Gurth, he is mine. He is alive, he is strong, and –" (for the first time I spoke the words), "I love him."

He sat, hunched over his hands, staring at the floor.

"Gurth, I beg of you, take us with you. I have to find Wulf. I have to!"

"You love him still?"

"Yes, I love him still. I never stopped. Gurth, if there is any chance he is still alive, I will find him. Then he can decide if he still wants *me*." My words were bold, but my heart was sinking. I held Gurth's eyes until at length he nodded.

My relief was so intense I almost groaned. I seized his hand and gripped it tight; then I told him how I had survived the last winter, how Steinunn's people had helped me, and what I was planning to do now that I was strong again. By the time I had finished, he was looking at me with some of his old respect.

Now we called the family in, brothers, wives, sisters, and told them the truth, as I had determined to do.

20

Naturally there were tears, after all the explanations. I begged forgiveness for what seemed to them like a lack of trust. Steinunn hugged me and promised to provide me and Ricberht with everything we needed for a journey. We feasted that night and told our stories in full. I heard that Gurth had ridden far to the north before meeting up with, and choosing, his current companions, most from the islands and coasts, far beyond where Wulf was marooned. Steinunn persisted in calling Gurth 'your man' and he smiled wryly and accepted it calmly.

Early in the morning we ate and saw to the loading of the horses. Our panniers were stuffed with provisions, and plenty of garments and cloth to wrap the baby. At my belt I hung a soft leather purse, with a few precious flints and my amber still in its carved box.

"Now you make sure to stop and rest," Steinunn admonished Gurth.

The leave-taking was painful. I had come close to these good-hearted people and could never repay their kindness and generosity. As we rode away, I cradled Ricberht, wrapped in a large, warm cloak, and wiped tears from my eyes. We retraced my steps, heading east, passing the little fold in the hillside, where I had endured the lonely winter and spring. I showed the eyot to Gurth. He and the other men were amazed, and I had to show them my hearth, the snares I had cut, even the remains of the midden. After that, it seemed to me that Gurth's followers treated me with a little more deference – they certainly eyed me with some admiration, and began to call me 'princess' as he did.

We bartered some lamb's meat and bags of hay at the settlement below the edge of the moor, needing a few more hides, in case we found no shelter on the moor-top. Then we turned north and began to climb.

Ricberht saw to it that we stopped whenever he was hungry, but the steady movement of the horse lulled him so that he alternately slept or lay gazing up at the sky. At the end of the summer, we were fortunate to have mild, clear weather. Even so, with the steep track, and the rough surface, we could not urge the horses to any great speed. We were on a high, breezy top as the day dimmed.

To our left ran a little stig, down into a tiny, steep valley. We turned down, hoping to be protected from the night winds, and found a shepherd's hut beside an empty fold. We called aloud, but had no answer, so we took advantage of the shelter for ourselves and our animals. Gurth pegged up a blanket to form a corner for me and the baby, but it did not muffle the sound of Ricberht's cries. I fear the men were roused twice in the night, and early in the morning.

I brought out floury cakes and nuts and we drank mead to give us heart, filled our flasks with water from the stream, and turned back up the stig and onto the path over the heights. A south-west wind at our backs urged us forward, and the only other sound, apart from the hooves thudding on the grass, came from the occasional crow we startled from the golden bracken, or a kite whistling overhead.

We made only about ten miles that day. One horse fell lame, wrenching its pastern in a hole on the uneven path, and had to have its leg bound. We came onto a vast, open expanse, with the sea glinting far off as it rolled from a darkening horizon to the east. I had never seen the sea before, and felt a thrill run through me at the sight. Below us we could see the road snaking down, and smoke rising from a settlement near the coast.

"Best to stay up here until morning," said Gurth. "We don't want to be on that slope as it gets dark." We turned off again to find more cover, and came to Ugglebarn, as its occupant told us. She was an extremely old woman, crooked with age, barely a tooth in her head, and her wispy hair as white as the cloth which covered it. Her name was Morwyn, she said.

She offered us milk and flat bread, soaked with honey and

sprinkled with nuts, freshly-pounded. We gave her meat and a flagon of mead. She apologised for lack of space to house the whole party, but the men were content to secure the horses on long tethers and to bed down on the springy turf in the lee of the narrow dale. Morwyn produced a hot cloth with a smelly poultice, which she applied to the leg of the injured animal.

I was pulled eagerly inside and given a stool, and she found an open box that served well for a cradle, lined with fleece. She clucked and chuckled over the baby and stroked his head gently, with fingers like hazel twigs, as he suckled.

Not wishing to retell my tale, I said we were travelling to meet my husband at the coast, and she was satisfied. Her husband had been dead for – she could not say how many years. I asked her how she managed on her own, thinking of my own fights for survival. Folk came to see her, she said, to ask for advice for cures, for charms and left her gifts of food, cloth, furs. She kept a few sheep: we ate some cheese. I slept well that night, later wondering what she had put in the warm posset I drank. Ricberht slept, too, waking only at first light. I felt rested and refreshed and ready for the ride down to the coastal cliffs.

I felt as if, at last, it was a real possibility that I could find Wulfgrim. I had no idea how much further we had to go, just longed to avoid the hardships of another winter on the road.

We bade Morwyn farewell, and led the horses up the steep gully back to the moorland road and made our way to the coast. One man, Gurth's appointed carl, whose name was Eric, had to walk the lame horse all the way, but that way was so difficult that he would be not long behind us. It began to rain as we clattered down the sheer, stony path to find accommodation. There was a cluster of houses, wharves and storage barns around the long, narrow harbour. This was edged with high cliffs and a look-out tower toward the mouth of the river as it met the sea.

It felt strange to be housed in a fair-sized hall, on a raised bed with a cradle, a chest and the use of the fire in the main room. Sometime after mid-day, we ate steaming hot fish and apple-cakes. Then, as the rain abated, Gurth said he would go to the mooring and see if we could ask for passage on a northbound ship.

"What can we offer in recompense?" I cried.

Gurth patted the leather purse fastened to his sword-belt. When he and Wulf had separated to try to throw their hunters off the trail, Wulf had shared out the little gold pieces, and some pretty stones he had acquired on his travels, and I had given him some more. So far Gurth had had little need of them. He had bartered with venison and fish he and his men had caught – even with skins from stolen sheep, cattle and goats, rarely parting with any treasure. As far as possible they had remained unobserved. Only now, with a woman and child to protect, did they need to find an easier, safer way to travel.

I sat, contentedly playing with Ricberht, amazed at how placid he was, gurgling as he lay on a lambskin, kicking his legs after I fed him. I was startled by Gurth's sudden return.

"Lady, we must pack up – swiftly, now!" He had had extraordinary good luck in finding a ship willing to take me, with the baby and two men. "It is not an easy voyage," he warned me. "There are dangers near the coast, and a strong current, which may turn against you at the river-mouths. I do not know if they will sail the seventy miles or so without putting in. Much will depend on the tide and the wind."

"Will you be with me?"

"No, there is more to tell you." By this time he had gathered one bundle together   and was pushing me into action.

"I will take four men and ride. The way is too rough for you and the child. There are moors, marshes and rivers to cross – but listen, princess – we have to make haste You must cover your head. Eadwacer might see you – "

"Eadwacer!"

"Yes. Raedwald's ship was entering the harbour as I was talking with the sea-captain. I do not know if he is seeking Prince Eni – or for what purpose. He will surely come here. You must pretend to be Eric's wife and cling to his arm. Hide your face."

He gave swift orders, passed a gold piece in settlement for our abbreviated visit and sent for the horses. The gold could be melted down to make a ring, or a brooch – ample payment for the innkeeper's trouble.

"Wait! Tell me, at least, where I am going. Where shall I find you, find Wulf?"

"Eric knows the island. It lies maybe seventy miles or more from here, about a mile and a half from the shore, covering the mouth of a river. It is a tricky place to enter, but you must meet me on the mainland, as close to the river mouth as you can get. Cocket, it's called – the river, and the island. The captain knows it. The gods go with you, princess." He looked at me calmly enough, but I knew how urgent was the need to be gone.

"I shall see you, Gurth. Wait for me."

"You have my word." They tightened their sword-belts, flung cloaks over their leather jerkins, mounted and galloped off, up the precipitous slope.

I wrapped the baby warmly in his lamb's fleece and with the two men, walked down towards the harbour, head down inside my hood. I was afraid. I had never been in a ship before. Wulf had told me that sailing north was hard, unless you were granted a wind from the south or southwest. And I wondered with dread what Eadwacer was doing here.

We turned a corner and a wind (from the south!) snatched the hood from my face. I was clutching at it with one hand, supporting Ricberht with the other, when Eric pulled me roughly to one side. Too late. We were face to face with Eadwacer.

I tried to duck past, but he recognised me, surprise turning to astonishment as he took in my companions, and the baby.

"Eric," I said, "go on to the ship. I must talk to this man – yes, I know him. I shall follow in a moment." He looked dubious but went ahead, leading the two horses. I saw his fellow wait several yards away, hand on sword.

I stemmed Eadwacer's questions almost angrily. Yes, I had arrived here in company and was making for the sea. He thought I must have changed my mind and planned to seek out Raedwald. My husband, he told me, had finally accepted that I would not come to him. He still planned to declare the marriage broken, and would look to wed again – a princess from across the sea, maybe; one with a great dowry and much treasure. Just what Raedwald needed.

"What will you do now, princess? And what of this child? Whose – ?" His voice trailed off, and I could see him trying to calculate.

"Oh yes, this child is mine," I told him, bitterly.

"Is it – did I – was it when we - ?" he stammered.

"This brat," I said harshly, "this whelp has no father." I told him I was taking it to lands across the sea, as far as I could go. "I belong to no man," I said. "I can do as I wish."

He tried to argue – begged me to stay a little, said he could protect me.

"I am in the protection of the sea-goddess. If she wishes, I will survive. Let go of me, Eadwacer! This creature is nothing to do with you." I held the child up, abruptly. "See! It does not even look like you!"

I could see my guard moving back towards us, nervous of this argument. "I shall be sailing east on this tide." As an after-thought, I demanded to know why he was here, and where he was bound.

"We have put in for provender. I am sent north." He hesitated. "It is my lord's concern. His brother – well, he is unfinished business. I am sent to put an end –"

"You are going to kill Prince Eni!" Now I knew this was his purpose. "Is he not dead already?" I gasped.

"That remains to be seen."

The guard was at my side.

"Is all well, lady? We must move on."

"Yes, the ship must be waiting. I am ready. Be well, Eadwacer. We shall not meet again."

"Niartha. Do not be so sure." His eyes followed me as I folded Ricberht closer and walked away.

I hoped, pleading with the gods, that he would believe I felt nothing for the child, terrified he would make some hold on me. If he thought I was heading east, he might not make haste to follow me.

I clambered over the ropes and rings on the wooden wharf and Eric gripped my arm as I stepped down into the ship.

21

I was surprised at how large it was, though later, tossing in the waves, it seemed perilously small. Ricberht and I perched on a low, plank seat below the wooden gunwale, in the middle of the ship. Eric tied some hides across at the high curve nearer the stern to the protective sides of the vessel, and lashed them down, making a kind of cave. Our packs of cloaks, blankets and food were similarly wrapped in various kinds of soft leather, to protect them from waves and weather. I moved there, crouched and nervous with my baby.

The captain, Lukas, was a trader, who regularly plied this coast. His ship was a good eighty feet long and had crossed the sea. A gnarled and wind-tanned hulk of a man, he came from the prow and asked if I was well. I thanked him, promised to keep still and out of the way. He turned aside and, after poking around in a sack, he pulled out a sheet of rough, but tightly-woven cloth.

"This has been steeped in goose-fat," he told us. "Use it to wrap the little one when we meet the waves."

The ship was lurching under us as the last sacks, boxes and bags were hauled on board and carefully stacked and tied. Three sheep and our two horses were tied to pegs and rings near the prow, fenced in with birch hurdles. Men coiled ropes, some seized huge oars, Lukas took the rudder oar in his large hands and began to shout orders.

I rose, bent from under my little awning, and straightened to observe our departure. Men on the wharf tossed our last ropes inboard, as planks were withdrawn. Oars shoved us away, until we were in the stream, then rowers pulled strongly. At the same time four men wrestled with the sail, until, unfurled, it took the wind and we surged forward. There was little need to row, but the skipper used six oarsmen to aid steering as we took the narrow channel towards the sea.

I sat down abruptly as we hit the waves of the open sea. Apparently it would have been a lot worse if we had not had the tide and wind in our favour. Even so it was an extraordinary sensation. The wind now completely filled the russet sail, and the oars were shipped. We seemed to fling ourselves to the open ocean, rising, leaping, sliding down, thudding onto the water. It felt much colder.

Wulfgrim had told me how some people were prostrated with sickness on the sea, but I felt exhilarated. Eric explained in his soft, northern voice how we had to keep at least a mile between us and the shore, and more in the hours of darkness, as this coast was edged with treacherous rocks and scars. If the current changed, we could be driven back, caught in tidal flows and battered to pieces or overturned. I shuddered, though not with the cold.

I asked Eric to thank the captain for his kindness. I did not think women were welcome on shipboard. He smiled. Warships were forbidden – women brought ill-luck. But traders were prepared to make concessions, one piece of merchandise being much like another. Few women, however, took long journeys.

Ricberht awoke and cried for more milk. I turned into the shelter and fed him, shy at first of the sailors' eyes. But they were all too preoccupied. We could still see the coastline behind us as we rose and dipped, spray hissing past.

Then there were cries of 'hold fast!' and Eric made me sit straight and cling to the rope hanging beside me. Ricberht screeched furiously as I covered my breast and cradled him tightly. The captain put the great oar hard over and turned our head to the north. We swung wildly up the side of a wave and settled. The buffeting eased as the strong, northerly current took us and we rode the waves, sweeping forward. It felt as though the ship were alive, in its element, its high prow lifting and falling, the wash flying away from its wide-curved sides.

A sailor brought us food and a horn of drink. I had not eaten since mid-day and I tore hungrily at the bread, and let Ricberht finish gorging himself. I cleaned him, rewrapped him against the chill of the late autumn afternoon and laid him on his lambskin in a rough basket, in the covered space.

"How long shall we be at sea?" I asked the captain as he made his way down the ship, relinquishing the steering to another shipman.

"All that's left of this day," said Lukas, "all the night and about mid-day tomorrow we should see our landfall. If all goes well." So soon! I had not thought we could go so fast. There was a long way to go, Gurth had said.

"Shall we sleep ashore?" I asked. He laughed.

"Nay, There is hardly a safe night-landing between here and the Cocket – and that is bad enough at any time." There came a cry from the man at the helm. I heard oaths, orders yelled and the men found each his place.

"What is it?" I asked Eric.

"The wind has dropped," he answered. "We must make what headway we can before the current turns against us." Sure enough, the sail was tightened to collect what breeze it could, and the oars reinforced our progress over the flat sea.

"Pray Rana that the wind does not change," said Eric. "It will rise again as the sun sets, you'll see."

"I watched as the turgid sea passed beneath us. Time seemed to pass as slowly. The sun was dipping to a cliff in the west, a reddish crag turning blacker as the shadows lengthened. I wrapped my cloak more tightly about me as I felt a chill. We turned this way and that, but seemed to do not much more than hold our position, level with the red scar on the cliff.

"West wind!" someone yelled. I was a little alarmed. I knew an east wind could drive us onto the shore, but would a westerly not take us out to sea? Now we were using the wind to take us forward more swiftly again, steadily at first, then more uncomfortably as we met the waves.

As the evening grew darker, a few stars gleamed in an indigo sky. We tossed from crest to crest, feeling the turbulence in the troughs; spray hissed over our heads. Men were set to baling out water with shallow scoops and bowls. Eric gave me a stout belt to fasten on, and tied my rope to it, as the wind freshened. He wedged the baby's basket tightly under the seat, the waxed cloth securely tucked round it.

"There are black clouds coming from the land," he warned me. "It will rain soon."

It did. The stars disappeared. I sat, knees bent to my chin, feet on the plank seat, as far under cover as I could get. I thought of Gurth riding through the same wet night. I thought of Eadwacer. Eric believed that he would not have dared to cross the tide at its lowest ebb. Whitby harbour mouth would have been impassable to Raedwald's great ship. I thought of Wulf. I was afraid, now that I was almost in reach of him – if he was alive.

I looked at my son's little form, sleeping so trustingly through the hurly-burly. I had never imagined the noise. Men called to each other raucously over the howl of the wind, the relentless booming of the black seas, the creaking of the ship's timbers and ropes straining, rain lashing on every surface. The horses neighed wildly in fright but the sheep fell silent, huddled in their fear. The sail crackled as it spilt the wind or filled again at the next turn. I was afraid, but drew some courage from the shipmen as they took action against the spirits of the air and water.

This went on for hours; two men at the tiller oar, others tugging at the sail, turning the yardarm. Eric was tending his comrade, lying sick in the bottom of the ship, too weak to cling to the side. There was no question of sleep. I slumped my head on my knees, exhausted, but roused myself to put the baby to my breast again, when he demanded it.

Eventually the sky lightened in the east, the rain stopped and our hearts rose. We moved northwest to find the land again, having braved the dark ocean to avoid the more dangerous shore. There were some arguments about our position – whether we had passed a treacherous river-mouth in the dark. Then one man spotted a headland jutting a quarter of a mile to the sea. In all these hours we had made less than thirty miles from our port of departure. We would have to battle through forty more.

We shook wet garments as dry as we could and ate and drank. The horses were fed. The sheep were thrown some hay, to take or leave.

We butted against the seas, wind against water, but the sun came up and warmed us. Our progress became more rhythmic and stable. The ship gracefully accepted the movement of the water and flew onward. It was hard to contain my rising agitation as the day drew on. Ricberht became fractious, and one of the sailors walked him up and down the ship to entertain him, cheerfully enduring the mocking laughter of his fellows. I had to force myself to eat, though I was glad to drink what I was offered, ewe's milk one time, mead another. The sun reached its height and was just visibly turning down its path when another shout had us on our feet.

We had kept a fairly steady distance from the shore, so I saw low cliffs: dark at the base, ridged with sandy stone and topped with grass, white foaming breakers at their feet, and even more frightening billows crashing onto the black rocks.

"Hauxley ledges!" called the lookout. Immediately the captain turned us further from the shore and they spilled wind from the sail to slow us down.

"Island ahead!"

I forgot my promise to be still and pushed my way to the prow. There, so close I could smell the land, lay an island. Waves broke on its rocky base; low, dark-grey cliffs rose towards the west. Closer now, I searched, hand brushing the hair from my eyes, for any sign of life. We sailed round to the south-east, and we saw a cleft in the rocks rising from a tiny shingle beach. In the lee of the island we slowed and the men roped their oars to the tholes once more. Cautiously we moved round the north of the island to see more crags lit by the westering sun.

It was agony for me to leave the island behind us. Moving to the stern I could see some walls – or were they rocks? – on top of the cliffs. I saw no sign of human habitation, no smoke from any fire.

Birds flew to and fro but their shrill screams faded as we ploughed north round some shoals and back in towards the river-mouth. The sail was dropped and men stationed to watch the water for hidden ledges and sandbanks. It was hard, dangerous and skilful work. The channel was narrow and to our right the rising swell was breaking on a rocky shoal. We rose and fell in the waves on the sand-bar at the river-mouth, and were at last inside the haven. There was a jetty for mooring and, across the dunes to the south, on a little rise, we saw a tiny hamlet. The occupants were out, three or four men, with weapons, to meet us, but seeing the trader, they called to their womenfolk.

I looked for any sign of Gurth and his men, but there was none. I knew he could not have reached here before us. Once again, I had to ask for shelter, saying my man (they thought I meant my husband) was riding to meet me. I think it was the baby who decided the matter and I and my two guards were granted hospitality.

Lukas completed whatever bargains he was making, summoned his men from their bottles of ale, and parted from us before the tide began to ebb. Though grateful, I was sad, and anxious, that he was leaving. How would we get to the island? So near now, and still I did not know if Wulfgrim were to be found there, nor if he were alive or dead.

Sharing their evening meal, Eric asked the locals about the island. It took a little persuading and the gift of a couple of gold pieces and a useful knife or two, but they had a tale of horsemen coming, several winters ago – there was an argument about it being three or four – no, it had to be three because that was when Ector's son had died. Eventually they returned to the story. One man had been captured by a band of marauding strangers. They were, of course, talking of the party of men with my uncle Edgar. These men had seized one of the fishing boats and braved the cold, rough seas to reach the island. They had returned without their prisoner, and had damaged the boat. It still rankled that they had made no reparation to the fishermen, but at least they had committed no worse crime. What these marauders did not know was that they had narrowly missed a second prisoner.

"Gurth!" I exclaimed. "Did you see Gurth?" They looked blankly at me. The villagers had spotted a man on the hilltop overlooking the sea, crawling among the tussocks of tough grass, but left him to make his escape.

"What of the man on the island?" I asked. "Has there been any sign of him? Has anyone gone to find him?"

"No-one could live there through one winter, let alone three," I was assured. My heart sank. "We do not go there except for birds' eggs on the low cliffs when food is scarce. The currents between here and the island are too fierce, most of the time."

But it was not just the dangerous tides, but the fear of ghosts that kept them away. The island was said to be haunted. A hundred or more years before, the island had been a look-out for a strange race of people, now long gone. Their tower was a tumbled ruin. Now and then flickering lights could be seen, or wisps of smoke, but these were certainly signs of spirits. No-one dared to land there now.

I glanced at Eric, who raised an eyebrow. My hope lifted.

WULF

I am forsaken. Gone is the love of father, brother, comrades. Never again shall I witness the ceremonies of the hall, where valour is rewarded, service is honoured. I shall not share again the joys of the hearth, nor the warmth of the bed: I curse the memories of past joys which come to taunt me.

The proud neighing of the steed, the clash of shining swords echo dimly in my mind.

The man I was has gone, changed into this gaunt, ragged stranger, who stares at me from the rain-water pools in the rocks, long hair blowing in the wind.

Why have the gods forsaken me? Why was I not granted the gift of death? If I had died in battle, I would be feasting in Valhalla. If I had been taken into the depths of the sea, I would have slept with the goddess herself.

I breathe the bitter air, feed on birds, their eggs and fish. I drink rain water, and store it in rocky scrapes. Once or twice I have been like to die for lack of it. I have chewed grass and found moisture in a few withering bilberries.

I gaze into the south, eyes following a flight of skuas heading for the warmer air as the days grow cooler. They skim above the water and suddenly rise, as if disturbed. A sail!

I stand transfixed by conflicting emotions. I have to know if this is my friend or my enemy – or merely another passing trading ship. As they approach I drop down flat, concealed amongst the drying tussocks of rough grass.

They dare not approach too near: there are dangerous currents here. I can see figures moving. The sail is shortened. Oars begin to pull. I cross the islet, crouching low, disturbing the occasional remaining tern or crow as I do so. The ship skirts round and enters the mouth of the river. I hold my breath as they edge past the rocks on the northern bank, then they turn on the curve of the stream and I see them no more.

I must keep watch from first light. Tonight I will not light a fire.

22

As dawn broke I walked to the headland and looked towards the island. It seemed so close. I searched it eagerly, hoping to see the figure of a man, or anything to show he was alive. The rising sun threw the low outline of the place into deep shades of blue. Only the words of the boatmen persuaded me that a man might not attempt to swim to safety. I did not even know if Wulf could swim! Then I turned and walked back to the house where I looked down at the sleeping child. Moving to the hearth, I found one of the women sitting there, quietly nursing her own baby. She smiled at me. Her name was Haesel.

"He is beautiful, your son," she said softly. "You are fortunate. This is my second daughter. My husband is displeased." We sighed, both of us knowing what it meant to be a mere girl.

"But she is lovely," I replied, touching the bright curls on the child's head. "Perhaps next time you may be lucky. Have you tried a syrup of apple and honey? It is very strengthening, they say, perhaps with a very little tansy."

We fell to talking of various remedies and cures, until Ricberht awoke and cried for milk. He sucked greedily as she prepared strips of meat in a pan, oatcakes soaking up the delicious fat and juice. Her family gathered for the first meal of the day, when we were interrupted.

"Horsemen!" shouted a lad, tumbling into the house. The men seized weapons: staves, spears, a sword, bows and rushed outside. The women followed, children held close and babies in arms. The men grouped across the narrow way beside the river.

Down the valley, and breasting the hillside came four men, drawing to a halt as they approached the men of the fishing village. The leader dismounted, holding up his hands in a gesture of peace. Eagerly I pushed forward, though Eric reached his friend first, embracing him in a warm bear-hug. I smiled – I had not realized how close they had become.

"Gurth! It is Gurth – he is known to me," I pleaded with the headman.

"Lady," said Gurth, delighted. "I hardly looked to see you here so soon." Then he greeted the fishermen courteously and begged their assistance and hospitality. Reassured, they accepted this new incursion.

We told our stories over the breakfast: Eric and I of the ship, and Gurth of their hard ride. Not merely had they contended with darkness, rain and appalling terrain, they had met with some outlaws, who promptly attacked them. One of Gurth's men was killed but their resistance had been fierce. They had cut down three and forced them towards deep water before they fled. Ailwyn was hurt, Gurth said. Indeed, he had a roughly-bound cut on his forearm. Before he could finish eating, he was taken in hand by the women. A poultice of bugle, burnet and dried moonwort was prepared and after the dried blood was washed away, this was bound firmly onto his wound.

Urgently, I used the time to exhort Gurth to find a way of reaching Cocket Island.

"They have fishing boats," I whispered. "We need their help. The currents are treacherous and there are rocks everywhere. We must hurry," I pleaded. "Eadwacer saw me. I told him we were crossing the eastern sea, but he is coming to find Prince Eni – we have to reach him first!"

"Very well, princess. I will talk with these people." But he looked exhausted, having ridden through the night.

"Rest first," I said. "We shall need your strength. It is early as yet." The men sat, or sprawled on rugs round the hearth, as Gurth told the tale of the prisoner on the island. When Eric told him of the lights seen there, Gurth's head lifted and he roused himself. He asked when was the last time they had been seen. There was some debate. Probably in the spring, maybe as late as the last frosts.

"Surely," said Gurth, "a man might do without light when the days lengthen and the moon is high." But one would need to cook, surely.

They were negotiating the use of a boat, with its master to pilot it, when, again, there were shouts outside. Two boys fishing from rocks at the base of the cliffs had seen a sail out at sea, coming from the south.

Gurth and Eric leapt up, and the fishermen raced to their small, broad boats, tied to staves on the muddy beach. Fishermen, Gurth and his men tumbled into the three tiny vessels, the last men wading as they shoved them into the water. Each boat had four oars and carried two of our men.

Women screamed, afraid of the sea, of the warship, of the ghost on the island. We stood on the sloping headland, watching helplessly as the great sail slowly came closer. Something strange was happening. Surely Eadwacer would circle the island as we had done, and would find the little landing on the east side. But the tide was now rising and the wind had veered from the east. The water between the river-mouth and the island was breaking badly. Eadwacer had left it late, someone said, to drop his sail, and we saw the shipmen fighting frantically at the oars. They began to pass the island at its south-eastern corner, and had to pull between its craggy cliffs and the rocky ledges below us. Very risky, said the fishermen's wives.

At the same time the fishing boats were tossing wildly as the stream met the ocean. Two broke off and turned to meet the warship – I hardly believed it; they could never hope to clash with her. But it served as a distraction. The third boat slid to the north-east, headed close behind the rough, black rock-slope of the island and disappeared from view.

Eadwacer did not ride down the small craft to their destruction. The great ship flung itself into the calmer waters, drove upstream, and was eventually beached near the mouth of the river.

I joined the other women, scurrying back to their houses. Desperately, I needed to hide Ricberht. Thinking of Eadwacer's last words and the look in his eye, I was afraid of what he might do. The other mothers were only too anxious to protect their own children.

"Who knows what these men might do, if we do not help them?" I urged. Two women and two older girls gathered up the little ones and the infants. I begged my new friend, Haesel, to take Ricberht too.

"I know the leader of these men," I said. "I can talk to him. We shall be safe." I ran back to the shore, to find an altercation already breaking out. The fishermen refused adamantly to pilot his ship out again. It was far too dangerous, they said, until the tide turned or the wind dropped. I wondered if they were telling the truth. Then Eadwacer saw me. He just nodded slowly, accepting my presence with no apparent surprise. He advanced towards me, leather boots crunching on the slippery sand and stones.

"Niartha." He looked around. "Your ship?" he asked.

"Gone about its business."

"And your business?"

"My business is complete."

"Indeed? And where is Prince Eni?"

"He has gone." Eadwacer turned and looked at the island, then swung back to me angrily.

I told him that we had taken the prince from the island the day before. I said that he was a changed man. I wept as I described how he rejected me and, furious at the way I had brought another man's child to him, he had torn it from my grasp, taken horse and left.

"He has taken our whelp to the woods," I spat at him. We could see the black line of a forest to the northwest.

"I shall kill him." I trembled at the quiet menace, but thrust my chin up boldly and glared at him through my tears. He thought they were of anger, not of fear. "The child is mine," he said. In my fury, I did not hear the menace in his tone.

"May you have joy of it," I spat. "It is probably already dead." I turned away, but he brushed past me, shouting to his men. He did not stay to bargain, but seized the reins of one of the horses tethered to some fencing. He galloped off along the riverbank, followed quickly by two of his men, leaving me shaking with relief, fear and fury.

My ploy had worked. But Raedwald's ship still lay beached, with its large crew around it. Even if Gurth found Wulf, even if they managed once again to cross the perilous channel, Raedwald's men lay in wait; and Eadwacer would return once he realised I had lied to him. I feared his wrath.

I returned to the house and tried to reassure the women of the village, though my own heart misgave me.

23

Voices rose by the shore and I saw fishermen gesturing toward the sea and then violently upstream. Some of them began dragging their smaller boats further up the beach, planting stripped logs below the hulls so that the boats rolled over them rapidly and onto the edge of the grassy bank. I felt the strength of the east wind, howling from the sea.

"The tide will turn!" shouted one man. "See! The water has changed already! The wind is wrong! Remember the last freak wave?"

Raedwald's sailors scanned the flow from the river-mouth. More arguing and arm-waving. Then they began slowly to drag the prow round until the ship stretched its great length along the shoreline, pointing upriver. Too late. Surging towards us from beyond the island came the first gigantic wave.

It broke, resounding, on the island, divided, remustered and hurtled over the rocks and promontories at the river mouth. Then it hurled itself, the full force of the east wind behind it, up the path of the river.

It was terrifying. Surely some furious god rode these waters, his raging spirit driving on. I could hardly hear the shouts, then screams of the men who clung to the side of the ship.

A few flung themselves on board as the upsurge lifted them, one sank under the prow as it lifted over him and pressed him implacably between water and harsh stones. A number struggled onto the high bank where I stood among the villagers, paralysed with horror, but some were undoubtedly drowned, snatched into the maw of that

157

monstrous, rolling flood.

The few men on board clung to the ropes, mast, hull. There was no time to grip the oars, and they would surely have been impotent. The ship reared and plunged forward like a warhorse, and tore into the river. The flow impelled it, and we ran up the shore, past the houses, in time to see the men striving to turn her head to the bend in the river.

But at this bend the tidal surge had broken, fallen and begun its return to the sea.

The strength of the under-tow seized the ship and flung it backwards and sideways so that it tilted, rose with a desperate heave and scraped shrilly up the beach on the far side of the river. It lay on its side, the next wave ripping from it and foaming back into the main stream. We saw the remaining crew – about ten of them – struggling hopelessly to right the ship, then a woman's wailing cry caught our attention.

"Norbert! Where is Norbert? His boat – did it reach the island?" It was one of the women who had been guarding the children. The whole group moved together. I took my baby from the arms of his protector. His whimpering echoed the frantic pleas of the women. No answer could be given.

We had seen the small craft rounding the island and one of the men said dubiously that he thought it would have had time to reach the landing. We remembered the force of the waves as they broke full onto the face of Cocket Island exposed to the sea. We had seen the spray flung high, even from this side of the island. I was terrified for Gurth and the men with him. I hardly dared to think of Wulf.

We had to wait. When the tide turned, if the wind dropped, then it would be possible to risk the crossing. Ricberht's yells became insistent. I took him inside, sat wearily on a stool and let him feed.

I changed the cloths that wrapped him and let him play. My hand absently tickled his soft, sturdy body so that he gurgled in delight, but my heart was oddly detached. My mind was repeating the words I had used to fool Eadwacer, and a quiver of doubt stirred: what if my lying words proved true?

If, in a matter of hours, Wulf and I came face to face at the end of these years, how would he receive this child? I myself had hated it for all the months of its growing inside me. Now I would defend him from anyone who tried to take him from me. The little hand clasped my thumb and pulled it so that it bumped the baby's nose. He laughed, a delighted chuckle and looked into my face. For the first time I responded by talking directly to him.

"Did you like that, little Ricberht? Do it again? Yes – funny, isn't it? Little sweet man!" I biffed his nose gently again, then bent and kissed it. I lifted him up and cuddled him. "I love you," I told him. For the first time I realized the capacity a woman has to love in varying ways. What of men, I wondered? Could they so open their hearts?

The waiting stretched out painfully. There was water to be fetched from the spring on the moorside. We cooked at the hearth, fed the men and the children and chewed a few mouthfuls. Every few minutes, one or another went to look towards the sea. Upriver, the crew of the warship were digging away at shingle. I wondered if their hull was still intact. I hoped they might be delayed by making good any damage. I prayed they would not cross the river and get to us. I fed the child again and laid him to rest as the day began to shorten.

"Will it be long to dark?" I asked one of the fishers, standing on the twilit promontory.

"Maybe the burning of two or three candles. Time enough yet."

People came out, gazed seaward and moved away. The women whose husbands and sons were crewing the little boat huddled closely, almost unmoving. I held a little apart from them, afraid to intrude, though sharing their dread.

The sun sank lower to our left, the reddish glow hanging over the black band of the forest towards which Eadwacer had ridden. I realized with a shaft of fear that he would likely return soon, angry at his fruitless errand. He would not willingly spend a night far from his ship. I feared for myself, for my child and for the kindly people who sheltered us.

As I turned back to scan the sea again, it seemed to me that one of the dark rocks at the base of the island shifted. I stared, then blinked. Then a man shouted, brandishing his arm and ran towards us. The babble of voices swelled and excited cries alerted the other villagers. We crowded to the banks and cliff-top, seeking vantage points.

Against the darkening sea, swollen with the slackening water, the shape of a small boat detached itself from the mass of the island, jostling below the cliffs. We could see the oars working and, as it fought its way towards us, the east wind ruffled the waves.

My heart thumping, I strained to identify the figures clinging to the tossing boat. It was impossible to see how many men there were as they heaved on the oars, leant back or lurched to grip the thwarts; movement, shadows and spray blurred our view.

The light was rapidly dimming; from the purple horizon beyond the island a great red moon was rising. Slowly, desperately heaving, the boat drew nearer and we moved involuntarily towards it as if compelling it. People began to shout, calling the men by their names. I could not make a sound, but in my mind I could hear the entreaty as if it were a scream: "Let them be alive!"

In terrible danger of smashing down onto the ledges below us, the craft seemed suddenly to hurtle past, slide past the dunes and into the river itself. Men threw ropes to them, which the crew made fast to wooden stanchions so that their momentum was slowed. Everyone helped and the little boat hove to and was tied to the tiny, battered jetty.

There was hubbub as two sodden men lurched from the gunwales. Women shrieked and clasped them frantically. I caught my breath as I saw Eric helping Gurth to clamber out, then someone thrust my baby into my arms and dashed forward screaming pitifully. One man, only too obviously, was dragged out and fell, unresisting, onto the beach. I could hear the woman who had cried out before, calling,

"Norbert! Where is he?" Someone, I think it was Eric, said in a voice blank with exhaustion, "He is dead. He is drowned," and her voice keened. But I was transfixed. Gurth and two of the villagers were helping another figure from the boat. He half-fell over the side, toppled to the shingle, but righted himself and stood as if dazed.

Wulf.

Around us the throng swirled. The ship must have been made fast. The dead man was carried away. The rest were taken into the warmth.

We stared at each other. I saw a man, thin-strung from lack of nourishment; his hair was long, unkempt and streaked with grey; his face was grey, too, under the wind-tan; his eyes seemed darker than ever, and had lost some of their gleam. His tunic, jerkin and cloak were tattered and he stood barefoot. The east wind blew the skirts of my kirtle around me and my mantle swirled so that I wrapped it round me – and the baby.

The movement seemed to jolt Wulf into action. He took a step toward me and lifted his hand. He cupped my cheek and lightly brushed my hair aside, gazing at me intently. I lifted my mouth, thinking he would kiss me. His hand lay on my shoulder and he looked down at Ricberht, his face inscrutable. I took a breath, but did not find words, just looked at him.

"Gurth said," his voice was low and rasping. I remembered instantly how rough my own voice had been, after weeks without speech. He had been silenced for years. "Gurth said you were here. However did you - ?" he stopped, slid his hand aside in a gesture of denial. "He said you had – you were..." His eyes fell on Ricberht again. "The steward's?"

"He is mine," I whispered.

He dropped his head for a moment, then looked up. His face was as blank as before, but his eyes were full of pain.

"Wulfgrim," I began. He shivered violently.

"All this time, through these endless, cruel months, I have thought of you. I remembered our love, our warmth."

"I, too," I pleaded.

His words swept over mine.

"I imagined that Raedwald might have kept you, in spite of all that happened. Or I thought of you waiting for me to return. I never thought of this." He looked as if he might drop down and I put out a hand to him. He flung it aside and staggered past me.

I cried out to him, but he disregarded me and stumbled on. Gurth, coming from one of the houses, met him and after a steady, silent look at me, he led Wulf inside.

I was distraught. I had been right to feel afraid. I had foreseen this renunciation – I had used my lying tale to deceive Eadwacer, but indeed it was true. Wulf wished my son had never been born. He despised me. He thought I had rejected him.

A year ago, I had stood on another river-bank and told the man who had betrayed me how my life had forever been full of pain, of rejection, of deprivation. I had let him comfort me, but the outcome was even more agony, even more loss.

Unthinkingly, I moved through the gathering darkness, and came to the little paddock where the horses stood. I laid Ricberht, unprotesting, on the grass. Then I harnessed a horse, lifting its saddle from the fence, tightened the girth and hoisted myself and the baby onto its back. I tied Ricberht inside my over-tunic and straightened my cloak to shield us. Then we moved away. My sight was blurred with tears and I let the beast move forward at its will.

24

I truly did not care where I went. The river narrowed and its path meandered. Dark shadows intensified around me but the harvest moon cast enough light for the horse to pick its way. My own misery was so great that at first I did not heed the wailing of the child: his cries voiced my grief. Of course, instinct prevailed and I drew rein and slid down onto a flat rock. I loosened my mantle and, unclasping my tunic, I gave him my breast.

The cessation of movement was enough to dry my tears, calm me sufficiently to deal with the baby's needs, and to make me completely aware of my unbelievably stupid action. I had never set out, even when escaping from Hardric or Oswald without some minimal supply of food, water or clothing. And now I had nothing, not even clothing or rags for the baby.

Ahead of me lay an unknown tract of country, hilly, forested, the home of wild animals and of men hostile to my tribe. My tribe! I nearly laughed. I belonged nowhere, so perhaps I had no enemies. I thought with longing of my friendship with Gerda, Hilda and Steinunn.

When Ricberht finished feeding I refastened my clasps and climbed from the rock. A rill trickled a yard or two away, and I pulled dry grass and moss to use to wipe him clean – he cried at the cold water, but calmed down when I found moss for padding, wrapped in a strip from my under-smock. I felt suddenly very tired, as the strain and grief of the day overtook me. I drank water, then sat in the lee of the rock and leant back. Gradually my body relaxed. I curled round, protecting the baby against my belly, and slept.

Someone shook me awake. Gurth.

"Lady!" he exclaimed. "What are you doing? We looked for you last evening. I have been fearful for you. We searched the shore." I sat up stiffly, amazed that Ricberht had let us sleep till daylight. Now his face crumpled and he began to complain. Gurth fetched water and I sat on the rock and fed the child.

"What were you thinking of?" he chided me. "You have no food, no blanket – and the child. You could die in the cold!"

"And who would lack me?" He was shocked.

"Your child, for one," he snapped. "And I, surely, who have sought you out so many times. Have I not brought you to the prince?"

My eyes filled with tears. Before I could describe Prince Eni's reaction, two things happened at once. We heard horsemen approaching from both directions and, just as Wulf and a party of men from the village reached us, Eadwacer and his two companions cantered round a curve in the riverside path and pulled their horses to a halt.

I clutched my mantle to cover myself, yet again tearing my nipple from the baby's mouth so that he yelled in protest. I lifted him to my shoulder and stood up. The eyes of both Eni Wulfgrim and Eadwacer took me in. Eadwacer was furious.

"So you lied, princess." He swore foully. "I have been on a wild goose chase. But now," he glared from me and the baby to Prince Eni, "I have found what I was seeking."

Abruptly he drew his sword and his two men urged their horses to separate Wulfgrim from the villagers. Gurth leapt forward, sword out, and Wulf swung himself from his mount's back and grabbed the proffered weapon. He made to cut Eadwacer's horse, but he reared back swiftly and his rider dismounted, too.

By this time the villagers had involved themselves in the fight and there was a short, violent scrap. But in the space they had cleared with huge sweeps of their swords, Wulfgrim faced Eadwacer. I wondered if he had even realized who it was who braved him, then Wulf spoke, with loathing.

"The steward."

Neither man wore a helmet, but Eadwacer had a mail corslet, while Wulf was covered merely with a leather tunic, not new, and doubtless, like his boots, provided by the fisherfolk. Eadwacer carried a shield but Wulf had none until Gurth dispatched one of the Seawitch crewmen with his long knife and, wrenching one from his dying grasp, flung it to his prince.

The two men circled, darting in and out, dodging the slashing, bright blades. Several times they clashed, shoving two-handed against each other, inches apart; then one would slice away, circling again.

I was terrified. Eadwacer was not the warrior son of a king, though he was trained in defence of his lord. But he was the stronger. Wulf had suffered long years of privation, struggling for survival. Without Gurth's swift actions, he would have been unarmed against his furious foe. Yet he had not lost his skills.

He struck, now high, now low, then he feinted and as Eadwacer swooped, he cut the sword arm. Eadwacer gasped, but his left hand relinquished the shield and clutched the sword from his loosening grip. Wulf paused for a fateful moment and as we watched, Eadwacer side-stepped, twisted and plunged his sword into Wulgrim's chest. He withdrew it slowly as his foe slid from the blade to the ground. Then he stooped beside the prince. He lifted his sword, though left-handed, and I knew he would use it in the act of ultimate dishonour. Beheaded and dismembered, a warrior's shade could not find its way to the hall of the gods.

I felt rather than heard myself scream and, thrusting my baby into the arms of the nearest man, I fell on Eadwacer, seizing his arm, and wrenched the sword from his hand to toss it at Gurth's feet. He kicked it aside and grasped Eadwacer round the throat, heaving him from Wulf's body. He flung him towards Eric, who gripped him fiercely.

On my knees I shuffled, gasping Wulf's name through my tears, and nursed his head in my lap. I believed him to be already dead, but as I sobbed his name, calling to him, "Wulf – Eni – Prince!" and begging him to speak to me, his eyes opened in a face gaunt with pain. I kissed him, forehead, cheeks and lips and heard him murmur my name.

"I loved you always," He barely sighed. "Even when I said –"

"I know, my dear one. Forgive me. If only I had come sooner. I'm so ashamed. Please –"

"Hush. The child is not –"

"I beg you, forgive me. It was my fault. I was so alone."

"Alone. I have been alone," his voice rasped.

"I know it. You have been forever in my thoughts. Look!" I fumbled in the purse-bag at my belt and tugged out the little wooden box, with the carved wolf and the amber nugget. "I held your gift dearly It was all I had of you. I thought you loved me!" I curled his fingers round the object I had treasured for so long. My tears fell. I wanted to tell him of the hardships I had undergone and how this belief in his love had given me the strength to endure them. I wanted to tell him I knew he had suffered, too. But his weight grew heavier, and his hand fell to the dirt on which we lay. His eyes widened and he seemed to gather power. He looked from me to Gurth, who crouched beside me. and smiled a little.

"Gurth knows," he whispered. "He found you for me. As for the child –" I laid my cheek close to his lips to catch the words he struggled to shape. "Take him to Rendilsham. Go to my father." He strove for another breath and his body convulsed. With a deep moan, his lips parted with a welling of blood and his head dropped on my breast. I clasped him, howling with despair, remorse and rage.

I do not recall much of what happened then. I was lifted from Wulf's dead body and made to sit before one of Gurth's men on his horse. Gurth took the child, in spite of Eadwacer, who had stood, bleeding and silent while he watched Prince Eni die in my arms. Outnumbered by Gurth's troop and the fisher-folk, he agreed to withdraw; he took himself off to his beached ship to have bound up the gash Wulf had inflicted on him. It would be many hours before my thoughts turned to him, though in the end they must.

25

I think I was crazed by grief. Sound, movement, sensation became a blur. Someone must have given me a drink laced with something soporific, for eventually I woke, head throbbing and weak with hunger, to find myself lying, wrapped in my cloak in a dim corner of a quiet house. I turned myself slowly and gave a low moan as my swirling mind collected itself, and memory returned.

"Ah, you are awake! Come now, drink this. You will feel better directly." Haesel handed me a horn beaker with a warm concoction of birch bark. "I added some honey to make it less bitter. It will give you strength and help the head."

I sipped at it and thanked her. "Is this your house, then?" I asked. "Does your husband mind? Who brought me here? Oh! Where's Ricberht?" I tried to stand up, but dizziness made me fall back.

"It's all settled. Rest now. The little one is fine, and I will bring him to you, just as soon as you are strong enough to hold him." She flushed and shifted in embarrassment. "I do not know how to tell you this, but I have had to feed him."

"What? He cannot take food yet! He is too young!" My voice rose in distress. She sat beside me and patted me soothingly.

"I was the only one, you see. I have plenty of milk, so I could wet-nurse him. No-one else has a suckling child just now."

I felt ashamed of my jealous flash of hostility and swallowed hard and thanked her. Then I looked about me. "Where is he? Where is your little girl?"

"Be calm. They are with Bertha, in the next house, so you could sleep."

"How long have I been here?" I asked, and recoiled in shock when she told me it was two days.

"But what about Gurth, and Eric? Where are they – oh, and Eadwacer. What has happened to -", but I could not think of Wulf yet. "Are we safe? I must -."

"You must finish that drink and have some of this broth before anything else. Then we will find you a clean robe and I will bring the others to you."

While I let her bustle about, I made her tell me how I had been almost literally dropped at her hearth, while the village men met with Gurth to discuss what had happened. They had other concerns, too. The dead Norbert had been their headman and they needed to choose a new chief. Before this could happen they had to bury Norbert. The man who had died in the skirmish out on the path by the river. Prince Eni. Arrangements were being made. I bowed my head.

Here Haesel's voice shook a little and she glanced at me sideways, afraid to speak. I would soon find that most of the people now knew my true story. Gurth needed to persuade them to join with us to withstand Eadwacer, who was still at his beached ship across the river.

"I am so sorry," she said. "It is the pity of it. That prince to be abandoned like that, and so near to us and for so long! And for you to lose him, and at the hands of that man!" She meant Eadwacer. I did not yet feel strong enough to think of him, let alone face him.

Someone called, at the doorway, and Bertha came in, carrying Ricberht, who was fretting.

"I think he is hungry. Look, little man! Your mother is awake and ready for you. Here, my dear." I accepted the small, heavy bundle, unclasped my clean dress and opened the shift beneath. I put my baby to my nipple and he began to suck and nuzzle at me, but too soon he cried tetchily. I tried the other side. I did not have the milk. The two women were sympathetic and helpful in trying to cheer me. I was under-nourished after my ordeal and the long, drugged sleep. Surely the milk would come again. But I felt sore and knew that I was dry. I gazed at the crying babe and began to weep, myself.

"Come now," said Bertha. "Give it time. There is help at hand, in any case." She lifted my son and put him in Haesel's arms. Quickly he settled and guzzled noisily. I turned my head, rose and gathered my cloak.

"I must find Gurth,"

"Come with me," Bertha offered. "I will get my boy to tell them at the hall that you are awake and need to talk to him." No woman, not even a king's daughter, especially an outcast from another tribe, could interrupt a hall-moot. It seemed as if Gurth was seen by these folk as being responsible for me, whatever our former relationship. I dutifully followed Bertha. I could do nothing here.

Outside, I perched on a tumble of logs in the space around the hall and shrugged off my cloak. It was a warm, bright day. Gulls screeched as they swooped near the fishing boats, women called to each other, and the smell of bread drifted from the bakehouse. I heard hammering from the beached ship at which I stared across the river.

Whether it was exhaustion from grief or the sleeping-draught I had been given, I felt numb. It was as if my strongest feelings were swathed in some heavy, blanketing cloth, deadened, muffled. I knew I had lost Wulfgrim forever and that I would never cease to mourn the loss of his love. I knew that I loathed Eadwacer and feared him. As for myself, I felt bitter remorse and contempt at my own weakness. If only I had found ways to come north more quickly; if only I had reached Wulf; if only I had not - but I could not now wish my son unborn! I had failed him, too, and he would survive only if another woman fed him.

Before this, I had been driven, impelled by love or fear or need. However vilely I had been treated, and into whatever foul plight I had fallen, there was a purpose. Now I had no aim, no goal. I was an outcast indeed. Too wretched even to cry, I slid to the ground beside the logs where I sat and hid my face in my arms.

WULF

The winds take me. I will do what I had planned: to come at last to the hall of my father, King Tyttla, at Rendilsham. I had longed to kneel in homage to him, to touch his knee with my head and my hand. Now I come, though he cannot feel my touch. My spirit roams through the oak woods, across the heath past the great burial mound of my grandfather, King Wuffa, and I pay him his due respect. I come to bend the knee at the newer pile that I now know covers my father. Maybe our shades will meet in Asgard. I lightly tread the slope to the ferry, cross the river and, unseen by men, take to a ship about to move from Wudubricgge to the sea.

If nothing else, my time on that accursed island taught me patience. I, who have seen once-grand cities lying abandoned and ruined, know that power passes. Where is now the warhorse? Where is now the rider? Where are the rewards of the hall?

My spirit can live without these things. Men take pride in their achievements: one man is clever at the board-game; one can draw music from the wood and strings of a lyre; another can craft intricate jewellery from gold and precious stones; yet another can twist and forge the mighty swords and shining helms. I can steer my ship of death over the waters, following the roads of the sea across the expanses of the ocean; I feel the pull of the tide; I raise my eyes to the stars and watch the moon as she swells and dwindles.

I lived so long without love that I have forgotten its ways. I mean nothing to my sons and they will tread their own paths.

Once I longed for human contact, now I crave it no more. I am restless, invisible, longing always for the surge of the seas.

The changing of the seasons, the busy life of the burgh, the duties of the hall – these are enough for most men; but for me, I hanker for the cry of the tern, the foam spilling from the prow of the ship and the freedom to follow my spirit to the uttermost limit of its daring.

The ship turns toward the sea. I feel no more the first cold rains of winter on my face, nor the east wind blowing through my hair. This will be no easy crossing but I do not fear it. Like the mighty sea-eagle, I make free of the winds.

26

After Eric had found me, he took me to the hall. The village men, he told me, had gone to busy themselves in preparation for the funeral rites. Some would put to sea as soon as they could, to get fish for the banquet. Older boys would set snares in the field edges for small deer and go hunting for waterfowl. Gurth would tell me more about the plans, said Eric. He meant, for Wulf's burial, but stumbled over the words, not wishing to speak the name to me. I nodded my understanding. He left me at the door of the hall and I moved inside.

It was smaller and dimmer than my father's hall, but its arrangement was much the same. No great settle here, the chief man sat on a wooden stool, unadorned by gilt or carving. There was even a small fire in a circle of stones in the single hearth at the centre. Resting against one of the tables where the elders would sit was Gurth. He moved swiftly towards me, hands outstretched, and gripped mine warmly.

"Lady! How glad I am to see you. Have you rested? Are you well?"

I did not know how best to answer him. I did not think I would ever feel hale again. He must have seen it in my face, so that he shifted a bench with his foot and sat me near the low-burning fire.

"I had to talk to the people here," he said. "it was necessary. They had to know the truth."

"Yes, I know. I understand. You were right. But what does it mean to them? I am an outcast. Prince Eni is – was – an exile, brought here

173

without their agreement. Eadwacer is an intruder. They could easily turn their backs on us all. They could kill us all!"

"No, no," Gurth held up his palm to hush me. "They are kindly folk. They have accepted you and the little one. They do not know – forgive me, Niartha (he had never called me that before), they do not know he is Eadwacer's. Only I know this. My men have never asked who fathered him." He looked at me inquiringly. I shook my head.

"No, the women have not yet asked that, either."

"They know we came to rescue the prince, and they know, of course, that Eadwacer killed him. They pity you. They plan an honourable burial for Prince Eni. I am sorry to presume, but they seem to regard me as his successor. I have had to make some decisions in the last few hours." He passed a hand over his weary face.

"It is all right, Gurth. No-one could do better. You have always been his loyal thane, and more, his loyal friend. And you have protected me as he wished."

"Not enough, I think!" His words were a little sharp. I was startled. "If I had found you sooner, then Eadwacer would not have –"

"Then little Ricberht would not have been born. I know. If I had not been alone and afraid to die, my death unknown and none to bury me, believe me, Gurth, I would have destroyed him before he quickened in my belly. But now – well, now he is mine and I want to rear him." Here I broke down and, clinging to him, told Gurth how I could no longer feed my baby, and how bereft I felt of hope.

He sat, strong arms around me, chin on my head, saying nothing till I quietened. He pressed his sleeve against my wet cheeks and, to my amazement, turned my hand and kissed my palm. It was not done with any disrespect. In fact, he rose and stood before me.

"All this may work in our favour, lady. If the fisherwife is content still to nurse your son, and if you will permit this, then we may stay here while I gather support. We can watch Eadwacer. If he makes that ship sea-worthy, he will swiftly reach Raedwald. If he does not, - if we can perhaps prevent it, then he must take the long and dangerous ways through the lands of our enemies, as I have done these past two years. And his crew is now depleted. That reminds me. One of his men lies dead after our encounter. I may be able to negotiate with Eadwacer, if we offer him the chance of a decent burial for his carl."

"Gurth, I have just remembered. When Wulf – when he – what he was saying – at the end. He said, 'Go to Rendilsham. Go to my father.' What did he mean, Gurth? Tyttla is dead. How could he ask such a thing? Why would he tell me to go to where Raedwald is? His own brother, who condemned him to island exile! Tell me, Gurth," I begged.

" It is true, Niartha. I know that is what the prince wanted – that you should take the child to king Tyttla. I had not told him his father had died. In any case, the child cannot leave here until it is weaned. And first, I must deal with Eadwacer. And then we must honour the dead. There will be time enough to decide."

"Who are you to say what I must decide?" I think grief and fear made me rude.

"I am the chosen thane of Prince Eni. I am – was his cousin, nephew to his mother, Tyttla's queen. I am the man who has ridden to and fro across these lands to find rescue for him. I have brought you here at his command. Woman, tell me who you are."

I stood, abashed and silent, and bowed my head in shame. He had not raised his voice, or threatened me in anger; he spoke in his usual calm, controlled manner. His courage and resolve came through, in spite of his exhaustion. I had given no thought to his grief.

" We will speak again of this. You have my word."

"Forgive me, Gurth. I was thoughtless. I know no-one I could trust like you." He relented, and took my hand. Before we left the hall, he gave me the wooden box taken from Eni's dead fingers. Neither of us found need for more words.

Tired though he was, Gurth dealt with Eadwacer, riding his troop of fully-armed men across the river, easily fordable at low tide. In return for his dead companion, Eadwacer agreed to leave the village-folk alone, unharmed. There would be no reprisal. It would be a cowardly act, in any case, to attack untrained men armed only with knives and arrows. In his turn, he asked for help in repairing the great ship. Craftsmen were needed to shape the timbers and caulk the planking, once in place. Eric told me that Gurth had agreed, seeing here a means of managing the speed of the work and controlling Eadwacer's movements. I asked what the fishermen thought of all this. Apparently they accepted Gurth's advice and were content to let him hold sway in matters beyond their experience. They felt safe in Gurth's hands, as I did.

27

The loss of Norbert, their headman, had left a void. In a fearful storm three years before, they had lost two men who might well have led them. Now they were bereft again. There were several elders in the little group of people, but one was losing his mind with age, one (a potter) was crippled with painful bones, and one was slowly dying, as so many old people did, racked with painful coughs. I had tried, myself to ease his chest, but there was no way to help him. Norbert's son was seven years old. The people were weakened and afraid, glad to follow Gurth. He was, indeed, a natural leader. He could draw men to his side. Bold in a fight, yet he kept control. His background meant little to these folk, but they respected him.

We left Eadwacer to bury his dead: so many who had drowned in the tidal surge or were crushed by their ship, as well as the man Gurth had traded.

As for our own, they were laid to rest in honour. Norbert's ashes were taken from his funeral pyre in a pottery urn the old man had crafted in his knobbly hands. It was quite unusual, having holes left purposely around its bulge. Haesel said this was to let his spirit escape into the other world after he was put in the ground. The two young men who had worked Norbert's fishing-boat with him helped his widow to place it on the headland, resting on a folded fishing net, together with his knife and the woollen cap he had always worn. To mark his chieftaincy, he had worn round his neck a torque of twisted metal, and his little son placed this on top of the ashes in the urn. Then the whole village, as well as Gurth, his men and I, built over him a cairn of rocks. After many years the grass, brambles and bracken would cover it and the hill would take him into her breast. That night all the people met at the hall, carrying in food and drink. Voices spoke of Norbert's skill in the boats, his courage and his sense of justice. He was a fair man and his folk had loved him.

The next day, the men, led by Gurth, carried Prince Eni in the simple wooden coffin they had made for him at his death. We followed him up to the headland again, not far from Norbert's cairn, to a place where you could see the river, the island and the sea. Gurth's carls had dug a pit deep in the difficult ground and they laid their heavy burden into it in silence.

The villagers seemed to retreat a little, leaving me with Ricberht in my arms, and Gurth. He signalled to his men and they stepped back.

"Niartha?" Gurth searched my face. I shook my head a little.

"It is for you. He was your kin. Say the words, Gurth."

So he did. He spoke of his lord, his cousin, his friend. He told how Eni Wulfgrim had sailed the ocean, how he had travelled into far lands. He had met with powerful men and represented the power of his own king, his father. He could fight, said Gurth, but preferred to negotiate peaceful alliances and open the ways to prosperity. He would have made a good king.

I waited for him to say how all had been lost. I feared he would say the fault was mine. He would hardly have been wrong. But all Gurth said was,

"He was betrayed. And his betrayer lies within my grasp." He looked back, across the river towards the smoke of Eadwacer's encampment. "I swear, I swear by this sword and, in the name of Tiw, I swear that I will take revenge. This promise I will keep."

Gurth drew the sword, the one Wulf had used in the fight with Eadwacer. He lifted its point high in a warrior's salute, and laid it on the coffin. He looked at me again. I handed my son to Eric, and felt for the purse-bag hanging from the girdle at my waist. From it I drew the wolf-carved box containing the amber nugget. So long ago, Gurth had brought it to me as a sign of Wulf's love. I knelt at the graveside and, reaching down, I let it drop onto the coffin with the sword. I stood again and gazed at the place where we had laid the man I loved. Its very plainness, the starkness of the wood, the unadorned sword, the humble gift, all seemed in keeping with the honest, straightforward nature of the man we were to bury.

I had no more tears to shed. Remorse was wasted here. I felt still and benumbed. Wherever I would go, however long I lived, my heart would stay in this place. I closed my eyes and, in my mind, I spoke to Wulf. "Be free, my love."

When I turned back to Gurth and the others I found I could smile calmly and take their hands with equanimity. I clasped my child to my shoulder. My heart was stronger than I knew.

Already I was feeling part of this small community, beginning to think in terms of 'us', 'we', and 'our' in the events we shared. To my amazement the women had collected enough provisions to hold a second feast, this time in honour of the strange prince they had seen so briefly. Such generosity was very moving, and Gurth and I said we would not know how to repay them.

Before the drink took hold, but with all present in the hall, the oldest man, he who was dying, stood and thumped his staff for silence. Children were hushed and the boat-owners and their wives gathered round him in support. This was obviously planned.

"Good people," he said, in his quavering voice, "we have to decide today who is the fittest man here to become our chief. We have had some hard times, and our need is for someone who will not be forever out at sea. We need a strong man, who can deal with the sort of men who trouble our quiet lives. It seems," but here he fell into a paroxysm of coughing and had to sink onto a bench, waving his hand helplessly. Surprisingly, it was Bertha who took up his words.

"Let me speak," she appealed, and although she was a woman, they let her go on. "Norbert was my father, as you know," she said. I had not known this and felt renewed gratitude for her warm care of me and Ricberht, when she must have been stricken herself. She told the whole group the full story of my search for the exiled prince, and how Gurth had found me, sought for help in regions far from his own, and how he had saved their village from the wrathful Eadwacer.

"Now, they wish to stay amongst us," she declared. "The child has found a wet-nurse." Indeed, Ricberht was being suckled in Haesel's arms beside the hearth, as she spoke. "We should be glad to welcome such as these. Are they not strong? Do they not have courage? Can you see here a man who is fitter to lead us than this one?" She pointed to Gurth, who had been sitting among his men, holding a drinking-horn. Now he stood up.

He looked astounded but I noticed that quite a few heads were nodding, men's and women's, and that the strangers he had brought with him, Eric included, did not seem so surprised. In the end, the din was so great, as voices were raised in support, that Gurth had to stand on the dais and raise his great hand for peace. He said he felt honoured. He shook his head in bewilderment. He asked for a night to think this through. He said he must consult with his men, and with me. At this the women cried out to me to beg him to agree. I rose and thanked them for this trust and friendship. I said we would speak in the morning. Gurth moved slowly through the crowd towards the door. Then he turned and caught my eye. I nodded. He pointed his finger upwards, and I knew we would meet on the headland to discuss the idea. Haesel smiled at me over Ricberht's drowsy head and I slipped outside, wrapping my cloak against the evening breeze. I suppose it was this rather obvious display of our close, but unusual, relationship that led to the assumption on the part of the fisher-folk that Gurth and I would wish to set up home together.

Gurth called the meeting next morning, to say that he would agree, provided always that when the time came, he could leave, with no hard feelings. It would not be for a few years, he thought, and he would make sure the young men now growing up from boyhood would be ready to take control. He was no fisherman, but he would do whatever else was necessary for the good of the people who had shown us such friendship. His men would do their share, but would be free to return to their homes at any time. I was happy to agree to all this.

I needed to be still for a time, for my own sake and for my child's. We were far away from Raedwald. Gurth was strong and reliable, and I felt sure he would try to protect me from Eadwacer.

When the menfolk began to talk of building us a house, and I found that I was naturally expected to dwell in it and be its keeper, I realized that they had other expectations of Gurth, and of me.

28

The folk here were too poor to offer a gold, or even a silver torque for their chief to wear, but they brought Gurth a circle of shiny, black stone, called jet. A woman might have worn it on her upper arm, but Gurth somehow managed painfully to squeeze his fist through it, so it became a bracelet. He would wear it to his death.

Gurth cleverly avoided embarrassing me by constructing a large, oblong house, almost as big as the moot-hall. He had partitions put down half one side, as one does in stables, and draped deerskins to give some privacy.

He built raised pallets of wood and gave us each, men, woman and child, a palliasse stuffed with soft wool to sleep on. The other half of the building was left, full width, as an open area to cook, eat and talk in.

His men now numbered six, as Ailwyn's wounded arm was causing so much concern that Bertha had taken him into her own house to be nursed. Gurth had the remainder stand guard, three at a time. One man watched on the headland, the other two were by the river, one near its mouth, the other a little upstream on our side of the river, above Eadwacer's camp by the broken ship.

When the house was ready, Gurth slept nearest the door, sharing his space with Eric. I moved from Haesel's home to take my place at the inner end, so I could sit near the fire to tend to Ricberht.

Gurth made a couple of forays into the forest to get food. Eric speared a wild pig, found she was in milk and got the village boys to help round up the piglets. They kept two of them penned, to grow on and breed. The rest of the meat was shared with everyone. This helped reassure the villagers that we would make a useful contribution.

I tried to help, too, though I was not as strong as Bertha or Haesel. It would take time for me to recover from the events of the past three years. But I could cook, sew and make medicines. I offered to show Bertha the Nine Herbs Charm I had seen my stepmother perform. You take mugwort, plantain, lamb's-cress, betony, mayweed, chervil and nettle. Have ready some fennel. You need the juice of an apple. Pound the herbs to make a powder, and mix this with a previously-used cream of soft wax, egg and honey. Add the apple-juice. Mix all this with a paste of water and ashes, boil it up, adding fennel. These herbs are sovereign against poison in a wound, and to treat pain. To ensure success, you must chant the words of the charm for each herb, three times; sing it again before you process them, and the apple; then sing them again into the wounded man's mouth, his ears, and over the wound.

Ailwyn had to be held down by Gurth and Eric as we performed the charm, and his scream when the hot poultice touched his suppurating wound was terrible to hear. Bertha quickly gave him a sleeping-draught, bound up his arm and covered him in a warm cloak. Time alone would tell, she said, and thanked Woden, god of healing, for my little store of herbs. I always picked stuff when I found it, and carried a small sack wherever I had gone. She looked at me with more respect. She must have thought me a poor, weak thing before. I felt our friendship strengthen.

Amidst this busy house-building and caring for my baby, I found that to be active kept me from distress. But I did mourn for Wulf when I sat quietly, or walked to the headland and looked on the island where he had struggled to survive. Several times Gurth or Eric comforted my tears; the greatest relief came in talking to Gurth of his life with the prince.

All the while, lurking in our minds, as he did across the river, was Eadwacer. Eric was often sent to observe the progress of repairs to the Seawitch, but it would take many weeks, and then the weather would turn foul. In any case, did they have enough crew to man her?

I was fearful that Eadwacer would come here. We could not be sure that he had not already sent word to Raedwald, though now we were watching for just such an attempt. I could not get out of my mind his savage words to me, when I had lied about Wulf taking our child. I had called my son 'whelp' and he had said, 'The child is mine.'

Had I so convinced him that indeed I loathed the child and that he was welcome to it? Would he try to take Ricberht from me? I never left the baby alone, never walked alone with him in my arms. I had come to rest here, like some wounded bird, but had found no peace of mind. We were easy prey.

Gurth had sworn to kill him, but could do nothing at this time. Eadwacer's men were too many and too strong. He could not put the village at risk, so he held to the pact he had made, and continued to work, watch and wait.

Some of the folk were equally suspicious of the men they regarded as invaders. I suspect it was Bertha who had the idea to protect the place from harm with a piece of time-honoured magic. A horse had died. It was not a war-steed, just an old wagon-puller once used to drag smoked fish to the burgh, just upstream. They made use of as much of the carcass as they could, hair, hide, hooves, teeth and meat. Bertha reserved the head. She boiled off the remaining flesh in a great iron cauldron and took the skull. She stuffed the cavity with heather and hoisted it atop a pole sharpened both ends. It was a grisly sight, the empty sockets black with menace against the white bone. The potent symbol of warning was stuck in the ground where Eadwacer could see it on the further shore.

I prayed with all my heart that the magic would work.

EADWACER

Unfortunately, Eadwacer was not in the mood to heed warnings. While they had been working and watching, so, too, had he. He had plenty of time to think. His mind was not clouded by hard living, exhaustion and grief. He had plans to make.

He must tell Raedwald that Eni Wulfgrim was dead. Should he tell the king that it was he who had killed him? There were witnesses to the words he had at Whitby, and here, at the Cocket, with Niartha. He, himself, had made the cause of his fury against Wulf all too apparent. It would be impossible to keep secret the fact she had born his child, and he believed that Raedwald, betrayed again, would surely seek to kill them all.

Somehow he had to take the child. Niartha would surely follow. Or would she?

She said she hated the creature she had born from their coupling. Then she would have to die. He would have to flee to the farthest north or find the lands to the west he had heard of in his fruitless wanderings, but the child must be with him. If he lost all else, he would have his son, though he did not know his name.

As for the ship, the crewmen were capable of dealing with that, better than he. If fit, they could return it to the Wuffing haven on the Deben river, or leave it here to rot. Raedwald would surely not wish to lose the Seawitch, however, so they would be fools to return without it. At all events, he would not be with them. He would take the child and flee.

He had no fear of the fisher-folk, but Gurth was another matter.

It was clear that he had become leader, over there, across the river. Eadwacer had seen the building going up so fast, and watched the movements that told him Niartha was now housed within it. On a still night, he could hear the cry of babies, and knew where he could find his own.

29

To relieve the sadness of the last few weeks, and to celebrate the success of the first fishing-trip the men had made since Norbert's death, Gurth summoned the village to a belated harvest feast. There was little enough, but the hay had been cut by the boys and women. Quite a store of wild plums and berries were dried, and apples stored for the winter. We had milk from the three cows, and there was a little flock of goats, so we had butter, cream and cheeses. Some of this new supply of fish would be smoked and taken to trade with the other people at the burgh in a few days' time to be bartered for more corn and wool, as supplies were running low.

Gurth's plan succeeded. Our spirits lifted in the busyness of the preparation. The celebration began on the shore. Garlands of the plant we call 'old man's beard' were laid on the fishing boats and the men danced a stamping dance on the planks of the rough wharves, against which the boats lay. We laughed, as the little boys tried to copy them. The sound was good to hear.

Then the villagers led us, still dancing and laughing, to the apple-tree we had saved for cider. We picked the fruit into wide baskets; if it was beyond reach, eager children were lifted to their fathers' shoulders, yelling with the fun of it, while the girls danced round and round the tree, singing. Everyone was clapping their hands.

As it was the holy month, a bull-calf was sacrificed to praise the gods for keeping us safe and fed. It was good to see Ailwyn gladly joining in, arm in a sling, but clear of fever. There was no priest, so Gurth presided. As the meat roasted over the fire lit outside the hall, people still drank, danced and sang, while the women turned the meat, catching the juices in wide pans. When Bertha pronounced it ready, we sat on benches and logs, or just the earth, and ate happily.

When a grey cloud blew up and rain began to fall, Gurth called everyone to the hall. There was no formal arrangement on this occasion. We all took food and drink from tables, men, women and children. Tired out by the excitement, and bellies full of milk, Haesel's little girl, Fritha, and Ricberht lay in their baskets, fast asleep under a table near the door, away from the sparks of the hearth.

People began to clamour for stories, and we listened to tales of these fishermen and their forefathers, of great storms, of weird creatures caught in the deep. I remembered Wulf's stories ; he would have enjoyed this. Now they demanded a tale from Gurth. To my surprise, he rose, perched himself on the singer's stool so all could see and hear, and began to chant. As if summoned by magic, Eric produced a small, reed pipe and blended its light notes with the deep voice of the singer. Ailwyn turned over a small keg, with his good arm, and joined in, drumming the rhythm of the words. They had obviously done this before.

Some of what Gurth sang was sad: the song of a solitary traveller, a man who walked the ways of the world, wandered over the waves, left lonely by his lord. I knew he, too, was thinking of Wulf. Then suddenly Eric passed his pipe to his leader and burst into a cheerful, bawdy song with a catchy refrain. Soon everyone was joining in, drunken men adding ruder and ruder words as they went. The dancing started up again, wilder than ever, and the noise was enough to waken the dead.

I thought it was also enough to waken a sleeping baby. I rose and went to the table to check on Ricberht, just as Haesel did the same. The baskets were gone. We began to search frantically, pushing through the crush in the hall. Our cries grew louder, until even the drunkards stopped to see why Eric no longer sang.

"What is it, Niartha?" Both Bertha and Gurth spoke at the same time. Haesel was by now hysterical with fear and I could hardly find the words. No-one here had the babies.

We dashed outside, sure the children must have played some prank, and everyone began to run in and out of houses, calling. Then I heard a cry, down by the river. We rushed to the spot and found one basket lying precariously on top of one of the great slabs of timber the men used to scrape and clean the fish, the babe in it completely unwrapped and screaming. It was Fritha. Haesel grabbed her naked child, sobbing in relief.

Suddenly I knew.

"Eadwacer!" I screamed, and fell against Gurth's breast, beating with my fists in panic and fury. "He's taken Ricberht! He said he would! Gurth, help me – help me! Get my baby back!"

Gurth passed me to Bertha, nodded to Eric and his men. They went for their weapons and their leather tunics and wrist-bands. Only Gurth had a helmet, and he bore it under his arm.

"Get the horses," he ordered. Ailwyn started forward, but Gurth's arm barred him. "No, you cannot manage this," he said. "I need you here to guard the womenfolk."

Ailwyn shrugged and held out his shrouded arm.

"It is your commonsense I need," Gurth told him. "See to it that the men and boys are armed, as best they can. Guard the boats. Watch the ship over yonder. Keep everyone together in the hall." He turned to me as I stood, tears streaming on my cheeks, and did what he had done once before. He lifted my hand and kissed its palm.

"I promise," he said softly, then swung himself onto his horse and led his small band of men up towards the river-crossing near Eadwacer's camp. I knew what he meant. He was promising two things: Ricberht's safe return and the death of Eadwacer.

I was restrained from following them, forced to a seat in the hall and made to drink something warm and sedative. Haesel's husband took her home, with Fritha, though she wanted to stay with Bertha by my side. I heard Ailwyn giving orders. All I could do was wait, staring through the open door toward the darkness.

Eadwacer

Eadwacer took one boy, Wilhelm, from his ship, a mere youngling, who was not likely to be much missed. He was easily cowed, Eadwacer had found, using him as a body-slave. He had, however managed to keep clean the cut that Wulf had inflicted, and it was practically healed. Together they had crept through the dark, wet shadows of the settlement. Wilhelm had slipped behind the tables near the door of the hall, as the people listened to Gurth's story. He would have missed the babies were it not that, crouching down to hide, he heard a slight whimper, muffled by a sucking sound , as the infant found its soothing thumb. He gently lifted both the rush baskets, clutching them to his bony chest, and slid out of the door.

"Why did you bring two?" hissed Eadwacer.

"I did not know which is the child you want, lord," protested Wilhelm. Carrying a child each, they moved swiftly away from the hall and knelt in the darkness by the little boats. Cursing softly, Eadwacer struck a flint and carefully lit a candle in the lee of his cloak.

"Quickly, boy. Unwrap them – let's see if they are boy or girl. Gods help us if they are both boys!" But the first child was a girl, and Eadwacer knew there were only two babies in the houses. Perhaps the girl-child was lucky that Eadwacer was holding the other child. He would have tossed her into the river in his haste to be gone and clear, but Wilhelm shoved her back into the basket, though she bawled in protest at the cold on her little body. Her cries were lost in the raucous noise now coming from the hall. Then the boy ran after his master, who was disappearing upriver, into the night.

Round the bend in the track that led upstream towards the forest, now invisible in the black night, Eadwacer found the sturdy horse he had stolen and tied to a tree. He pushed Wilhelm up onto the beast's back and handed him the basket with Ricbehrt in it, amazingly still asleep. He mounted in front of the boy and urged the horse forward. He had to reach the shelter of the trees before Gurth came hunting for him. It was no use risking the horse on this stony track in the pitch dark, but the same caution also held good for Gurth.

There was, too, the problem of feeding the child. If he could get to shelter, he could stave off its first pangs with water from the skin he carried.

He had once seen a child fed from a small bladder, after its mother died and no wet-nurse was to be found. He would have to find homesteads where he might send Wilhelm to beg milk, or take it from the cows as they grazed. At the worst, he would have to return and take the mother, herself. Eadwacer may have been watching the fisher-folk closely, but he did not know that Niartha's milk had dried.

Soon, he thought, he must acquire a slave, some girl to care for the infant while it was weaned and as it grew. That would hardly be a problem: he held enough gold at his belt. They could continue their journey towards the high mountains and the western seas, where none could find them. Wilhelm would not be a problem, either, Once he stopped being useful, he could easily be disposed of, one way or another.

But his thoughts were rushing too far. First he had to put sufficient distance between himself and his pursuers. As the clouds parted on a pale, watery moon, Eadwacer urged the horse to a trot. Ricberht slept on, oblivious, as they passed the place where Eadwacer had killed Wulfgrim. Wilhelm shivered, afraid of the silent man.

RAEDWALD

Raedwald had listened with increasing anger to Eadwacer's account of his finding Niartha at Barmby. He had overcome his initial fury at her betrayal because, as everyone had said, she was only a silly girl. He blamed his brother entirely for seducing her and his wrath hardened against Eni Wulfgrim. When he sent Eadwacer with the token to offer Niartha forgiveness and a place by his side as queen, he had convinced himself that he could love her again, remembering her beauty and her gentle care of him when he was hurt. He closed his mind to the image of her in Wulf's arms. Now her rejection hurt his pride and he determined to divorce himself from her formally and look elsewhere. Eadwacer eagerly advocated this proposal.

First, however, Raedwald wanted to deal with Wulf. He had to delay, however. First, persistent, strong north winds, and then westerlies, prevented an immediate voyage. Then came the winter months, when no man of any sense made long journeys on sea or land. In any case the ship needed some refitting, as sails and ropes were frayed, and the planking had to be recaulked. In the spring there came another delay, as he was called to attend the funeral of a king of the East Saxons. However, eventually he was able to put his plans into action. Raedwald chose the crew for their skill at sea, having heard how dangerous was the approach to Cocket. Eadwacer, his emissary, also needed the backing of strong men, who could fight when necessary. After all, they were in a remote part of the land, ruled by a warlike king, Saxon though he was. As usual, Raedwald planned carefully.

Eadwacer seemed rather withdrawn since his return. Perhaps the encounter with the outcast princess had upset him? It would do him good to be put to employment. Raedwald hoped his man was capable of the final act, if Wulf was found alive. Could a man survive three winters on such a place? The king was not sure that Eadwacer had the stomach to kill Wulf, though he had been the one to betray his association with Niartha. Raedwald privately briefed the sea-captain. He would be waiting for the news that his brother was dead, by whatever means.

Eadwacer had left, a month after Midsummer Day, unaware, of course, that Niartha had given birth to his son. He made his way up the coast, to arrive in Whitby. From there he sent two men overland to report to Raedwald that they were near, and then he came face to face with Niartha, and the bright-haired child. Even as these men came to Raedwald, disaster had struck the Seawitch. Raedwald heard of that three weeks later, when a trader let fall the news as he unshipped a chest full of jet and amber near the mouth of the river Deben. Raedwald was visiting his wooden look-out tower on the hill above the tiny hamlet by the ravens' wood, and immediately forgot his interest in the exotic goods. The trader, whose name was Lukas, spat in disgust, repacked his cargo and headed south. Maybe he would have better luck in Kent.

It was not a simple matter for a king to leave his lands and travel through other men's territories. Raedwald was fortunate in having a strong and close relationship with his neighbouring kindred, and he had followed his forebears in honouring agreements and alliances. His cousin at Helmingham would act as regent till his return.

He raised a troop, large for the purpose, of one hundred men and set off, first to the west, though he avoided the court of King Aescgar, for the good reason that he had brought with him Edgar, Niartha's uncle. He had come to respect the man for his wise counsel. Besides, Edgar knew exactly how to find, overland, the place where he had marooned Prince Eni. The troop rode north, up the ancient route built by the Romans centuries before, now broken, worn and covered with weeds, grass and brambles, but still a good enough horse-path to the north.

They passed peacefully enough through Deira, negotiating passage with an eorlderman, but once they reached the borders of the Bernician kingdom of Aethelfrith, the notorious king of those vast, combined lands which formed Northumbria, Raedwald sent forward a small group of twenty men to act as emissaries, led by Edgar, to request a safe passage through the land. He wished, they told Aethelfrith, to deal with a purely private matter concerning only his own kin; there was no ill-will toward the Northumbrian people; Raedwald would leave them in peace. When Aethelfrith seemed perturbed, they even offered to leave a man hostage as a token of good faith. He chose Edgar. He gave Raedwald's men an escort to rejoin their king and to guide them to the coast, There were stipulations. As this ferocious, young king was a force to be reckoned with, Raedwald wisely conceded. King Aethelfrith would make too formidable an opponent. Raedwald left fifty of his men to wait at the northern border of Deira (the southern half of Aethelfrith's mighty kingdom), and another ten were to attend Edgar, also hostages, at Hexham, one of Aethelfrith's strongholds. Aethelfrith obviously believed that the permission he had given constituted a debt to be repaid at some future date. He was busy raising an army against the British to the north and west, and had no particular enmity with Raedwald's people. After all they were of Anglian blood like himself. Nor was Raedwald threatening his land, or his throne.

So, after over two weeks' delay, the diminished troop of sixty men, with the twenty of Aethelfrith's, moved on, by hill, moor and dale, until they reached a track wriggling east towards the mouth of the Cocket, still some hours away, as their guides assured them. On the second dark, showery evening, they made camp in the western fringes of a great forest of fir, oak and ash. Maybe Raedwald uttered a prayer of thanks to his favourite god, Thunor, for bringing them to the place he sought. It was, after all, the holy month. Some guards killed a deer and brought it to the fire, so they certainly ate well before they slept.

Next morning, Raedwald ordered them all to be watchful, and to move on quietly. He sent out-riders, fanning out ahead of the main group, whistling signals to each other like strange birds.

A sudden, piercing call brought all parties together at a canter, dodging through the trees. The men who had alerted them held captive a boy, no older than ten or eleven years.

"What is this?" demanded Raedwald. "What has this boy to do with us?"

"My lord," said the man gripping the youngster's shoulder, "he ran straight into our path and when we grabbed him we asked him where he was from."

"Well?"

"My lord, he said he was from the Seawitch."

Raedwald dropped from his horse and stood before the boy. The lad seemed to brace himself, then bent his knee to the ground, head down. Then he raised his eyes and looked at the king.

"It is you!" he said. "I mean – I – my lord. I have seen you at the ship. That is, when you –" he faltered to a halt.

"What is your name, boy?" Raedwald asked, gently enough.

"Wilhelm. My father is – he was – oh, my lord-" and he burst into tears. Raedwald gestured to the men to step back, and he pulled the boy down to sit beside him on a fallen tree. They sat, shoulder to shoulder, while the boy's sobs subsided, then the king drew from him all that had happened, as far as the boy knew. Wilhelm's father was the sea-captain, killed when the tidal wave beached the Seawitch. He told of how the man they called the king's messenger had taken him as a servant.

"Eadwacer," interjected Raedwald. Wilhelm nodded. He said that Eadwacer had had a furious quarrel with a woman – all the sailors said it was about a baby. Then he had gone racing off into the forest. When he came back a day or so later, he had a cut arm and was in a fury.

"Where is the king's messenger now?" asked Raedwald.

"Oh, please don't send me back to him," begged Wilhelm. "He beats me and he wants me to steal milk for the baby, and it's not very well, and I hate him!"

"Calm yourself," Raedwald ordered. "You are quite safe, I promise. Is the word of your king enough, young man?"

Wilhelm stood and bowed his head. "Sir, I thank you," he said, with quaint formality. Then he took Raedwald's hand, much to the king's amusement and began to lead him through the trees. The troop followed, one man holding the reins of the king's horse. A low, eastern light glinted ahead of them between the leaves.

They came shortly to the edge of a small, steep dell and looked down at a crude shelter made from branches and leafy twigs. Sitting by a low fire, holding a child of about three months old, was Eadwacer. He stood up, slowly, and then stayed, as if rooted, gazing up at Raedwald. His face was white. The baby was screaming.

Just as Raedwald took a step forward, there came the sound of thudding hooves, and, crashing through the sheltering bushes at the far side of the dell, burst a group of horsemen, dragging their horses to a standstill. Their leader's horse nearly unseated him as it reared, but as its hooves dropped the man slid from its back and drew his sword.

"By Thunor!" swore Raedwald, "It is Gurth!" He gestured with his hand, left and right, and his troop of men, reinforced with Aethelfrith's guides, swiftly encircled the area, closing in round Gurth's band, swords and spears at the ready.

30

I had not slept, nor swallowed food, all that long night. Haesel came to me in the morning and pressed her cheek to mine. No-one knew what to say to me.

Ailwyn paid a visit to the Seawitch at day-break, but the men there had no knowledge of Eadwacer's whereabouts. Now they discovered that the boy, Wilhelm, had gone, too. No-one cared much. The king's man was not popular, and now they were left to deal with the final repairs themselves. They were disgruntled. "What baby?" they asked in blank bewilderment. What in the name of any god would they want with a baby? Ailwyn returned to the hall, where everyone was waiting. There was obviously no threat from the crew of the Seawitch, he reported. He thought it wise that nobody strayed from the village, certainly not to go to sea. Bertha's proposal that they got on with cleaning and smoking the fish was agreed and people busied themselves with these tasks. At low tide, some of the youngsters took baskets to the rock-pools. Mussels gave food and sometimes pearls. Whelks produced a strong, lasting, red dye.

After a while, I moved out into the hazy autumn sunlight and began to drift about, listlessly. All I could think about was my baby. I went to our little bedspace in the house and picked up the tiny clothes Steinunn had sewn. There was a small, soft blanket he loved to clutch and to chew with his toothless gums.

I held it to my own mouth and wept with frustration.

Outside again, I wandered aimlessly to the silent boats where Fritha had been found, then along the path where Gurth and his men had ridden into the darkness. I felt useless and bereft.

Ailwyn came to me. "Lady," he said. "Take heart. If any man can find him, it is Gurth."

"I know it, Ailwyn, but I should have gone, too! How can he feed my baby? What does he know of the care he needs? Eadwacer will kill him, I know it!"

He drew me back into the hall, sat me by the hearth and pushed a beaker of milk into my hand. "It would only have slowed him, lady, if you were there. That is why I had to stay, too. We must be strong."

I did not feel strong, but acknowledged his kindly encouragement. Later, when no-one noticed, I stole away and climbed the slope to the highest part of the headland, shivering in the wind and pulling the hair from my eyes as I looked to the island. I had lost everything now, husband, lover, child. I had met kind friends, but truly belonged nowhere. If Gurth failed to return with Ricberht, if he did not keep his promise to kill Eadwacer, then I knew what I would do. I gazed down at the sea, fuming and seething on the lurking rocks below. Not yet...

A sea-bird shrieked overhead and I turned back towards the hamlet. Something caught my eye – movement far up the riverside track. Sunlight glinted on metal. Horsemen! I hitched up my skirt and ran.

Hearing my cries, everyone rushed to gather outside the hall, wiping hands on aprons and tunics. The air was pungent with the smell of fish and smoke, the people grubby and tired. This was not Gurth's little band of men – there were dozens, surely! But yes, in the midst I saw his massy frame. Then I saw Eadwacer. I rushed forward, screaming my child's name, recklessly thrusting my way through the horses. Eric caught my arm, bent from his horse and handed down to me a little bundle wrapped in his cloak. Ricberht. Too dazed with shock and joy, I clutched him to my breast and turned to move out of the press of men and beasts.

The tall figure of the leader blocked my path. I had not even looked at him. Raedwald. For the second time in my life, overcome by conflicting emotions and weak with anxiety, I fainted. Apparently he caught me, and the child as well.

Raedwald recognised Gurth's standing in the village and let him call the people to some sort of order. Gurth reassured them that this was not another invasion. They seemed at least as scared of Aethelfrith's men as of Raedwald's. The hall was prepared to house the king and his chief thanes. The horsemen would have make some sort of camp. Our house was used to hold Eadwacer, under the eyes of Eric and Gurth's men. I was, again, in Haesel's care. While I turned from swoon to sleep, she fed and cleaned my baby so that, when I woke, I found him apparently quiet and contented. He gave me his wide, gummy smile and I kissed him from head to foot, unwrapping him to make sure he was not harmed at all.

It was not a feast, but Bertha had seen to it that everyone was fed, from king to slave. She took Wilhelm under her wing, treating him, he told me later, just like one of the village boys. Her kindly, rough, confident handling was just what he needed. It had certainly worked for me.

As darkness fell, Raedwald called a council in the hall, now set out as I remembered my father's court had been. The women were excluded, of course, though I was told to attend in order to be questioned. I no longer felt afraid of Eadwacer, nor of Raedwald. I had my son again, and felt brave enough to face them all. I sat in a place not far from the guest-stool, now the position for those bearing witness. To my surprise Wilhelm was brought and made to sit next to me. He looked scared, so I briefly squeezed his hand and smiled. He shifted uneasily, but sat straighter and lifted his chin.

Raedwald had summoned the crew of the Seawitch, the ten of them who were left. They stood at one end of the hall. Gurth's men Eric, Ailwyn and the other three stood together in a small group. The elders of the village, and the boat-owners, sat watching, still in awe, and suspicious, on the benches of their hall.

Surrounded by Radwald's thanes, Gurth waited, and Eadwacer, several feet apart. Aethelfrith's men guarded the doors of the hall. Raedwald, bathed, freshly-dressed and as relaxed as ever, took the stool on the dais. He laid his sword on the small table before him as a sign that the proceedings were to begin.

He had obviously held conversation with Gurth and Eadwacer, but this was an open court so that all could hear. Then Raedwald would decide what actions he would take.

31

I thought Raedwald would begin by questioning Eadwacer, but after a long, straight gaze from one face to the other, he chose Gurth, who moved to his place opposite the king in the middle of the crowded, little hall. Raedwald gestured to him to sit.

"Cousin," said the young man (and now I became aware for the first time, that he was, indeed, a king), "tell me why you are here. What are you doing in this place?"

Gurth admitted, in a straightforward way, that he came in the first place to rescue Prince Eni from his island exile. He added, not without pride, that he was currently acting as headman for the fisher-folk.

"You know the penalty for aiding an outcast. You are, yourself, an outlaw."

"Yes, lord. From your lands. Here I am in another country."

"Are you under the protection of King Aethelfrith?"

Gurth replied that he had not yet chosen that option. He had been too much occupied with travelling in order to find help, and in doing Prince Eni's bidding.

"What was that?"

"He wished me to ensure the safety of the king's daughter."

"My wife." The fishermen of the Cocket stirred at this, gasped and murmured, to be quickly silenced.

"If, indeed, she is, lord. I thought you had rejected her."

"Did you bring her to this place? Where did you find her? When?"

Gurth gave a brief account of his travels, first to evade capture, then to track me down. He described how he had journeyed north to recruit some support. He had then traversed the fens and crossed the moorlands till he found me again. By this time I had a child, but he had promised Wulf –" he was interrupted. "Ah, yes this child. Whose is it?"

"Niartha is his mother."

"Do not play the fool! Are you the father?"

"I, my lord? Indeed not. Cousin, you know I prefer the company of men."

Scales dropped from my eyes. How naïve I had been. I had not thought of this, though it was common enough; now I understood the relationship between Eric and Gurth. I had always felt safe with them, never feared Gurth's virility. He had taken me into the house built for us here, but ensured my privacy, which he never invaded. Always respectful and considerate, he had never shown a hint of sexual desire. True, Gerda had found him attractive. Perhaps he had indulged her. Some men liked to enjoy both men and women. Such proclivities were normal enough. The gods were not offended. But I believed she had never been in his bed.

"Then who got this child on her?"

"That is for her to say, king, not I."

I thought Raedwald would be angry, but he glanced at me, like everyone else in the hall, and said merely, "Indeed." He looked thoughtfully at Gurth.

"What were you doing in the forest this morning when we met?"

"I was searching for the child. He had been abducted last night. We all knew who snatched him, and they could not have gone far in the dark. We heard the baby's cries."

"I shall come to that shortly. Return to the matter of my brother." Raedwald drew out an account of the rescue of Wulf from the island. Gurth had not seen what happened to the Seawitch, struggling as he was for survival on the island; others would have to tell that tale. He described how he and Wulfgrim had ridden to find me (he did not say why I had fled) and how they had encountered Eadwacer. He described the fight and Wulf's death. Raedwald listened, impassively.

204

He even told the king how Eni had insisted the child be taken to the court at Rendilsham.

"He spoke of your father, Tyttla, as a wise ruler. He told me the night before he died that he hoped the child would find protection there. My lord, I had not told him of your father's death. He was distressed. He had suffered too much privation. I think he had forgotten that the child would be in more danger –." He stopped abruptly.

"From me!" Raedwald gave a short, sardonic laugh. "The child cannot have been his, surely. She cannot have reached the island."

"No, cousin, but he felt they needed protection. They still do," he added softly.

Raedwald sat in silence for a minute, thinking. Then he stood and held up, not his sword, but an ivory wand with a gold ring around it.

"Your life," he told Gurth, "is in my hands, and your actions have broken the laws of our people. Your loyalty to my brother, who made you his chief thane, is manifest. You have acted justly, according to your lights, in the matter of this woman and her child. I shall give my judgement in due course."

He signalled Gurth to return to his place among his guards. Then he turned to me.

"What shall I call you?" he mused. "You have no standing in any man's hall, lady. You have betrayed me, wife, twice it seems, first with my brother and then with whoever fathered your child. Princess you are not, and you spurned my proposal to reinstate you, make you my queen. Is that true? Did you reject the token I sent you with my messenger a year ago?"

"It is true."

"Speak louder, Niartha, let all hear your words."

"It is true," I repeated. "I could not return to you. I was seeking Wulf – Prince Eni."

"How old is your child?"

"Three months. He was born at Midsummer."

"So the seed was planted a year ago, from which he grew." I stood silent.

"Eadwacer told me," said Raedwald, "that he found you in an inn in a remote spot, acting as a servant."

What did he want me to say? I just nodded.

"Well, then, was it the innkeeper who took his pleasure? One of the travellers? Were you raped?" Raedwald sat on his stool, legs sprawled. Suddenly I found the sort of courage with which I had faced my stepmother some two and a half years before. Angrily I replied.

"A woman outcast and unprotected has to make her way as best she can. I have found shelter, sometimes at a friendly hearth, but I have been reviled, exploited and –yes, king- raped. But my son, Ricberht," (it seemed somehow important to use his name) "was not born from the act of rape. Seduction, maybe. I was tired out, weak, anxious and alone. When Eadwacer was kind to me - " I could not go on.

"Eadwacer!" Raedwald was on his feet. He crossed the space to me and gripped my face in his strong hand, staring into my eyes. "By Thunor! That's it," he said slowly, still holding me, but twisting to look at his messenger. "By the gods!" he exclaimed, shoving me aside so that I nearly fell. "You were in this together! Your father told me that a man who deceives one master may deceive another." He snatched up his sword and, for a second I think he meant to run Eadwacer through. But he collected himself. The hall quietened as he sat again.

"When did you tell Eadwacer that you had his child?"

"He met me at Whitby. No, it was not an arranged meeting! He was the last man I wanted to see. And then he said he was going to kill Wulf. Raedwald," I urged. He glowered at me. "King," I said. "I told Eadwacer after he – after we – when we lay together. I told him I never wanted to see him again. I tried to mislead him." I told them of my lie about Wulf taking 'our whelp' to the woods, so that he left on a fruitless chase. In tears, I confirmed what Gurth had told them of Wulf's death. I praised Gurth for his courage and the wise way he had dealt with the people. Then Raedwald made me tell of the stealing of my baby, and how Eadwacer had said, 'He is mine'.

"It's all true, my lord," piped up a child's voice. Everyone stared as Wilhelm planted himself beside me." He made me take the baby. Well, there were two, but we found which one was the boy-baby, and we rode off into the forest." He looked up bravely. "You know the rest, lord."

After a pause Raedwald spoke. "It is late. We shall sleep tonight. Let this man," he pointed to Eadwacer, "be guarded as before. You, Cousin Gurth will stay with me. All others may go to their beds. We meet again tomorrow."

32

It was not a quiet night in Haesel's small house. Fritha was coughing and Ricbehrt had griping pains in his belly and kept vomiting and soiling himself. I did my best to hush him for the sake of my hosts, and asked their pardon as day dawned. I was, in fact, very anxious. What had Eadwacer given him for food? Had he even poisoned him? When Bertha came in with young Wilhelm, I thanked him for speaking up in the hall. Then I sent him to get a message to Raedwald, begging that I might be excused from the hall-moot that day, as Ricbehrt was very sick and I dared not leave him.

From my pack I took a few of the little pots and twisted sachets of cloth, and began to mix a paste, or salve. I hoped that, if Haesel smeared this on her nipple, when she suckled him, he might take in some of the medicine. I made a honeyed liquid to soothe Fritha's cough, and another to try to stop my baby's flux. I knew that an infant could die in hours, if his body continued to lose liquids like this. Maybe I should work the Nine Herbs Charm on all three of them, so that the evil could not pass between their body openings. This would take most of the morning and I was tired already. But I had to try.

When a voice called from the doorway, we expected a reply from Wilhelm's errand. Indeed, that is what it was, but in the figure of Raedwald himself. Haesel began to rush around in a state of agitation: a king in her house! Everything was in a mess and the babies began to whimper. Bertha wiped a stool with her apron and offered it to the king, but he politely declined, looking round, apparently distracted by the sound of crying.

"Shall I take the babies to my house, lord?" suggested Bertha.

"Not yet. I heard that the baby is sick. I need to know if it is because of what happened, when it was taken away at night. Niartha?"

"They are both unwell." I described the signs of their illnesses, and said I was afraid Eadwacer might have poisoned my son, after stealing him from me.

To my surprise, Raedwald took Fritha from her mother's arms and gently felt her head. Then he listened to her breathing, putting his ear to her tiny chest. He smiled as he returned her to Haesel.

"She should do well. Perhaps a soothing draught to quell the cough and help her sleep. Now for this young man."

I held Ricberht, who was lying listlessly, too tired to cry lustily. His gown was smelly and stained, his skin pale and clammy. Raedwald bent over my shoulder and gently stroked his head.

"Is there a healer in this place?" he asked.

"No," said Haesel and "Yes," said Bertha at the same time.

"Well, fetch him," ordered the king.

"She is here, lord," answered Bertha. "Niartha has the skill. I have seen her heal a festering wound, cure a throbbing head, soothe –"

"Very well," he said. "I should have remembered." He said to me, "If you need anything, send word to me at the hall. I will question Eadwacer now." He left.

At noon, Raedwald called for a break and Eric was sent to me to ask after the children's health. Ricberht had screwed up his face at the strange taste as he fed, but took in a little milk. Then, after I had dropped tiny spoonsful of the other mixture into his mouth, he had fallen asleep. I used small shears to cut away his dress, unwilling to disturb him. I wiped him gently all over with warm water; he grunted, but did not rouse.

"What did Eadwacer say?" I asked. "Did Raedwald find out if he gave Ricberht anything to poison him?"

"He says not, and the boy, Wilhelm, bears out the story. He had some water in a small bladder, and then he sent the boy to find some milk. He never got far enough. Perhaps the water was not clean. But he swears that he saw no poison."

"Tell me more! What else did he say? Did he tell the truth?"

Eric related the interrogation of the king's man. Eadwacer

confessed to having got me with child a year ago, but denied it was rape, claiming I embraced him eagerly. That was true of the moment. He agreed that he had kept this act from his king, but declared that he knew Raedwald would annul our marriage once he knew I had rejected his proposal of reconciliation. Eadwacer denied that this was treachery. He had taken the child because he was its father. He had the right, he said. He did not even know its name, I said to Eric. I was terrified. Eadwacer made it all sound so irreproachable, and we were all at Raedwald's mercy.

He acknowledged that he had killed Prince Eni, but, again, it was because Raedwald had told him to. Yes, the Seawitch was damaged, but that was because there was a freak wave. Ask the villagers!

Questioned, the spokesman for the fishermen described the event, but said it was poor seamanship. It had cost a lot of lives. Raedwald heard how the folk here were afraid of Eadwacer, having seen his fury with me and with Wulf. They also told how Gurth had dealt with the king's man to keep things peaceful.

That afternoon, said Eric, the king was going to see the sites of the burials of Norbert, and of Eni Wulfgrim. Then he would cross the river to inspect his ship and see where his men had been buried. After the evening meal, the council would meet again. If I could leave my child, I should attend.

While we talked, Ailwyn had, on Gurth's instructions, persuaded Bertha to remove the horse's skull on its post. It would be prudent, he suggested. It disappeared, but I do not think she destroyed it.

I watched my child closely all day: he did not vomit again, and the flux abated a little. He had a more natural colour, and took the breast again for a brief feed. I felt he was recovering, but made Haesel swear to call me if he worsened or was in distress.

I had to hear what Raedwald decided to do now. I dreaded the outcome for Gurth, for me and for my child, if the king accepted that Eadwacer was blameless. Food dried in my mouth. I wrapped myself in a shawl, pinning it at my neck with a brooch. I kissed Ricberht, sleeping again, and hugged Haesel. Bertha, who had been sent to fetch me, said she was permitted to come with me to the council. Gurth had told his cousin that she was the wise woman of the village (which I suppose she was), and that I needed her support. She led me, clinging to her arm for support in my fear.

RAEDWALD

As he surveyed the headland where his brother was buried beneath the cairn, with the man who had rescued him lying nearby, and then moved down the slope and across the dunes to the beached Seawitch, Raedwald was accompanied by his thanes, the chief of Aethelfrith's men, Gurth and the more able-bodied of the village elders – the potter. At each site he asked questions, took in the answers, then moved away from the group, thinking.

He had matured, of course, in the more than four years since he was chosen for the Midsummer rites. Then he was a careless youth. Like all the other young men he knew, he had fought his first battles and lived through the pain of wounds. The hurt of his wife's betrayal and his anger against his brother had put an end to play. He felt he had acted with mercy, even magnanimity, in extending his forgiveness to her, one of his first acts after taking up his father's crown. She rejected it.

As he stared out at the grim little island, he felt a surge of wrath. Here were three people who had created this turmoil. He had the right, surely, and the power to kill them all in revenge, here and now. However, here he was in another man's country: perhaps he should take them all as captives back to Rendilsham, and deal with them there.

When he looked at Gurth, he could not help admiring the loyalty he had shown to Wulf, the skills he had employed in evading capture, and the leadership and consideration he showed in his handling of people. Such a man was to be esteemed. Compared to

213

him, Eadwacer seemed self-seeking and untrustworthy. Yet Gurth was an outlaw in exile, and Eadwacer had done everything his king had required of him. He had also lain with his lord's wife and tried to abscond with the child.

His wife. If he kept her and brought her back to his hall, he would surely lose the respect of his people. He had wanted her dead when he learnt she had let Wulf take her, newly wedded to himself, his brother. To hear that she had born a child to Eadwacer filled him with disgust; but he had watched her anguish at the baby's loss turn to joy. He had seen her care of the infant, and remembered the gentle skill with which she had nursed him, when he broke his leg.

And she was so beautiful – his body stirred in response to his yearning. He had, of course, taken many women to his bed, since returning to his father's hall. Not always in bed, either; he half-smiled as he remembered one girl complaining of pine-cones in her back on the forest floor. Niartha was a different matter.

His anger grew again at the sight of the Seawitch propped on beams as men refitted her. It was harder to pin blame here, and the crew was struggling, after losing so many comrades. Thanks were due to Gurth, for calming a potentially acrimonious situation. Eadwacer had done little to make things better with the fisher-folk, and his snatching of the child from their hall was an offence.

Raedwald ate alone, keeping a quiet space around him in the hall, deliberating over his decisions.

When everyone had gathered, Raedwald called forward the fishing-boat owners, the elders and, much to her embarrassment, Bertha. He thanked them for their hospitality and, he said, their courage. Faced with an incursion of so many powerful strangers, they were to be praised for the honourable treatment they had given. He promised they would soon be left in peace.

He summoned Gurth to stand, once again, before him, as he held the ivory wand of the Wuffings.

"Cousin," he began. "My former ruling stands. You are outlawed and exiled from my lands. You have not attempted to return, but sought to aid, and indeed to rescue, the man I condemned to island exile. Therefore, I still hold you banished from my kingdom. I will not, however, claim your life.

"I have taken note of your leadership here, and accept your

election to the headship of this village. It is not, though, for me to concede to the wishes of these people. You are in the realm of King Aethelfrith, to whom I shall shortly return. If he accedes to my request, you will remain here. You may be sure, however, that he will need the strong arms of you and your men, in his actions against the British in the west. Do not look for a quiet life."

Gurth bowed his head, saluted his cousin, with a fist clenched to his heart, then looked across at Eric and his men, with a calm smile. As he moved to join them and the fishermen, he paused and patted the shoulder of Niartha, whose eyes were wet with relief at what seemed to be Gurth's reprieve. She could not have heard what sort of king was Aethelfrith.

Eadwacer was called. He stood, facing the king, his face white with tension, one hand fiddling nervously with his belt.

"This man," Raedwald declared to the gathering, "came into my service, by my choice. He has performed every task I demanded of him. He did carry a message to my wife, with a token, both of which she rejected. I told him to come to this place, to find Eni, my brother, on Cocket Island, and to ensure that he was dead. If necessary he was to see to it that he died. Again, this he did. I can hardly blame him totally for what happened to the ship, but it is largely thanks to the efforts of my cousin, and the help given by the men here, that the repairs are almost done. So far, I pronounce him blameless."

In the hush of the hall, everyone could hear Niartha's little gasping cry of distress. The king ignored her. Bertha put an arm round her to quieten her.

"What is less forgivable is firstly the way he concealed from me his bedding of my wife. She has admitted it was not rape, rather an action she immediately regretted, but he took my place, before the marriage was annulled. Finding out that she had born a child as a result seems to have – what should I say? – shaken him?

"Since then his actions have been driven by a kind of wildness. He was apparently attacking my brother when Wulf – Prince Eni – was unarmed and unprepared for a fight. He was also about to dismember him. I did seek my brother's death, and for good reason, but I did not seek to deny him his place in the halls of Asgard. Eadwacer's fury took him too far. It was for me to seek revenge.

"I believe it was jealousy of the love Princess Niartha bore for my brother, and that she had, as she admits, lied about her son, that made him so angry. This passion led to his abduction of the child, and his attempt to escape with him. As a result of this action, two infants are today unwell. Undoubtedly, the child would have died out in the forest, being not yet weaned. This was an inhuman act. Eadwacer may, ultimately, have some rights to the child –"

Niartha screamed and stood, shaking from head to foot. "No!" she yelled, waving her fist. "Raedwald, no! Not my son! No!"

"Be silent!" he thundered and she stood like a carved figure. "I decree that by taking the child from his mother, Eadwacer has forfeited his all these rights. Therefore -"

Eadwacer sprang at Niartha, one arm round her neck, dragging her back towards him. In his other hand he held a knife, blade at her throat. He glared round.

"The child is mine! I am its father! Don't move!" he snapped as Raedwald made to go for his sword on the table. Eadwacer thrust stabbing gestures toward the men trying to surround him and then put the blade again to Niartha's neck.

He made to drag his victim towards the door, but Gurth blocked him. It distracted Eadwacer. In a flash of movement Bertha's arm swung with all her strength. She had removed the long bone pin, tipped with bronze, she wore on her shawl, and plunged it right through Eadwacer's arm.

He gave an outlandish yowl, dropped Niartha and slid to the floor, as Bertha wrenched out the pin. Blood streamed from the puncture wounds. Gurth raised up Niartha, looked to Raedwald for permission; the king jerked his head and the big man lifted her in his arms and carried her out of the hall, returning a few minutes later.

Ironically, it was Bertha who tried vainly to staunch the flow of blood, kneeling by the man and ripping strips from her skirts. The pin had ripped into the wound Eadwacer had taken from Gurth when he attacked Wulf, and the damage was severe. Bertha rose and, ragged and bloody-handed, she knelt before the king and bent her head in submission.

Raedwald looked at her. He seemed tired, and spoke almost tonelessly. "Let no-one here think to blame this woman. She has shown courage worthy of a man, and acted to save her friend, when we were powerless. Go home," he told Bertha. "We shall finish these proceedings after breaking fast tomorrow. Let all attend, as before."

The injured Eadwacer was carried back to the house, still under the guard of Gurth's men. The man's action now forced Raedwald to alter his decisions. It was impossible to entrust the return of the Seawitch to him, and the only other man capable was the king himself. He could not leave Edgar and his escort in Aethelfrith's hands, so had to return, to prove his friendly intentions toward that king. Provided Eadwacer was held securely captive, then he could leave the village for a few days, to trade Gurth's fealty, as he had already suggested, in return for the release of Edgar. That would suit well with his plans for Niartha and her son. Meanwhile, he would have to entrust their protection to the fisher-folk.

33

To my relief, I found that Ricberht was sound asleep, when Gurth carried me into Haesel's house. He returned immediately to the hall, wishing to witness the outcome of Eadwacer's attack on me. Bruised and shaken, I told Haesel what had happened. Her husband, who arrived from the hall after the hasty end to the council, confirmed what I had hardly been aware of, that it was Bertha who had saved me.

"Is she safe? Surely she cannot be blamed!"

He reassured us that the king had praised her. Eadwacer was under guard, he said.

"Rest now," he urged. "We shall hear more tomorrow." Indeed, I was glad to lie down, beside Ricberht's little cradle, and let the bone-weariness melt away into sleep.

Raedwald called me to him next day before the hall-moot began again. He told me his plans for the next few days – I had not even understood that my uncle was a hostage to the Northumbrian king. Raedwald told me how Edgar had left my stepmother and her brother, and joined him. I wondered how he would feel at seeing me again. How would he deal with me? I had always liked him. I could not blame him for capturing Wulf – he followed orders. Raedwald praised him.

"He is a trusty advisor," he assured me. I was pleased. All of a sudden it felt good to be talking to Raedwald like this. I felt more relaxed in his company, though I did not yet know what his plans were for me. He enquired about the babies' health, and I was happy, as I told him they were now well.

The hall began to fill, though Eadwacer was left in the hands of Eric and the others of Gurth's band. Raedwald called for order.

"There are matters still to settle here," he told us, "but I can do no more until I have met again with King Aethelfrith. "Gurth," he beckoned his cousin, "you will accompany me."

Gurth stiffened, and as he seemed about to object, Raedwald said very quietly, so only Gurth and I could hear, "The alternative is to share Eadwacer's captivity, and face a new judgement."

"And what of Eadwacer, king? Who will guard him if we are gone?" Gurth spoke so that all could hear.

"Cannot your men be trusted?"

Gurth glared. "Certainly, cousin. Will they not be with me?"

"No, they will await your return."

"If Aethelfrith permits it."

" I will speak to him, Gurth. Your presence is necessary, if I am to persuade him to release those I left hostage with him.

"Lord king." It was the quavery voice of the old potter, who stood, cloth cap in his crooked hands, ducking his head, as he dared approach.

"Beor, isn't it?" Fancy Raedwald learning the old man's name! "What is it?"

"Lord king, what shall we do if you take away our headman? Who will save us from the mad one?"

"Do not fear. He will not leave the house in which he now lies. Gurth's men will guard him, and I will see to it that these men (he indicated the crew of the Seawitch) will take their turn." He raised his eyebrows at the bosun, who pulled off his cap and bowed his head in acknowledgement. "I ask you, men of Cocket, to provide the same care of this woman, Niartha, and her child. Will you protect them till my return?"

"Happy to, master," said the old man, forgetting protocol and grinning at me with his gappy smile. "She's done my bones a power of good, with her salves and such."

"When I return, "Raedwald resumed, "I plan to refloat my ship. I shall be glad of your help in this, and your skill to help us put to sea. Now," he said decisively, "we shall prepare to depart."

"Raedwald," I spoke up. "I mean, king! You have not yet made known what you purpose for me and my son, Ricberht. I beg you –"

"Niartha," he answered, "I shall not be able to come to a decision until I bring your uncle here. We shall need to speak again, you and I. Until then, be patient. You have nothing to fear." He summoned his thanes with a lifted finger and they swept out, purposefully. Gurth paused a moment to speak to Beor and his fellows; then he saluted me with his usual charming kiss of the hand and set off after the king, together with Aethelfrith's escort.

We watched as, a few minutes later, they rode off up the riverside track. I turned away from the riverside. The king had still not told me what he planned for me – nor did we know the fate he had in store for Eadwacer. I longed to go back to my place in our house, but dared not go near. I would ask Bertha if there was nowhere else they could guard Eadwacer. – perhaps the hall, now that the king and most of his men had gone. She could ask the elders. If I said I needed to have a space to make my salves and potions, they might well agree. I had imposed so long on Haesel and her family, but Ricberht still needed her, of course.

Before I could look for her, Bertha sent Wilhelm to find me. He said it was to do with his master. I looked at him blankly for a moment, unsure who he meant, then realized it was Eadwacer. I said I would talk to Bertha outside the house.

When she found me, she was unusually agitated. Eadwacer's arm, doubly wounded, was inflamed and she feared he was feverish. Such signs were dangerous, and could lead to a painful death.

"I need your help," she begged me. "If the man dies, your king will be angry when he returns. I am afraid of what he could do to us. This is my fault!"

I told her the king had cleared her of blame, and that I did not think he was very likely to take action on Eadwacer's account. I refused to go near the man, especially while he was in my house.

"Move him and his guards to the hall, out of my sight," I begged, "so that I can prepare some ointment. I will give you what is needed. Do not ask me to come near him," I pleaded.

She bustled off, and I saw the men lifting him on a hurdle across the space to the hall. He was groaning in pain, and would not let them touch his arm. After moving my few possessions, and my son, into our house, I kept my word and set to the tasks of grinding, boiling and mixing the various medicines needed for Bertha to use. Wilhelm went to and fro, willingly enough, though, like me, he feared Eadwacer.

In between times, I played with Ricberht or took him to Haesel to be suckled. It was comical to see the two babies reaching toward each other, rolling on the blanket we laid down for them, and making babbling noises and little crowing sounds.

"These two are going to be great friends," laughed Haesel. I smiled, but in my heart I wondered if they would be given the chance.

I had been asleep for several hours, when someone shook my shoulder. A candle shone in the darkness, and Bertha urgently whispered my name. I sat up. She told me that Eadwacer was delirious, skin burning and the wound was turning bad. It couldn't wait till morning, she said. I had to help her now. I looked at Ricberht, fast asleep. I could not leave him, and the village was asleep.

"When you are dressed," said Bertha, "Eric says he will come and watch over the child. He can call you or Haesel if need be. Quickly, I beg you!"

I dressed, in response to her plea, but felt a strong dread at the thought of going near this man again. Reading my thoughts, Bertha squeezed my arm. "Do not be afraid. He will not know you are there. He is raving in his heat. Now, what will you need?"

We collected potions and salves in a basket, then some cloth from Bertha's house, a jar of water and a sharp knife, and stumbled over to the hall, our steps lit only by the guttering candle. The moon had waned to a sliver overhead.

There was some light in the hall, though men were sleeping in shadows at the far end, and Eric stood up from the bed they had made for Eadwacer on one of the tables. A torch flamed from a bracket on the wall above.

"Are you all right?" he asked me softly? I nodded. "Then I will go to your son. Call me, if you need me."

I looked down at the restless body, tossing on the flimsy mattress stuffed with bracken. Part of me wanted to walk away and leave him to die, but I knew I could not do that to anyone. So I set down the basket and Bertha and I began to fight for the life of the man who had done his best to destroy mine.

RAEDWALD

Luckily, Raedwald had delayed no further in his return to Aethelfrith. The Northumbrian king was ready now to set off on his campaign to assert his power over the British tribes in the mountainous country to the northwest of his lands.

He had the courtesy to offer Raedwald a seat at his table in the hall, and the meal was a good one to set up the warriors before they left on the battle-trail. The two young men talked earnestly, then Raedwald sought out Edgar and his fellow-hostages, while Aethelfrith questioned the men he had sent with Raedwald to Cocket.

He called for Gurth. Raedwald, watching at a distance, had misgivings as, initially, the encounter looked as if it might be confrontational; Gurth stood rigidly before Aethelfrith and the red-haired king leant forward on his stool, jabbing his forefinger. Eventually the burly figure bent his knee and laid his hand on the king's sword. As the hall hushed, all eyes on the pair, Gurth swore fealty to Aethelfrith. Then, given permission, he rose and came to Raedwald.

"Cousin," he said quietly, "all is well. King Aethelfrith has approved me as headman of Cocket. In view of recent events he has given me permission to return there, for the time being. I think he wants to watch how things work out, once the fisherfolk are left in peace." He put his hand on Raedwald's sleeve, to placate him. "No offence, cousin, but we have drawn his attention to the fact that he is vulnerable from the east, as ever. I am to keep a look-out, and to warn him of any other incursion. Later, maybe, he will call me to fight."

Perhaps, years later, the two men would remember these words.

Next morning, the two kings parted, amicably enough, although Aethelfrith had hoped for physical support from the Wuffings. Raedwald, for his part, was impressed by the great muster of men gathered for Aethelfrith's fight. This man, he felt, would, indeed, make a formidable enemy.

Now he could, without the 'escort' provided by Aethelfrith, retrace his route to the Cocket river, accompanied, to his satisfaction, by both Edgar and Gurth. Eadwacer could be dealt with, easily enough. As for Niartha, his decision would have to wait.

34

Four days after they left, Raedwald rode down the winding Cocket valley, surprising us all at the speed of his return. While he was gone, the men of the village had constructed a small hut inside a tight palisade. They were not entirely happy at using their hall to house a captive, especially as it would be needed again for Raedwald and his men. The hut had a broad shelf to serve as a bed, behind a chest-high partition, held shut by a beam of wood. There were two stools and a small hearth for the guards in a slightly larger space inside the outer door to the lock-up.

They asked to move Eadwacer here that very morning, though he was still weak and pale. We had lanced the pus from his wound, and after stunning him with smoke and a sleeping-draught, I had scraped the area as clean as I could. We washed it, applied a poultice of mugwort, plantain and fennel, and bound it up. Bertha forced him to drink a tisane of mayweed and nettles; it tasted vile, but his fever abated quickly. In his delirium he had often called my name, sometimes with desire, sometimes with loathing. I was mortified and yearned to stop his mouth, but could not bring myself to put my hand to his face. At one time I could have tolerated him, but since he had killed Wulf and stolen Ricberht, I detested him.

I took my turn sitting beside him, two days after Raedwald had left. We had kept him sedated so that his body did not succumb to the shock of pain. I was sewing, in a shaft of sunlight, Ricberht safely in Haesel's arms, at her house. Making a baby's dress for Fritha from the cloth Haesel had woven seemed small enough thanks for her kindness.

I was startled by Eadwacer's voice.

"Princess." I leapt up. I had intended to be gone before he regained full consciousness.

"Wilhelm!" I called. "Fetch Bertha!" The boy jumped up from the place near the door, where he had been playing a game with some stones. He took one look and darted off.

Then Eadwacer became aware of his surroundings. The last thing he remembered must have been when he seized me so viciously in the hall. The bruises on my neck were still visible.

"Niartha, forgive me. I should never have –"

"You should never have come near me! You should never have taken my child!"

His eyes flashed a little. Then, as Bertha's shadow fell on him, memory returned in full.

"You!" he exclaimed. "It was you!" He was agitated and becoming angry. "Get away from me!" he shouted.

Eric and Ailwyn plunged towards us and pushed him back onto the bed, none too gently.

"Be still! These women have saved your miserable life! Feel thankful, or you would now be dying in agony, as you deserve."

From that moment, they took on the task of administering to the man in their charge. They hauled him to the midden, brought his food and water, and watched over him as he slept. I sent in what medication seemed meet, but kept away. Once the rough lock-up was ready they came to ask me to take a look at Eadwacer to see if he could be moved. Reluctantly, I stood at his feet and considered his colour. At my request, Eric felt the man's forehead.

"Cool," he pronounced, "and the clamminess has gone."

"Can he sit up?" Upon the word, Eadwacer swung his legs to the edge of the table-board and sat up suddenly. I stepped back, but Eric was there, between me and harm.

"He will need some care, still," I said. "But take him. The king will need this hall again."

A few hours later, Raedwald returned.

We were all delighted to see Gurth riding behind the king. The villagers crowded round him eagerly. Could they go to sea again now? The smoked fish had to reach the market soon! Come and see the lock-up we have made for the mad one!

I stood with the women, holding Ricberht. I felt shy of meeting my uncle again. He dismounted, stiffly, and looked round, a tall man with long, grey hair and dark brown eyes. Like most men in his forties, his smile revealed worn teeth with gaps in them, but it was warm and embracing.

"Niartha!" he cried and strode towards me, arms outstretched. He hugged me, child and all, and I had tears in my eyes, as the years flew back. I could have been a girl again. I wondered what Raedwald had said of me, now that my husband had found me again. Ricberht grabbed hold of a lock of grey hair and would not let go. Instead of withdrawing, Edgar reached out his hands and lifted the child from me. The round blue eyes looked up at the wrinkled brown ones and the two of them smiled.

"Will you take me to your house, niece?" asked Edgar. "I need a drink, and we have much to tell each other."

For the next few days, Raedwald busied himself with the final work on the Seawitch, and preparations to refloat her. He needed the local knowledge of the fishermen to judge the tide and wind. He must use the current wisely if he was to moor the great ship at the rather flimsy wharf prepared some way downstream. Turning the ship, everyone told me, would not be easy, but she would have to meet the waves as they returned to sea. That challenge would be met in due course, if, indeed, travel proved possible this late in the year. First, he had to decide who would join her crew.

He appeared to give no thought to Eadwacer for the next week, content to leave him under guard in his small jail. Eric and Ailwyn reported to me that the man was recovering well from his severe illness, and that he was chafing at his confinement, demanding to see the king. I, for one, was afraid of the results of their encounter.

Raedwald's seamen, aided by the village men, all supervised by Gurth, cleared a swathe of ground at the place where the Seawitch lay beached. Next morning, they carefully inched her round, small boats stretching ropes upstream, from her stern, while horses and men heaved her prow up onto rollers, lifting her clear and shifting her head round. Then she was backed into the water, and she slid with the current, crossing the river, to lie alongside the rickety wharf, where she was moored fast. Raedwald and two seamen leapt aboard to check she was waterproof. She would float for two days to make sure her planks were riveted and caulked tight.

There was plenty of beer drunk that night, though we did not hold a feast. Men ate at their hearths and foregathered at the hall to share in the merry-making after their hard work. One man, with a flagon of his own, was left to guard Eadwacer.

With the menfolk gone, I cleared up the meal and put up the cooking pots. I swept up the crumbs, fed the fire and put some water to warm. When Haesel brought Ricberht back after his evening feed, I gave her the little dress I had made. Her face lit up.

"Fritha will wear it tomorrow," she promised. We spent a few minutes discussing whether it was time to give the babies some thin broth, to supplement her milk, and decided to ask Bertha the next day.

"Good night!" she said and left me to bathe Ricberht. Moments later, there came a tapping at the door-jamb, and someone lifted the leather flap.

"May I come in?" Raedwald paused for my permission, then dropped the flap. He came to the hearth and stood, looking down at the naked child. Raedwald crouched down and splashed him gently, so that Ricberht gurgled and smacked the water with his tiny hands, spattering it onto the king's face and clothing. He toppled back, laughing.

I hastily lifted the baby and swathed him in a warm cloth, cuddling him and tickling him as he dried. I swaddled him in a pad of wool in soft linen, tied at each hip. That task was not easy, as he was wriggling and trying to escape. Then I slipped a soft tunic over his damp head and wrapped him in a woollen shawl, his little piece of blanket in his fist, rocking him gently to and fro, crooning a little song Steinunn had taught me after he was born. I sighed. How long ago it seemed! How much had happened, and how harrowing!

My eyes met Raedwald's. I had almost forgotten him, sitting there quietly watching us. I began to say something, but he put his fingers to his lips and pointed to the baby. Together we watched the child's eyes close and the red-gold lashes fall. I gave it a few moments before laying him softly in his basket-cradle. I tidied away the bath and discarded clothing. Anything to keep busy and delay the moment when I had to face Raedwald. But I brought him a stool, saying,

"Forgive me. You should not sit on the floor."

"Niartha," replied Raedwald, "that is exactly what I wished to speak of – forgiveness."

I sat down on my own low stool to face him and waited for his next words. He paused.

"Did you love my brother?" he asked. I felt a shock of surprise. Why did he think I had come here, through hardship and danger, so far north, if not to find the man I loved?

"You were not found in his bed that day. No-one saw you coupling. Was Eadwacer telling the truth about your love?"

"Yes," I said flatly. "We were lovers. I came here to find him."

"You wanted to find my brother, condemned to island exile? Even after I had sent word to you that I would take you back?"

"Yes."

Raedwald sighed. "Did you understand what Eadwacer told you – that I would reinstate you, make you my queen? That I had forgiven you?"

"I understood."

"Then –why?"

"I loved Wulf, always. He was kind to me. I was not just another woman to him. He loved me."

"You were married to me."

"Yes, but that was a political arrangement to suit my father and King Tyttla. You never gave a thought for my feelings, or–"

"Well?"

"Or for my desires."

Raedwald got up and moved around the room, his feet shuffling in the ferns laid on the floor, and his face half-lit by the torchlight flickering in its wall-bracket. He stood over me, looking down.

"And now. What do you desire now? Tell me."

I sat, gazing at the glowing hearth, thinking what to say.

"I want some quietness. I want to find somewhere that is safe for me and my son. I want to have time to think, and to remember." I could feel tears welling up.

"Would you have done what Eni wanted? To bring your child to Rendilsham?"

"He did not know your father was dead. Gurth says he hoped he would protect Ricberht."

"From me?" He spoke with irony.

"I don't know!" I cried. "Does he need protecting from you?" My tears began to fall. "He has had enough to fear from the man who fathered him!"

"Niartha," Raedwald said quietly. He sat beside me. "Listen, now. I will see to it that you are safe, and your baby, too. First, you must understand one thing. I could not now take you home with me as my queen, not with another man's child. My people would not respect me, nor accept you. I will formally annul our marriage. I will choose another woman to sit beside me in my hall. You will be free again. For the time being, I shall leave you here. Your child has a wet-nurse and you have won friends here. Gurth will protect you. If he has to leave, he will ensure you are guarded."

"What about Eadwacer?"

"Leave him to me." I wondered what that meant.

"Now, I wish to ensure that the child has a secure future." I looked up in surprise. "I have it in mind that once he grows towards manhood, I shall place him where he may learn a skilled craft. Maybe with a scop, to learn music and old tales."

"Whose tales, lord?" I asked. "Those of my people, or of yours?" I was not hostile, merely seeing no virtue in this idea.

"Very well, then. Let us think of a jeweller. There was a skilled man in Lindsey - perhaps he or his son could take him on, make him proficient. Any king will be glad of such a man. Maybe, even I."

"Raedwald, you are kind to think of such a thing. But I could not leave him! He is all I have!"

"Yes, I understand." He took my hand and looked at me closely. "I hope that you will also develop your skills as a healer and a woman of wisdom. Such a one can also be used."

"Have you spoken of this to Gurth? Or my uncle?"

"Yes, but the answer is yours. Gurth is very willing to keep you here. He will give you house-servants to help with the keeping of this place. He will see to it that little Ricberht learns mastery of weapons and horsemanship as he grows. I have asked Edgar to make his home with me. I value his wisdom, and I hope that one day you could bring your son to his house, to serve me. You could tend Edgar in his old age, maybe?"

It was my turn to get up and pace restlessly to and fro.

"You seem to have thought it all out," I said. "I have been thinking you might give us both to Eadwacer, or worse, that you might have us all killed. Could you not have spared me this fear?" I demanded angrily.

"I beg you, Niartha, to consider this. I needed time to think – I am sorry, I did not see it all through your eyes." He stood beside me. "I do not seek to harm you, or the child. I can offer the help that my brother desired for you both. If he was prepared to care for the child, then so can I. It needs no action now. For now, you can stay here safely. Later, we can decide."

"How can we be safe? Eadwacer –"

"I said, leave him to me."

"But you saw him, Raedwald. He tried to run off with Ricberht, and he tried to kill me."

"He will be in no position to hurt you, or the child, again, I give my word. Please, think of what I have said. Talk to Gurth and to your uncle. We can give your son an honourable future. Give me your answer in the morning. I will call a meeting tomorrow evening. Good night, Niartha." He leant toward me, kissed me lightly on the forehead, and left me to my whirling thoughts.

EADWACER

The whole village assembled, together with the shipmen and Raedwald's thanes and horsemen. The little hall could not hold everyone, but Gurth had had fenced an area around it to form a kind of forecourt. Tables, benches and stools were brought out, and lanthorns augmented the light of the almost full hunter's moon. The night was dry but chilly, so people huddled in cloaks and shawls.

Raedwald disclosed to the whole company the proposal he had made the night before to Niartha; he did not ask for their approval, he told them. It was her decision to make.

"Come forward, Niartha," he bade her. She stood beside him, cradling Ricberht, asleep in her arms. "Now tell the folk here what you have resolved to do." He already knew, of course, as she had spoken to him earlier.

"I have spoken to Haesel, wife of Osmund, to Gurth, our headman, and to my uncle, Edgar," said Niartha. "Now that I know their minds, I am content, if the folk of this village agree. I can think of no people I would rather live with. You have shown kindness and generosity in your hospitality and care of me and my child. I know Gurth agrees to see to Ricberht's upbringing until he is grown enough to learn a skill.

"King Raedwald has shown the greatness of his heart in promising to support us later. I have no wish to cleave to our marriage. I seek only a time of peace, rest and safety. Will you let me stay?"

There came a great clamour of approval, Bertha embracing the girl, and old Beor clasping her hand in his excitement. When

Raedwald held up his hands for quiet, he asked if anyone was against the idea. Not a voice was raised.

"There is no priest here," said Raedwald. "Therefore, I summon as witnesses, my cousin Gurth, your headman; also the elders of this place; and my thanes and Edgar, uncle to Niartha.

"I formally declare that, from henceforth, my marriage to Niartha, former princess of Wedresfeld, is set at naught. Each of us is now free: we may marry whomever we wish. Herewith, I give to you this in place of the due portion of the dowry gifted to me by your father." He beckoned, and one of his men stepped forward, bearing a bronze bowl, containing an assortment of objects: gold, silver, ivory amongst them.

None of the fisher-folk had ever seen such wealth. Again, there were cries of approval, and Niartha knelt to kiss the king's hand, overwhelmed at his generosity. He raised her up and led her to sit beside Haesel and Bertha. He gave a signal, and Eric and Ailwyn unbarred the door to Eadwacer's tiny cell.

Raedwald stood behind the table on which lay his sword and the ivory wand of the Wuffings. Eadwacer, guarded at each side, and at the rear by Gurth's men, was brought before him. He had been searched for hidden weapons, but his guards were armed.

Once more, Raedwald recounted the service this man had done him. Then he reminded the listeners that, while not guilty of rape, he had lain with his lord's wife, knowingly. Furthermore, he had threatened her; he had abducted the child, though it was still a suckling infant, and had tried to kill Niartha with a weapon, banned in the hall.

"I declare this man, Eadwacer, formerly of Wedresfeld, latterly of my household to be guilty of felony. His life is forfeit to me, but I will not have him killed here and now. I have spoken with Aethelfrith, king of these lands, and to my cousin Gurth of Rendilsham, now of this place, and have their agreement in this decree."

The king stood now, before the table, holding his wand of office.

"Eadwacer, you are condemned forthwith to island exile. You will be taken at dawn to the island yonder, for a period of five years. Thereafter, you will be banished from all lands of the eastern seaboard. Your path will be north or west or across the seas. Return him to the lock-up."

Two voices rose in response to the king's words. One was Niartha's, exclaiming,

"No! Oh, no! He is too close!"

The other was Eadwacer's own. He uttered a kind of strangled groan, followed by a bellow of wrath. He might have been weakened by illness, but fury lent him force. He swung Ailwyn by one arm, flung him against Eric and, as the other men reached for him, he grabbed a short sword from Eric's belt and plunged it into Ailwyn's chest. As he tugged out the blade, his victim slumped to the ground, blood gushing from his mouth. In the seconds it took for the men to react, Eadwacer leapt onto the table before which Raedwald stood. He planted his foot on Beorhtfyr, the king's sword, and stood poised with Eric's gory weapon, ready to strike again. The instance of silence was followed by hubbub.

The women grabbed their children, someone pulling Ricberht from Niartha's arms, and pushed their way through the throng, screaming in fear and shock. Only Niartha and Bertha fell to their knees by the dead man, The guards rushed toward Eadwacer, and Raedwald's thanes hauled the king back, out of reach. Eadwacer stepped forward, and the table (a board laid on trestles) toppled, sliding to the ground. He landed on his feet, swaying and waving the sword to keep his balance.

He encountered Gurth. Before Raedwald could utter a cry of command, Gurth sprang forward, his own sword in hand. The blades clashed, silver in the moonlight, one held against the other, wheeling in a great loop, separating, then clanging again. The metal hissed as they slid, hilt to hilt, then Eadwacer stabbed forward, Gurth parried, caught the next stroke high, disengaged with lightning speed and sliced a back-handed stroke that cut straight through the neck of the man who had killed Eni Wulfgrim.

Niartha gave a wailing cry of horror and fell to the ground, her face covered below her outstretched arm, clutching wildly at the earth. She struggled and screamed hysterically, as Bertha raised her, so that the woman slapped her on the cheek to bring her to her senses. Gurth lifted her onto her feet, shielding her from the grisly spectacle of Eadwacer's removal.

"I kept my promises, princess," he whispered, "all of them."

Raedwald demanded silence. He accepted, he told them that Eadwacer had called down his own death. He acknowledged Gurth's right to fulfil his vow of vengeance for the death of his former lord and. of course, his kin.

Once she had recovered from her terror and revulsion, Niartha admitted that now, at last, she could feel safe. To have known that Eadwacer was so close, on the same island where Wulf had struggled to survive, almost in view, wondering if he would die before his five years were through – all this would have been intolerable. Now Gurth had spared her this, and she was grateful to him, as ever.

Yet the horror of Eadwacer's death subdued them all. Raedwald ordered his body to be buried outside the boundary of the village in the wild wood, with no formal rites or ceremonies, that very night. Gurth had Ailwyn's body watched over in the little guardroom, awaiting an honourable funeral pyre on the headland.

The next day, the wind and tide were set fair. Raedwald sent thirty of his riders back through Aethelfrith's kingdom to make their way home with what speed they might. They would meet up with the men left at the borders of Deira. After a hasty farewell, all the rest took to the ship. A large crew would be needed at this late time of year. The Seawitch, piloted by the fishing-boats, was rowed to the river-mouth and turned, for the wind to catch the sail. She leapt southwards, riding the water, as the entire village watched from the headland. Pray Rana, they would reach the Deben river, so far to the south.

After Ailwyn's funeral, Gurth allowed two of his men to return, as they wished, to their home, even further north. Then he set about restoring order to the village, and keeping his promise to Raedwald that he would care for Niartha and her infant son. Now, he trusted, the people dwelling by the Cocket could live their lives in peace.

Now, perhaps, Niartha could look to the future with hope.

35

In order to keep his queen happy, Raedwald held his great winter feast on the traditional Mothers' Night, at the shortest day of the year, not on the new holy day prescribed by the Christian priests. Garmund, the high priest of Woden, presided here, but we heard he would be leaving soon, along with many others to travel to the northern lands from which our people had originally come. Some had already taken the ways from there to the cold, eastern forests, rather than bow the knee to the new god Raedwald had agreed to worship four years before. Now, quiet men in long robes, wearing crosses as pendants, took wine and bread at another altar. The people did not altogether trust them, but obeyed the king reluctantly. He seemed uncertain himself, but left the arguments to the disputing priests.

It had been a shock to me, when Raedwald had suddenly sent word that my uncle, Edgar, was stricken with a palsy and needed my care. Ricberht had just turned thirteen, and I knew that his boyhood was ending. Gurth had often sent messages with our friend, Lukas, so that Raedwald was aware of how our lives progressed.

I had known, ever since Raedwald proposed it to me, that he would send for us one day, but to learn that I was to board Lukas's ship next day and take my son to Rendilsham struck me with something like fear.

We had enjoyed over twelve peaceful years. True, Gurth had gone twice to fight for Aethelfrith, but had returned safely, Tiw be thanked. He kept his word, and taught Ricberht, Wilhelm (who remained in Bertha's care) and the other village boys to handle angon, spear and short sword. He taught my son and two other boys to ride and to manage a horse. The others he let the fishermen teach to handle the boats, the nets and the baskets. The tiny village had strong young men growing up. If some were called to serve their king, others would remain to guard the rivermouth and provide fish for the local communities.

For my part, I had enjoyed a peaceful existence, serving the people as a healer, and practising with pleasure the domestic skills I had learned in hardship. I sought no man's bed, and none dared to, or cared to seek mine. To leave the people of the Cocket was a huge wrench. To leave the quiet, grassy resting-place of the man I loved was heart-rending. Yet the future of my son lay in Raedwald's power, and we owed his safety to him. We certainly bore no allegiance to Aethelfrith. And my uncle needed me.

So we packed our belongings into chests. I left gifts with Gurth, Eric, Wilhelm, Bertha and Haesel, in gratitude and love: pieces from the treasure Raedwald had given to me. If times proved hard, they could be traded richly. I was showered with gifts of cloth, hornware, pots and food for our journey. Ricberht was overwhelmed with pride and joy when Gurth gave him his old sword. I knew it was the one that the big man had used to kill Eadwacer, father of my boy, but realized it was an important gift and a reminder of promises kept. In a year or two, the boy would have the strength to wield it properly. I wept at leaving my faithful Gurth, wondering if we would ever meet again.

After many days at sea, putting in at several ports to trade, we disembarked on the banks of the Deben, a pleasant river, with useful saltmarshes and views of woods and meadows as we rounded the bends. What amazed me was the sight of the huge, monumental mounds on the ridge, the burial-place of the Wuffings, beyond which lay their royal hall. Our possessions were loaded onto wagons. When the fore-runner met Raedwald's scouts, he was alerted and came riding out to meet us, with a welcoming escort. I felt honoured.

We were taken straight to my uncle Edgar's house, one of a group in a clearing dominated by a huge oak, not far from Raedwald's hall. True, Edgar was weak, with trembling hands and tottering steps, but his face lit with joy to see us, and his servants were well-prepared to receive us. He made it clear that I was the lady here, in charge of the household, and by now I was used to such a position.

The king gave us a week or so to settle in, before sending for us all to come to his hall. My uncle could not ride, so we travelled in a wagon, while Ricberht trotted proudly beside us on a small, sturdy horse, given to him by Edgar. We were feasted that night and housed in the guest-rooms. Next day Ricberht was to meet the man Raedwald had chosen to teach him his craft. For the first time in three years, my son crawled to lie curled beside me, too nervous to sleep. I had not realized that from now on he would be housed at Rendilsham, not at the oak with me. In the morning, he faced the day with boyish bravado. I had to let him go.

So it was on the Mothers' Night that we met again, after five months, when Edgar and I came again to the hall for the winter feast. Like everyone else, we bore gifts. The hall – already grander than anything I had ever seen - was adorned with the usual holly and ivy and glowed with candles and torches. The Yule logs blazed gloriously. I looked round eagerly for my son, and gave a cry of surprise when a tall youth, strongly-built, stepped forward rather shyly and bent to kiss me.

"Ricberht!" I exclaimed. "You've grown so much!" He smiled and introduced me to his master, Diuma, who, though white-haired, had a firm grip and bright, grey eyes under bushy brows and a deeply-wrinkled forehead. I kissed my son and smiled at the old man. I knew him to be skilful, for otherwise Raedwald would not have employed him. Now I saw he was also kind.

"Is he working well, master?" I asked. "Are you happy with him?"

"Indeed, lady, he is learning fast. Show her, young Ricberht. Give your mother the gift you have made for her."

Ricberht fished in the pouch slung from his belt and pulled out something wrapped in a piece of cloth, he held it out to me. A flash of memory held me still for a moment, then, in response to his questioning look, I took it from him and unwrapped the gift with care.

It was a pendant, made of gold, impressed with a knot pattern, encircled by twisting threads. On the back were the runes to spell my name –Niartha. It was suspended on a thong of soft doeskin.

"I have not learnt to make a chain yet," he said. I showed him how thrilled I was, how clever I thought him, and he began eagerly to describe the process involved in its making. Diuma smiled quietly, patted the boy's shoulder and nodded to me. He slipped away, leaving me to enjoy the moment with my boy.

For this moment, it seemed as though all would be well. Raedwald's queen had born him two sons, one in the first year of their marriage, the other two years later, after the king returned from battling in Elmet and Lindsey. The elder child, Raegenhere, was now eleven, and the younger, aged nine, was called Eorpwald. When I asked Ricberht if he had the chance to meet the two princes, he shrugged. Raegenhere was a pleasant boy, quick at swordplay and with a ready smile, like his father. They sometimes rode out together, said Ricberht. He did not, apparently like the younger one much: he was given to sulking and could be spiteful. I told Ricberht it was probably due to the child's age, and a thwarted desire to be as skilful as the older boys. He shrugged again and then the horn sounded for the start of the feast.

King Raedwald and his queen (whom I had not yet met) were bountiful and splendid. I sat beside Edgar to help cut up his meat and pour his drink; he was too shaky to pass round the drinking horns, but supped from a silver cup given him by the king.

As I fell asleep some time long after midnight, I thought that things had not changed that much since the Christians had arrived in the lands of the Wuffings. Our traditional Yule-tide and the sacred Night of the Mothers seemed much the same. Some would celebrate the birth-mass of Christ in four days' time. Perhaps one more god would not make much difference. Years later, I would discover how wrong I was.

For now, at least, I was content.

BACKGROUND READING

St. Bede: (trans.Ecclesiastical History of the English People (Penguin) Sherley-Price/Latham)

Old English poems:The Wife's Lament; The Husband's Message; Wulf & Eadwacer; The Wanderer; The Seafarer; The Ruin; Deor; Widsith; Men's talents; Men's Fortunes; The Panther; Riddles (all in the late 10th century Exeter Book). Beowulf.

S.A.J.Bradley (ed):Anglo-Saxon Poetry (Everyman).

Richard Hamer: A Choice of Anglo-Saxon Verse (Faber)

Dr. Sam Newton:The Reckoning of King Raedwald (Red Bird Press) The Origins of Beowulf (Red Bird Press)

S.Pollington:The Mead-Hall (Anglo-Saxon Books)

Bill Griffiths:Aspects of Anglo-Saxon Magic (Anglo-Saxon Books)

John Blair:The Anglo-Saxon Age (in A Very Short Introduction series) (OUP)
G.R.Owen-Crocker:Dress in Anglo-Saxon England (The Boydell Press)

Kathleen Herbert:Looking for the Lost Gods of England (Anglo-Saxon Books)

Angela Care Evans: The Sutton Hoo Ship Burial (British Museum Publications)

Martin Carver:Sutton Hoo: Burial-Place of Kings? (British Museum Publications)

Francis Simpson: Simpson's Flora of Suffolk (Suffolk Naturalists' Society)

Oliver Rackham:The History of the Countryside (J.M.Dent)

W.G.Hoskins:The Making of the English Landscape (Book Club Associates)

Culpeper:Complete Herbal (Wordsworth Reference)

The Editors: The Macmillan and Silk Cut Almanac 1990 (Macmillan)

T.L.McAndrews:Amble and District (Sandhill Press)

Cadwallader J.Bates:History of Northumberland (Sandhill Press)

Lightning Source UK Ltd.
Milton Keynes UK
09 January 2010

148354UK00002B/4/P